A Second Chance for Love

A Second Chance for Love

A SEA GLASS BAY ROMANCE BOOK

CAEZIK
R O M A N C E
ARC MANOR
ROCKVILLE, MARYLAND

SHAHID MAHMUD
PUBLISHER

www.CaezikRomance.com

A Second Chance for Love copyright © 2021 by **Arc Manor, LLC.** All rights reserved. This book may not be copied or reproduced, in whole or in part, by any means, electronic, mechanical, or otherwise without written permission except short excerpts in a review, critical analysis, or academic work.

This is a work of fiction. Any resemblance to any actual persons, events, or localities is purely coincidental and beyond the intent of the author and publisher.

Sea Glass Photo copyright © by Ellen Josina Lowry

Mom Wanted copyright © 2021 by **Anna J. Stewart**
Father Wanted copyright © 2021 by **Kayla Perrin**
Hero Wanted copyright © 2021 by **Melinda Curtis**
Family Wanted copyright © 2021 by **Cari Lynn Webb**
Epilogue copyright © 2021 by **Cari Lynn Webb**

ISBN: 978-1-64710-023-0

First Edition. First Printing.
1 2 3 4 5 6 7 8 9 10

CAEZIK
ROMANCE

An imprint of Arc Manor LLC

www.CaezikRomance.com

Contents

Mom Wanted

by Anna J. Stewart

1

"Miss Claire, it *has* to be purple." Six-year-old Lindie Vaughn caught Claire's hand seconds before she touched the paintbrush to the little girl's cheek. "I *only* like purple butterflies."

"Understood, little miss." Claire bit the inside of her cheek to stop from laughing. If youthful independence had a photographic example, it would be this little, tenacious take on life, full-steam-ahead girl. With her crookedly braided dark hair, even more crooked smile, and a twinkle in her bright blue eyes that could've put any bit of sea glass to shame, Lindie was rarely seen without a book in her hand or a skip to her step. "Just keep in mind, butterflies come in all colors, all shapes, and all sizes. Perhaps it's best to say you like purple best. Not only."

Lindie's mouth scrunched into that familiar "thinking about it" way she had. "I guess that's okay." She heaved a little girl sigh that wrapped around Claire's heart. Lindie had been coming to Claire's ArtSea Classes and Creations tent at Sea Glass Bay's historic town's weekend market ever since she and her father had moved to town two years before. Claire's offerings of art classes, projects, and un-official childcare duties (because, according to Lindie, no one called it babysitting anymore) provided a safe place for the kids of parents who were shopping, working the market, or—in a lot of instances—hoping for a break. One would think Claire would be the one looking

3

for a break, considering she taught art at the local grammar school, but far from it. If anything, the weekends Claire spent here, rain or shine, summer straight through the seasons, reinvigorated and inspired her. There was nothing like the open, hopeful mind of a child.

With a delicate touch, Claire painted a pair of purple butterflies onto Lindie's pink-tinted cheek. A dab of black outline and accent here, a splash of pink on the wings there, and she was done. "One of my masterpieces."

Lindie grabbed the hand mirror off the table and angled it this way and that to get the best look. "Ooooh, it's perfect. Daddy's going to love it."

That remained to be seen, Claire thought with another silent chuckle. Sully Vaughn was nothing if not wrapped around his little girl's finger, but the man had to have his limits. Not that Sully's limits were any of Claire's business. Still, it was hard not to think about the handsome single father who had set more than his fair share of hearts fluttering. With those Hollywood blue eyes of his and that curly, close-cropped sun-kissed hair, add in the physique of the qualities romance novel heroes were made of and, well…. Claire sighed.

Sully was spoken for; his entire life was focused on his daughter, which, since Claire approved, was how it should be. But that didn't mean Claire, her close-knit circle of friends, along with half the female population of Sea Glass Bay, didn't frequently offer a thought or comment on the subject of one of the town's most eligible single fathers.

"Speaking of your father." Claire glanced at her watch, then pulled on her sweater as the late afternoon breeze turned chilly. She was due to meet her friends, Jazzy Dunbar, Paige Duffy, and Leah Martin, at The Tipsy Table for their weekly wine and whine ritual. "He's late."

"He doesn't mean to be." Lindie shrugged it off even as she began to help Claire clean up the remaining art supplies. She was such a little go-getter, always eager to help and learn and try something new. She was also one of the shrewdest individuals Claire had met in her thirty-five years and that included more than fifteen as a teacher. Something Claire needed to remind herself about frequently. "He's just really good at his job and he gets a lot of customers."

Claire couldn't argue with that logic. Sully was the town's "jobber", meaning he could get anything for anyone at any time—for a price of course. A scrounger, by some definition, resourceful to the point of miraculous and, as far as Claire knew, had always come through in a pinch.

His history with picking his daughter up at Claire's tent on time, however, left a lot to be desired. She was really looking forward to that glass of wine.

"So what are you reading this week, Lind?" Claire slid her paints and brushes into their containers and set them aside. The market workers would come by later and clean up, break down the tents and tables, and then reestablish everything the following Saturday morning.

"It's a biography on Amelia Earhart." Lindie's already wide eyes sparkled with excitement. "She was ah-may-zing! Did you know she was the first woman to fly solo across the Atlantic Ocean in 1928?"

"I think I did know that, actually." Claire's heart pitter-patted at Lindie's thirst for knowledge. Their town library had a stellar reputation for their programs and selection for all ages, and Lindie's teachers, thankfully, recognized a mind eager to learn.

"I think it would be cool to fly a plane. Did you know you lose eight ounces of water for every hour you fly? That's so weird and cool." Lindie, satisfied the cleaning up was finished, tucked herself into one of the white plastic chairs and hauled her backpack into her lap. She didn't, however, pull out a book on Earhart, but a rather substantial hardbound book on aviation. "Amelia Earhart and Eleanor Roosevelt went flying together, did you know that?" Lindie set the book in her lap and hefted it open to her bookmarked page. "They snuck out of the White House one day. I wonder why they had to sneak." Lindie bobbed her head from side to side. "If I wanted to go flying, I'd just go. 'Cause I can."

"Yes, well, you no doubt can because Eleanor did." It surprised her, Claire thought as she touched her fingertips to the paper-covered table, that the sadness could still strike with such sharp teeth. It didn't happen often these days, and normally it was when she was alone in her little cottage by the beach that she was reminded how empty her home and heart were.

A little knowledge-sponge like Lindie was never going to be hers. She might still have the time to have a child of her own, but not the ability. Filling her life, her hours, her days with her students and her friends' children sufficed most days. Others?

5

They didn't come close to eroding the loneliness.

"Eleanor Roosevelt did a lot of things," Lindie agreed in that matter-of-fact way she had. "I read a book about her, too, and Eleanor wasn't even her first name, it was her middle. I wonder if I should use my middle name instead?"

Curious, and more composed, Claire faced her. "And what would that be?"

"Imogene." Lindie's pixie nose scrunched. "Never mind."

"Never mind what?" The male voice that joined in the conversation had Claire spinning around and Lindie diving out of her chair.

"Dad! You're late." Lindie launched herself at her father and into Claire's wounded heart as Sully Vaughn wrapped his arms tight and hoisted his daughter into his arms. "I told Miss Claire you would be because you always are, but then you always turn up." She linked her hands behind his neck and leaned back to study him. "Did you do a good job today?"

"I did an excellent job." Sully said with a firm nod. "I got Mrs. Perkins' rose bushes for her and found a good deal on new windows for the Chattingham's remodel. And made my usual stall deliveries of course. How did you do today?" He freed one hand and touched her cheek. "New artwork. Are you testing out tattoos?"

"No." Lindie laughed. "We were waiting on you and Miss Claire suggested it."

"Hope it's okay," Claire said, clicking her art supply cart shut and grabbing her bag. "It'll come off with baby oil."

"It's fine," Sully said with a grin. And oh, what a grin.

Claire cleared her throat, ignoring the fact her cheeks had gone beach bonfire hot. "Great, well, I guess I'll see you next week, Lindie."

Sully angled a look at his daughter. "You didn't tell her?" Lindie caught her bottom lip in her teeth and shook her head. "Lindie, we talked about this."

"I know, but I don't want to stay with Mrs. Filbert from now on. She has creepy animals and she smells funny."

Claire turned her face away before she was caught laughing. Elderly Mrs. Filbert maintained her late husband's taxidermy collection and did have a tendency to smell like…well, a certain medicinal herb

Claire was glad Lindie couldn't identify. "What's going on with Mrs. Filbert?" she asked Sully.

"I've been asked to help with the supplies and prizes for the Mother's Day carnival." Sully set Lindie back on her feet and gestured for her to get her things. "It's going to eat up a lot of my time and I won't be able to get over here as easily. My schedule's about to become quite unpredictable and Mrs. Filbert's only two doors down from us."

"Oh." Claire couldn't quite process the disappointment. "Oh, sure, that makes sense I guess."

"It's not just the weekends. It's after school, too. We just have to start a new routine. And I'm doing it for yard work trade," he added. "Can't beat that daycare rate."

"Daa-aad." Lindie shot him a look.

"I didn't say babysitting," Sully responded. "Anyway, Lindie was supposed to tell you this was her last day at the market. Sorry about that."

"Yeah, me, too." Claire's hand clenched around the strap of her bag. She shouldn't. She really, really shouldn't, but the words slipped out anyway. "You know, if anything changes and Mrs. Filbert doesn't work out, I'd be happy to help you with Lindie."

"Oooooh, really?" Lindie's eyes went wonder wide. "Dad, did you hear that? That would be awesome!"

"I don't think Miss Claire knows what she's getting into," Sully said with a tight smile. Claire's stomach knotted. Obviously Sully didn't think her spending more time with his daughter was a good idea. Probably just as well. She was already far too attached to the little girl. Claire wasn't entirely sure what had possessed her to make the offer anyway. Still...

"It actually makes more sense for me to help out," Claire blurted out. "I'm at the same school already, I can even pick her up in the morning if you need me to. And you can swing by my house to get her when you're done for the day. Lindie's always a big help to me here on the weekends and I wouldn't charge anything, either." Now it was her turn to shrug, much, she thought, in the way his daughter did. "Something to think about."

"Daa-aaaad."

"No whining," Sully commented gently, touching his hand to his daughter's head where she clung to his waist and beamed up at him. "I appreciate the offer, Claire. I will definitely consider it."

"Bye, Miss Claire!" Behind her father's back, Lindie gave Claire a look that reminded her just how clever the little girl was. Sully, she'd bet, was going to have his hands full this evening.

"Sorry I'm late." Claire took a seat at one of the patio tables at The Tipsy Table, the four friend's designated meeting place once the market shut down for the weekend. "Thanks for ordering for me." She plucked her usual glass of Syrah up, took a sip, put it down, then, with a wide smile at Jazzy, she held out her arms, wiggled her fingers. "Gimmie."

Jazzy laughed, the action sending her springy black curls bouncing around her face. She shifted her three-month-old son Caleb from her lap into Claire's arms. The little boy's big brown eyes went wide as he settled into the crook of Claire's arm, snuggled, and let out a content baby sigh that had Claire's heart skipping a beat. She pressed her hand against the baby's chest, felt the last of her tension melt away.

"Everything okay?" Leah Martin, owner of The Flower Girl flower shop in Sea Glass Bay, shot her a curious look over the rim of her glass.

"Yeah, fine." Claire glanced up at the responding silence, found Jazzy, Leah, and Paige Duffy watching her. "What?"

"Nothing." Paige shrugged and grabbed a handful of marcona almonds. "We were just betting on what was keeping you. Didn't you have Lindie today?"

"Yes."

"And Lindie usually means Sully isn't too far behind," Jazzy added with a bit of a smirk as she sat back in her chair, her eyes rarely moving from her son.

"Uh-huh." Claire narrowed her eyes. "He was late picking her up."

"So the man has one fault," Leah waved off Claire's criticism. "I'm sure his other attributes more than make up for it."

"You guys must be really hard up if you're obsessing over my nonexistent love life." Caleb squirmed a bit and let out a huff of breath that told Claire he was tired of being ignored. She shifted him up and over her shoulder, felt a tug as he grabbed hold of a bunch of her hair and shoved it into his mouth.

"Oh, Caleb, no. That's not—" Jazzy leaned forward, but Claire waved her off. The bright flower print of her blouse reminded Claire of one of Jazzy's amazing pieces of art that she sold in her stall.

"It's fine. Baby drool doesn't hurt anything." But that snuggly, warm, baby smell fixed so much. "Can we please," she said to her friends, "focus on something, *anything* other than Sully Vaughn? I'm sure there's lots of other things to talk about, like maybe Leah's ex's upcoming wedding?" She batted her lashes.

"That's just mean," Leah grumbled. "You know I'm dreading having to go because Owen's in the wedding party." She glanced toward the playground where her four-year-old son was about ready to dive-bomb down one of the slides. "I think that might be its own circle of Dante's Inferno."

"No arguments from us," Paige agreed. "And before we fall too far off the Sully track—"

"Oh, for—" Claire patted Caleb's back to keep herself calm.

"I'm just saying, with you helping on the design of the booths for the Mother's Day carnival and Sully now on board to help with supplies, you two might be running into each other more than normal." Paige sipped her wine. "Couldn't hurt to test the waters out a bit, huh?"

"That's one current I'm not dipping my toes into," Claire assured them. She'd seen in on Sully's face when she'd offered to watch Lindie. He wasn't interested in either him or his daughter spending more time with Claire, and if there was one thing Claire had perfected over her thirty-five years, it was how to take a very obvious signal.

"This isn't fair." Lindie slumped into her bed as Sully drew her covers up. "We're a family, and families decide things together." She crossed her arms over her chest and glared up at him. "I don't want to go to Mrs. Filbert's."

It had been five years since Sarah had passed away, but he'd recognize that stubborn locked jaw a mile off. Like mother like daughter, he reminded himself and bent down to smooth Lindie's hair back.

"It's my job to do what's best for us, Lin, and this is it. Do you want a bedtime story?"

"No. I want Miss Claire to take care of me after school." She stuck her lower lip out.

"Then this is probably a good reminder for you that we don't always get what we want." He bent down, kissed her forehead and traced a gentle finger over the butterfly on her cheek. The knots in his stomach felt odd, misplaced, and definitely unwanted. His daughter's attachment to Claire Bishop had been growing more intense by the week and it was something he couldn't let continue. Not if he was going to do his main job and protect his little girl. "Last chance for a story."

"No story." Lindy shoved herself onto her side and squeezed her eyes shut. "I'm mad at you."

"You go right ahead and be mad."

"If you didn't take that stupid job then I wouldn't need someone else to take care of me," Lindie said as he headed for the door. "I could have kept staying with Miss Claire at the market."

Even at six, she knew how to twist the knife.

Sully hated how much time his job took away from his daughter, but his reputation was growing and their income was rising. His stupid job kept a roof securely over their heads and Lindie in a town with one of the best school districts in the state. If he had to take a job working twenty-three hours a day, he'd do it if it meant giving Lindie the life she deserved. "I made a commitment, Lindie. When you accept a job, you do it, no matter how difficult it is. A person's word is the most important thing they have. Good night, Lindie."

He closed the door but didn't latch it. Heading into the kitchen, he opened the fridge, pulled out a bottle of beer and slapped the cap off, drinking half of it in practically one gulp. He could hear the gentle roar of the ocean a few blocks from their house, along with the tinkling of neighbors' wind chimes and yard ornaments squeaking against the cool, night breeze.

He walked out the back door of the kitchen, stood against the porch railing and closed his eyes against the darkness and doubt. Sea Glass Bay had been a fresh start for him and Lindie after Sarah had died. Someplace without the memories that threatened to drag him into the future he'd had planned out for his family. The little two-bed-room house had been a bit run down when he'd found it, but it had charm and character and, more importantly, he could envision Lindie growing up here. Safe, secure, and planted in the knowledge that he would always, *always* put her first.

Sully scrubbed a hand down the side of his face, around his neck where the tension sat like an anvil on his shoulders. It was better, he told himself for the hundredth time, to break Lindie's attachment to Claire now, before any of them got too close. He knew how much Lindie longed for a mother. It was in every drawing she ever made, in every imaginary story she whispered to her toys when she thought he wasn't in hearing distance.

It hurt that Lindie had no memory of her mother. Sarah had been the best person Sully had ever known, and when Lindie had been born he'd thought life was as perfect as it could get. He'd been wrong.

He knew how it felt to lose someone he loved. He had felt it in his marrow to the point he didn't think the pain would ever end. It had lessened, but it had also become a part of him, settling into the corners of his heart he didn't allow himself to access. He couldn't allow anyone other than Lindie to ever access it again.

It didn't matter that Claire was one of the most beautiful women he'd ever met, with her long, curly strawberry-blonde hair and bright green eyes that sparkled like the morning grass glistening with dew. It didn't matter that her laughter made him smile or that when he looked at her the memories of Sarah he continued to cling to faded even deeper into his mind. It couldn't matter that in the late hours he found himself wondering and longing and wanting…

He drank, deeply, waiting for the exhaustion to creep over him as the night settled around him.

The idea of his daughter becoming close enough to feel the pain of loss with someone who had no real connection to either of them, simply wasn't an option. Mrs. Filbert was safe for his daughter.

Claire Bishop was not.

Not for his daughter's heart. And not for his.

2

"Claire, do you have a moment?"

A stack of her student's origami art projects in hand, Claire glanced up at her classroom door. "Sure, Melanie." Melanie Studdart, Sea Glass Bay Elementary School principal quickly stepped inside and waved Claire over. Only a few years older than Claire, Melanie wore her platinum blonde hair bobbed short and sharp, almost as sharp as her brown eyes that hadn't missed a student's trick in all her years as an educator. "Something wrong?"

"Not wrong, exactly. You know Lindie Vaughn, don't you?"

"Sure. Is she all right?" Panic seized Claire's chest. "I just saw her the other day at the market."

"Oh, she's fine, fine," Melanie quickly assured her. "Mr. Kozwalski has informed me that Lindie has gone on strike."

Claire blinked. "Excuse me?"

"You heard me." Melanie's lips twitched. "She came into school this morning, sat at her desk and pronounced she was on strike. "Mr. Kozwalski was hoping come lunch time she'd give up, but apparently she has made up her mind. When we asked her why she was on strike, she said her father would understand and that she'd only talk to him or to you."

"To me?" Claire could feel something akin to dread circling inside her. "Um, why me?"

"She said you'd understand. She mentioned Mrs. Filbert and her collection of creepies?"

"Ah." The light dawned. "Lindie's father's having Mrs. Filbert look after her when he's at work. Lindie was less than pleased at the prospect."

"Would you mind speaking with her? Her father isn't answering his phone and I'm thinking it's not a great idea for the other students to get the idea to strike their way out of their education."

"Yes, of course." She set her papers down and followed Melanie down the hall and across the outdoor corridor into pre-K through second grade building. The second she stepped into the classroom, she could only empathize with Mr. Kozwalski.

Lindie, wearing a denim jumper dress and bright pink sneakers, her normally crooked braids even more out of skew, sat at her desk, arms folded across her chest and her little jaw set like granite. The instant Lindie saw Claire, she was out of her chair like a shot.

"Hey, what's going on, Lind?" Claire bent down before Lindie latched onto her like a barnacle. "I hear you're on strike."

"I don't want to go to Mrs. Filbert's." As Lindie spoke, her dark eyes filled with tears which plopped onto her chubby cheeks. "Please say I can stay with you, Miss Claire. *Please?*"

"I'll leave you two alone," Melanie whispered and backed out of the room.

"Come here, Lindie." Claire led her over to the reading corner and, after taking a seat, drew Lindie up and onto her lap. The way the little girl curled into her, her little body shaking as she cried had Claire struggling to breathe. "Hey, now, nothing's that bad, little miss." Claire wasn't about to tell Lindie she was overreacting. Children needed to feel whatever they were going to feel, whether adults agreed or understood it or not. "Mrs. Filbert's a very nice lady, Lindie. I'm sure she's going to take good care of you."

"But I want to stay with you."

"Lindie." Claire waited until Lindie lifted her chin. "I think maybe your father knows what's best for you."

"Don't you want me to stay with you?"

Of all the things the little girl could have asked, it was the one question that sliced her heart in two. "I would very much like that, but this isn't up to me. It's up to your dad. It's his job to take care of you."

"Dad said last night that when someone takes a job, they have to do it no matter what. No matter how hard it is."

Claire nodded. "Your father's right."

"So if you took a job, even if it wasn't what someone wanted, you'd have to do it, 'cause you promised, right?"

Not entirely sure where this conversation was headed, Claire hesitated. "Yes. I suppose that's right."

Lindie brightened. "So if I hire you to be my after-school adult, you'd have to do it."

"Ah, that's not exactly what I—"

"I'm the one who needs watching. Why don't I get to choose who it is?"

Logic, especially when presented by a child, often posed its own roadblocks in arguments. "Lindie—"

"I brought my treasure box." Lindie jumped off Claire's lap and raced back to her desk, pulled it open and brought over a seashell and sea glass-decorated box she'd been gifted by her Dad from Ellen Lowry's Timeless Seaside Creations stall at the market. "Here." She pushed the box into Claire's hands. "It has all the money I've saved from my allowance. It's all I have in the whole world. I was saving up to buy a tortoise, but this is more important. Besides, Daddy said I could have what I want for my birthday and that's what I'm going to ask for."

There was no trace of the tears that, only moments ago, had run unchecked down the little girl's cheeks. It was as if she'd been waiting for a particular door to open and somehow, Claire had opened it.

Claire clicked open the box. Inside lay three crumpled single dollars and a collection of coins and bits of sea glass collected from the beach.

"Is it enough?" Lindie asked. "I can go to the beach and get more glass. Maybe you can use them in one of your projects?"

Claire sighed and closed the box. "I can't promise anything," she started and had to catch Lindie before she started jumping up and down. "Let me talk to your father and see if we can work something out." She wasn't entirely sure she wanted to know Sully's reasons for not taking Claire up on her offer yesterday, but it was clear she was going to find out.

"Yay! Thank you, thank you, thank you!" Lindie launched herself at Claire, locked her arms around her neck and squeezed. "Maybe now you can come with us to the Mother's Day carnival. I've never been with a mom before."

And that was it—her heart shattered against the rocks like an unruly wave. "Hold on there." Claire set the box down and caught Lindie around the waist, held her firmly in front of her. "Lindie, we'll talk to your father *only* about me taking care of you after school and on the weekends when he works. Let's *not* talk about the carnival, okay?"

"Okay, not now." Lindie nodded. "I'm going to go to lunch now. I'm starving." She sagged and sighed so dramatically Claire thought she might just crumble to the floor like a Hollywood diva. "I'll come to your classroom after school. Bye!"

Stunned, and feeling more than a bit manipulated, Claire sat in Lindie's classroom and looked down at the treasure box. She'd walked right into it, hadn't she? Lindie had laid a trap, baited it with her teacher and the principal, and *bam!* Caught Claire exactly where she wanted her.

"Well, Sully," Claire got to her feet and brushed her hands against her flowered skirt, "looks like we've both got our hands full now."

It took some doing, and more time than he'd excepted, but Sully managed to track down a collection of imported beer tap levers Hank DeLeon was hoping to install at his bar. The morning had been spent locking down a supplier of custom, wood carved toys in need of some serious promotion opportunities. Another hour or so of haggling over the price of the beer pulls had him acquiring the items at an amount that would net him an acceptable profit and keep both his customer and the supplier happy.

"Never burn a bridge you might need later," Sully said to himself as he headed to his car for the hour drive back to Sea Glass Bay. Mid-April in Northern California could not be beat, and that was saying something considering he'd spent most of his formative years in San Diego. But everywhere he turned there he had memories of Sarah and the life that should have been. No, the move north had been exactly what he and Lindie had needed.

Lindie. Sully sighed the sigh of a beleaguered, guilt-ridden father. That girl of his could hold a grudge tighter than he could squeeze a dollar. The silent treatment had continued through breakfast, after which Lindie had, perhaps for the first time without being asked, set her cereal bowl in the sink and filled it with water. He'd spent five minutes shouting through the house for her to get a move on only to find she was already in the car ready to go.

No eye contact. Not a word. Barely a sound.

It was not, Sully thought as he'd watched her stride into school, thumbs hitched into the straps of her backpack, the way he liked beginning his day. Now it was the end of the day, he was contemplating another dose of silent treatment from his child, so he dug out his cell phone, opened the door to his banged-up SUV then cringed. He'd completely forgotten to charge his phone last night. It must have died while he had been haggling prices. Muttering to himself, he slid inside and plugged in. No sooner had he started the car than his alert tones began to chime.

Ding! Ding, ding, ding.

He slammed the car back into park, heart thudding when he recognized the number to the school on his voice mail. Without even listening to the messages, he called back, glancing at his watch. Swearing again, he hung up.

It was almost five. No one would be in the school office this late.

He scrolled through his contacts, located Mrs. Filbert's number and dialed, all the while trying to keep the panic at bay. "Mrs. Filbert, it's Sully Vaughn. I wanted to check in about Lindie."

"Lindie?" The older woman's voice sounded oddly detached for a moment. "Oh, yes, of course. I had a lovely visit with her earlier this afternoon after school."

"Visit?" The word echoed in the cab of the car. "Isn't she there?"

"Not anymore, no. That lovely Claire Bishop offered to take her. And you know, it's a good thing, too. My sciatica has been acting up something fierce and, frankly, I don't think I'm up to taking care of a whirlwind like Lindie."

"Lindie is with Claire." It was a statement more than a question.

"Yes, dear. She left me her number in case you called." She rattled off the information, including Claire's address. "I hope you know I was more than willing to lend a hand, but—oh, well. I suppose the yard work can wait until my next Social Security check comes."

"There's no need for that." Sully forced himself to breathe. "I've blocked out some time on Wednesday afternoon if that's good for you?"

"Oh, my, yes. That would be lovely. Thank you, Sully."

"You're welcome." It took him a good few minutes after he hung up to wrap his brain around what came next. Obviously he'd be picking his daughter up at Claire Bishop's house, at which time he and the can't-take-no-for-an-answer art teacher were going to have a chat about boundaries when it came to *his* child. "Yeah," he muttered. "That should go over really well."

"So I carry the number one here?" Lindie's tiny tongue stuck out from between her lips as she hunched over her math homework while sitting at Claire's kitchen table.

"That's right." Claire stood over her, moving the empty glass of milk out of the way. "Now count them up in the line like the book shows."

"Five, six, seven…" Lindie tilted her head. "Nine." She scrunched her face and tilted her face up. "Right?"

"We'll find out. Let's write it first." She tapped a finger against the answer line. Outside she heard the slam of a car door. Her hand tightened around the back of Lindie's chair. "You keep going, okay? I think that might be your father."

" 'Kay. Come on, Friday. You can help me." Lindie patted the chair next to her for Claire's ginger cat to hop up. Friday, giving Claire one of his "Really, must I?" looks did as he was instructed and joined his new biggest fan at the table, promptly plopping his plump backside on the homework page.

Claire let out a slow, controlled breath as she hurried down the hall to the front door. She could feel the vibes already, irritation and anger pulsing against the front door before she pulled it open.

Sully stopped briefly, one foot on the walk, the other firmly on the bottom step of her porch. The setting sun caught against those glorious highlights in his hair and the don't-mess-with-me glint in his eye.

Instantly, Claire raised her hands. "I can explain."

"Uh-huh. Is she in there?"

"Yes, she's doing her homework." Claire stepped outside and pulled the door closed. "I've been helping her with her math."

"Well that just fixes everything then, doesn't it?"

Okay, he was more upset than she expected. Actually, she hadn't been able to imagine Sully Vaughn angry at all. He always gave off such a relaxed, easy going, nothing-bothers-me attitude. She should have known little Lindie would be his trigger point.

"We had a situation at school. The principal asked for my help and I agreed. Honestly, Sully, this just sort of happened."

He paused. "What kind of situation?"

"Lindie went on strike."

"*Strike?* What does that even mean? How does a six-year..." he trailed off, lifted a hand and pinched the bridge of his nose. "*Newsies*. We watched *Newsies* the other night and she asked me to explain what a strike was. Who knew she was taking notes?"

Claire did her best not to laugh, but it took ducking her head and pressing her lips together. "She is a bit of a sponge when it comes to facts." When she lifted her gaze to his, she saw the anger begin to fade. "I didn't do this on purpose. I was willing to respect your decision for Lindie to stay with Mrs. Filbert, but she just wasn't having it. She refused to do any schoolwork or participate in any activities until she talked to me, at which time I agreed to talk to you about alternative care options for her."

"So you let her win."

"No." Claire frowned, trying to see this from his perspective. "No. I let her know she was being heard. I've kept my end of the deal. We're talking and, for today, she's with me. But she knows that might not be the case in the future."

He sighed. "Yeah, well, as far as Mrs. Filbert is concerned, she's off the option list. She's convinced Lindie's too much for her."

"Oh." Claire swallowed a bit of guilt. "Yes, well, that might be partly my fault. We stopped for an ice cream after school on our way to Mrs. Filbert's and, well, sugar certainly does have an effect on Lindie, doesn't it?" She'd honestly thought that was an urban myth.

"Actually, no, not normally," Sully said. "Getting her own way, on the other hand does tend to bolster her energy level. Man." He let out a long breath and, after a glance at the door, shifted his attention to the old-fashioned porch swing at the end of the porch. "I'm going to sit for a minute, that okay?"

"Yes, sure, of course. Do you want something to drink?"

"Arsenic with a foxglove chaser would be good."

Claire chuckled. "I can do milk or soda, or I made iced tea this afternoon. Raspberry iced tea."

"That actually sounds really great, thanks."

"Be back in a second." Claire hurried inside, nearly bashing Lindie in the nose with the door when she opened it. "Nosy little miss," she chided and steered the little girl back into the kitchen. "You're supposed to be working with Friday on your addition."

"I got stuck. And I wanted to know what Daddy said."

"He hasn't said anything just yet because he's trying to understand why you're here and not at Mrs. Filbert's."

"Oh." Lindie slid back into her chair, picked up her pencil. "Then I will keep doing math. You can talk to him."

Claire retrieved the pitcher of tea and some fresh raspberries from the fridge. She poured two glasses and, when she turned, found herself mesmerized by the image before her. A little girl doing homework at her hand-painted turquoise table, the scarred white chair she sat in oversized enough to make it look as if Lindie had been caught in a doll's house. It was, she realized in that moment, the most perfect sight she'd ever seen.

How was it, she asked herself as she withdrew to take Sully his tea, that the reality of the moment both broke and soothed her heart?

She found Sully, his legs stretched out, hands folded over his chest, looking up at the twilight sky as the day came to an end. Another perfect image. One that, for a moment, she thought she could get easily used to—having someone to come home to, or someone coming home to her. But complicated didn't begin to describe her odd relationship with Sully Vaughn. She'd twisted herself up in knots over both father and daughter and it was clear she needed to remedy that right now.

"I'm sorry it all happened this way," she said as she approached. "I'll be happy to help you find someone to take care of Lindie when you can't be with her. I know a number of former students who would be excellent baby—"

Sully's head tilted up and he looked at her, brow arched.

"Ah, childcare provider," she quickly corrected herself. She handed him a glass, which he happily accepted and drank. At his nod of approval, she lowered herself into the opposite end of the swing, tucking one foot up and under her thigh. "I want to say I didn't mean to take advantage of the situation, but I suppose I did. I'm sorry. Your daughter is a bit of a light for me and I guess I wanted it to shine a while longer."

The remaining tension on Sully's face eased. "I get that." He sat up, leaned his elbows on his knees, held the glass between his hands. "Her mother called her a cardiac tornado, just whipping into people's hearts and spinning there endlessly." He smiled at Claire's questioning look. "Sarah, my wife, was a nursing student. She was hoping to work in the cardiac care unit when she got her degree."

"You don't have to tell me." She could see the topic of his late wife caused him pain. It was written all over his face, in the shadows of his eyes. It was, perhaps, the greatest regret of her life, that she'd never loved anyone as much as Sully had clearly loved his Sarah.

"I know. She's been gone almost five years now." He shook his head. "Some days it feels like yesterday and others…" He trailed off.

Uncertain how much to push, she asked the only thing that came to mind. "How did you lose her?"

"Stupid freak accident. She'd gone away for the weekend with her girlfriends. A few hours' drive to a winery. They went on a bicycling excursion up through the hills and her bike blew a tire. She was wearing a helmet, but," he shrugged, "the fall was too severe. She was put immediately on life-support and they'd hoped to repair the damage to her spine but…." A shake of his head told the rest of the story. "She never woke up. That was a month before Lindie's second birthday."

Claire had no words. All she had was the surrogate grief wrapping its way around her heart. She reached out, lay her hand on Sully's arm and squeezed.

"There's this fog that descends," he spoke as if from a distance. "This mind-numbing, all-encompassing fog that just blankets you with paralyzing fear, but I couldn't let that get to me." He turned and looked in the window of Claire's living room, to where the kitchen light shone through the lacy curtains. "I had my little girl to take care of. Thank goodness. I think she saved my life."

It both surprised and humbled Claire that Sully didn't pull away from her touch. "What about family? Your parents? Hers?"

"All gone. It's just been me and Lindie ever since." He shifted his focus toward the hint of beach peeking around the corner of the house. "This place, it's been healing. It's let me start over and begin to build something really solid. For both of us." He hesitated. "But the more I build, the harder it is to stay on top of everything. She needs so much, and I want to give it all to her."

"And sometimes you feel as if you're pulled in twenty different directions at a time." She caught his look of surprise. "I'm a teacher. I have parent meetings. I hear things. If you need help with Lindie, we'll find it."

His gaze softened. "I suppose you want to know why I don't want that person to be you."

She could lie and say it didn't matter. But it did. Far more than she wanted to admit. "I'm sure you have your reasons."

"Lindie loves you."

"Okay." Claire's throat burned against the rush of emotion. "Should I apologize?"

"No, of course not. But I can see it, hear it every time she talks about you. Miss Claire said this. Did you know Miss Claire can do that. Oh, you should see what Miss Claire had us do today at the art tent."

"Again," Claire forced a laugh. "Sorry?"

He covered her hand, still on his arm, with his. The cold from the icy glass glazed his skin and it was that, not him touching her she told herself, that made her shiver. "I know what it is like to lose someone I love. As her teacher you're...temporary, Claire. You're a part of her life now, but what about later?"

"I don't have plans to go anywhere. I am not a fair-weather friend. And, if it helps, I can let you in on a not so well-kept secret." She untucked her leg and scooted closer. "I love Lindie, too. If I can help you, help her, I wish you'd let me."

"She needs stability, Claire. She needs someone she can count on. But I don't want her getting so attached that, if she loses you, she's dropped into that same pit of grief it took me so long to pull myself out of."

"So instead of teaching her to take a chance on love, you're telling her to walk away from it before she gets hurt." It would be easy, so easy, to touch his face, to trace those lines of grief until they faded beneath her touch. "I didn't know your Sarah, but I don't think that's the lesson she'd want her daughter to take from her death. If I had a child, it's not what I'd want them to learn."

21

Sully looked at her, really looked at her, to the point Claire found herself resisting the urge to shift in her chair, knowing she should move away even as the urge to lean even closer wove through her. Her gaze dipped to his mouth, to the lips she'd found herself thinking about far too often in recent days. Lips that now were only a breath away from her own...

The front door swung open and Lindie bounded out. "Twenty-nine!" She landed like Supergirl poised to launch off the top of a spire, hands on hips, braids sticking out of each side of her head. "I got the answer and I checked it with subtraction and it is twenty-nine!"

Claire pushed back to the other side of the swing, tempted to fan her face against the flush in her cheeks. Heaven help her, if just the promise of kissing Sully Vaughn caused this reaction, what would the actual act do to her?

"Did Miss Claire tell you, Daddy?"

"Tell me what?" Sully set his glass down and pinned his eyes on his daughter. "And you're speaking to me now?"

"She wasn't speaking to you?" Claire echoed.

"Nope. Silent treatment. She could give classes," he muttered out of the corner of his mouth. "Lindie? Tell me what?"

"I hired her," Lindie announced. "To take care of me. I gave her my treasure box for payment. The one we got from Miss Ellen at Timeless Seaside Creations."

"You *hired* her?" Sully looked from his daughter to Claire. "She hired you?"

"Yeah, I was getting to that." Claire held up her hand and got to her feet. "Lindie, how about you go get your things together so you and your father can head home."

"Okay." Lindie narrowed her eyes as she walked away. "Do I get to come back?"

Claire turned an equally expectant gaze on Sully. "That's up to your father."

Sully's jaw tensed; she could see it, even in the dimming light. "I never really stood a chance, did I? You're two of the most stubborn and determined females I've ever met in my life."

"Now that," Claire declared as she followed Lindie into the house, "is a compliment indeed."

3

"Can we go sea glass collecting when we get to your house?"
Lindie asked, her hopeful voice floating from the back seat
of Claire's car. "I want to create a new treasure box and you
live soooooo close to the water. There had to be lots of sea glass there."

"That will depend on how quickly you get your homework finished."
Claire couldn't quite rationalize how easily she, Sully, and Lindie had
fallen into a routine. Granted it had only been two days since Lindie
had bamboozled her father—and, to an extent, Claire—into getting
precisely the after-school care she wanted, but they all just…fit. Like
finding pieces of a puzzle Claire didn't know she'd been waiting to
construct. She swiveled her car into a parking spot down the block
from The Flower Girl, Leah Martin's shop, which was located right
beside Tank's Bar & Grill.

Their little town was everything Claire loved—small, compact,
and filled with all the amenities she ever needed or wanted. Having
friends like Leah, Jazzy, and Paige only added to the benefits, as they
always had leftover items from their own artistic creations that Claire
could use in her classroom.

"I don't have any homework today," Lindie declared as she un-
hooked her seatbelt.

"Really?" Claire didn't believe her for a second. She knew Mr.
Kozwalski, and even if the first-grade teacher didn't give them written

homework, his students were obligated to read fifteen minutes a day outside of school. Not that that was a hardship for Lindie. Claire glanced at Lindie in the rearview mirror. "You do know teachers speak with one another, don't you, Lindie?"

"Yes." Lindie grumbled and twisted her mouth. "I meant I only have a little bit so I can be fast and we can go collect glass." Clearly she didn't appreciate being caught in a lie.

"Well, before I can play, I need to do *my* homework. Come on. Let's see what new flowers Leah has in her shop."

"All right." Heaving a heavy sigh of burden, Lindie pushed open her door as Claire climbed out. She reached up and grabbed Claire's hand and skipped beside her as they made their way to the store, then set the bell to dinging when they pushed open the door.

"Ooooh." Lindie's eyes went wide at the sight of all the flowers and plants, the ever-so-faint trickle of a small water fountain soothing them both. "It's so pretty."

And a breath of fresh air, Claire thought. Literally.

Leah popped her head out of the back room. "You're early," she chided Claire gently and waved them back. "I was just getting these together for you. Hello there, Lindie."

"Hi." Lindie grabbed the edge of the metal working counter and peered over it. "What are you doing?"

"I'm getting these older flowers together for Claire."

"They're for this weekend's market projects," Claire told her, looking around the space. "Where's Owen?" Leah's four-year old son was usually zooming around here about this time.

"Taking a nap. I hope," Leah muttered. "He came back from his father's crankier than usual this time. I'm hoping he'll sleep it off."

"Oh, right. Eesh. These are gorgeous." She plucked up a handful of wilted tulips. "The colors—wow."

"Think they'll survive a shellacking?" Leah chuckled at her own joke.

"I'm not shellacking all of them," Claire corrected. "But they're perfect for paintbrushes."

"Paintbrushes?" Lindie didn't look convinced. "We're going to paint with *flowers?*"

"We are." That reminded her, she needed to stock up on some of her paints. "What have I told you in class?"

Lindie rolled her eyes. "Always see the potential in everything."

Leah chuckled and retrieved a box from the back shelf. "Here, Lindie, help me place all these flowers in here."

" 'Kay."

"So, Sully changed his mind, huh?" Leah murmured when Lindie was out of earshot. "What did that take?"

"A very determined six-year-old," Claire told her. "And maybe me as an unwitting accomplice." Sully's warnings about hearts being at risk hadn't really sunk in until this afternoon, while Claire was walking across the corridor to pick Lindie up from her classroom. It had felt so right, so natural, so absolutely perfect. She hadn't just opened her heart a little to the child, but had flung the door so far open it may never close again. But, as Claire had told Sully, love was worth the risk, for however long one might have it.

"You're a natural with her," Leah said. "Just as you are with Owen and Caleb."

"Some things just feel right." And children had always felt right for Claire. Her body, on the other hand, had other ideas.

"What about Sully?" Leah asked. "How do things feel with him?"

"Don't start that again." This time when she chided her friend, however, it lacked its usual punch of authenticity.

"Huh." Leah stuck her tongue in her cheek and reached for a pile of lilies. "Slightly irritated tone, inability to meet someone's eyes, a pink tint to your cheeks. Something tells me things are feeling pretty fine with our sexy single father."

"Can we discuss this later, please?" The last thing she wanted was for Lindie to get ideas about Claire and her father.

"Oh, absolutely." Leah's grin hinted at a very focused conversation over wine after the market this weekend. "In fact, you can count on it. Hey." She touched Claire's arm, her expression shifting to concern. "You know we are just playing around. If this is serious with Sully—"

"It's not," Claire cut her off before Leah got carried away. "I get what you all are trying to do, and I appreciate it, but that just makes it more difficult to deal with. Just..." She struggled for the right words. "Just let me be with this for a while, all right?"

25

"Yeah, sure." Leah nodded. "But that won't stop me from sending out good thoughts that you and Sully have some serious alone-sexy time."

"What's alone-sexy time?"

The two women looked down to find Lindie standing beside them. "Uh—" Leah glanced to Claire, who took a deep, frustrated breath. "Just something adults do when they're bored," she explained before Claire could find the words. "You know, like in fairy tales?"

"I liked Merida," Lindie announced as if alone-sexy time was forgotten. "She's my favorite. But I don't remember something called alone-sexy time with her. She had a bow. And crazy hair and her brothers to take care of. She didn't have time to be alone." She seemed to be thinking hard on that. "Are there more flowers, Miss Leah?"

"Ah, no, I think that's it." Obviously she was trying not to laugh. "You guys going to get some ice cream?" Having heard about the aftereffects of their last trip to SeaSweets & Treats, Leah was no doubt getting a kick out of sending them there for a double sugar dose. "I heard there's new flavors today."

"Oh, can we?" Lindie asked, bouncing on her toes. "I promise I'll do my homework first thing when we get home."

Get home. To Claire's house. Had it really happened that fast? Had Lindie become so attached she considered Claire's house... home? Worry she didn't dare acknowledge niggled at the back of her brain. Worry and the words from Lindie's father who knew, far more than Claire, how quick and sharp heartbreak could come.

Being distracted was not a good state of mind for Sully. Not only did it interfere with his productivity as a negotiator and salesman, but it left him wanting to be doing anything other than the job he typically loved.

He had the lumber and supplies locked down for the new booths they planned to construct for the Mother's Day carnival. It would be cutting it close, but he'd built in a few days' buffer to ensure the carnival committee had the time they needed. Besides, he'd gotten the price knocked down twenty percent from what was budgeted, and no one was going to blame him for saving money. As good as those results were,

Sully found himself anxious to get home. Not only so he could spend the rest of the afternoon and evening with his daughter, but also…

He was anxious to see Claire again.

That odd, barbed knot in his belly tightened and he wondered, not for the first time as he climbed into his car to drive home, how this had happened. After Sarah, he'd never found himself remotely interested in pursuing anything resembling a relationship with a woman. How could he when the only female in his life demanded constant attention? Not that a relationship was in the offing. While he didn't know a lot about Claire Bishop, he knew enough to suspect she wasn't particularly casual about her dating life.

He hadn't even given her dating life much thought. At least not until a few days ago. Since then, he'd been thinking about it. A lot.

Sully stopped at a café drive-thru for a double jolt of coffee, checked his phone before jumping on the freeway for the hour and a half drive north. His contacts were growing, in everything from landscaping to construction, to event supplies, and his list of acquisitions and promised commitments from others in payment were also growing substantially. He was about ready to finalize the deal with Gavin Cole, a local charter boat operator, for him to build Lindie a one-of-a-kind playhouse in the back yard. It would require some extra leaps and bounds on Sully's end, but Lindie was worth it. That imagination of hers couldn't be boxed in and anything he could do to bolster it and set it free…. There wasn't any price he wouldn't pay for that.

Claire had been right the other night. He hadn't been setting a very good example for Lindie by trying to protect her from getting too attached to Claire. She already was, and trying to put a wedge between them was only going to alienate his daughter and create problems he didn't want. He'd just have to make sure boundaries were set…both for himself and Lindie.

Yes, he told himself as he hit the gas and sped toward home.

Boundaries would be a very, very good idea.

It was that resolve, as well as blasting classic rock out of his speakers, that had him making the drive back to Sea Glass Bay in record time. He bypassed his own house, a few blocks away from where Claire's cottage sat amidst the beachside homes. He pulled into the driveway behind Claire's compact.

27

He sat in his car, window rolled down, the spring air flowing around him as the tinkling of wind chimes danced against the breeze. Her saltbox cottage siding had been painted in hues of pale blues and greens, reminiscent of the ocean that lay just beyond. With the bright white porch and colorful pillows arranged on the swing he'd occupied only a few nights ago, Claire's personal space really did evoke tranquility and escape. It was easy to forget there was a word beyond this place, a world that Sully knew could be harsh and unfeeling.

But the woman who lived here, the woman who had dedicated her life to education and promoting art and beauty to her students and the small-town residents of Sea Glass Bay—she really was a bit of a haven in a storm. Perhaps it was time to accept that and see where the tides took him.

He climbed out of the car, stepped onto the porch, only to hear the familiar, excited squeal of his daughter being carried to him by the ocean breeze. He walked around the side of the house, clicked open the wooden gate leading to the walkway down and around to the beach. As the wind whipped up and the waves crashed, he found his daughter twirling and spinning about a few feet away from the shore. Claire, her hair blowing against her face, sat on the sand, knees drawn up, a small plastic bucket beside her.

"Daddy!" Lindie whooped and hollered, half jumping her way over to him, her bare feet kicking up sand as she went. "You're early! Claire said we could hunt for sea glass when I finished my homework." She locked her arms around his waist and beamed up at him. "I got to play with a puppy a few minutes ago. Oh, Daddy, she was so cute! Can I get a puppy, maybe? That would be so so so cool!"

He thought he'd done pretty well staving off her desire for a cat. A dog was definitely going to be tougher to deny, especially since he'd always had one growing up. "We'll talk about it later." He rested his hands on the top of her head, looked down into her glowing face. She looked so happy. So utterly without care and worry. It really was all he wanted out of life. "How was school?"

She shrugged. "Okay. Come see Claire, keep her company while I keep looking for sea glass for my treasure chest."

"You're having trouble finding some?" Near as he could tell, the sparkling, pastel glass pebbles dotted the entire beach.

"No," Lindie laughed. "But I want *special* ones. Come on." She grabbed hold of his hand and dragged him over to Claire, who looked up at him with a smile, catching a strand of wild hair to tuck behind her ear. "Daddy's early, Miss Claire."

"So I see. Pull up some sand." She patted the beach beside her. "I try to come out here at least once a week and watch the sun set." A glance at her watch had her sighing. "Maybe not tonight, since we're early."

"I'll be back." Lindie raced off, kicking sand up and around her flying feet.

Sully sat, the bucket of tumbled sea glass pieces sitting between them. They really did look like rainbow stones.

"Everything go okay for you today?" she asked in a way that told him she was searching for a safe topic of conversation. He'd be lying if he said he hadn't been thinking about their almost kiss the other evening, when they'd been sitting on her porch. It had felt like the most natural thing in the world in that moment, leaning into her, wanting to taste her lips, to plunge his hands into that thick, curly hair of hers and hold her against him. And yet, he hadn't. And right now, he regretted that more than anything.

"Today went pretty well. I finalized a couple of deals. The carnival construction committee should be getting their supplies in the next few days."

"As a member of that committee, I thank you." She turned her face to smile at him, a smile that had her green eyes sparking against the late afternoon sun. "The old booths are so rundown and faded. It'll be nice to have some fresh, bright color to display on the pier. Lindie's looking forward to the carnival."

"Is she?" It had always been a bit of a bitter pill—a Mother's Day carnival when his little girl didn't have a mother. But he'd made the best of it. "I have gotten the feeling she has plans for us this year."

"Oh, she does, at that. And before you worry too much, I've already told her I'm working at the carnival and won't be able to go with her. Yes, she did ask."

He'd been afraid of that. "She's gotten to that age, when she understands what she's missing out on."

"It must be difficult, not being able to do something about it."

"It is what it is. It's more difficult thinking that Sarah only got to celebrate two Mother's Days. It was one of her favorite family holidays."

"Moms are special. Whether they're here or elsewhere." She glanced up at the sky. "I remember the first one after my mother passed. It didn't feel right, having any kind of celebration. Then I realized she'd have wanted me to remember the good times and honor her that way. So that's what I do now."

"You asked me the other day about my family." Sully leaned back on his hands, stretched out his legs. "What about yours?"

"It was just me and my mother for most of my life. She was a teacher, too. Music," she added with a soft chuckle. "I did not inherit any of those abilities. The artistry apparently comes from my father's side."

"He's not in your life?"

"No." She shook her head, but he didn't see a trace of regret. "My mother always said he wasn't the settling down sort. I had my grandparents early on, but they died when I was about Lindie's age." She fidgeted with one of Lindie's sea glass stones.

"What about a family of your own? No one special in your life?"

"No one who's ever wanted me as I am." Her smile was wistful. "I'm quite independent. Very set in my ways. That's not easy to work around when you're trying to build something with someone. Besides, I'm getting a little old to keep believing in happily-ever-afters."

"Oh, yeah, you're a real Methuselah," he teased. "What are you? Thirty? Thirty-one?"

"Thirty-five." She reached out and pushed her hand against his arm.

"You've got plenty of time."

"No, actually." She glanced away, seeming to find solace in the sea. "As much as I would have loved a house full, children aren't in my future. I had severe endometriosis when I was younger, followed by early menopause. I was twenty-seven when that door closed on me."

"I'm sorry." And he was. She was such a natural with kids. He hadn't only seen it with Lindie, but with all the children who came to her tent at the market on the weekends.

"So am I." There were no tears, only sadness, but even that seemed couched in resignation. "There's no changing it, so there's no use dwelling on it. So I live my life on my terms, where and when I can."

"Sometimes it seems like the people who want and need children the most are the ones who aren't blessed with them."

"Well, I get a new classroom full of them every year. In fact, I should have Lindie in a few years."

"If we're still here." While he'd wanted to set roots, it wasn't the first time he'd given thought to moving on beyond Sea Glass Bay, if things didn't work out. It was, however, the first time the thought gave him pause.

"Oh?" Claire frowned.

"Given what I do, there's a whole world out there for us. The owner of the house we're renting told me today he's thinking about selling, so maybe I'll take that as a sign." Or maybe the almost-kiss on the porch was the sign he should follow?

"Does Lindie know you're thinking of leaving?"

He'd have had to have been deaf not to hear the strain in her voice. "No. I haven't talked to her about it and I won't. Not unless it's a certainty. I don't want her going on strike on me or anything."

Claire's lips twitched ever so slightly. "Well, she'd be missed." She looked back at him, met his gaze. "So would you."

"I appreciate that." It didn't feel right, at all, to be discussing this with her. In fact, the more he turned the idea over in his mind, the more he wanted to discard it all together. He checked to see his daughter was engrossed in sea glass selecting farther down the beach. "I didn't bring it up to upset you." His fingers itched to reach out, to touch her, touch her face. And, because he'd never been one to easily resist temptation, he did just that.

Her skin was soft, slightly chilled by the ocean air. As he'd imagined, he slipped his hand behind her neck into her thick waterfall of curls, pulled her toward him and lowered his mouth. He kept his hold gentle, giving her whatever space, whatever time she might need to pull or turn away. She didn't. She leaned in, offered her lips to his and, when he claimed them, he found himself falling into that swirling tidal pool of desire he never thought he'd feel again.

Kissing Claire was, Sully thought, as if she met him beat for beat, breath for breath, stroke for stroke—as close to a perfect moment as he'd ever experienced. The world that felt so harsh softened and brightened and, when he pulled away long enough for them both to catch their breath, he found the same awe and disbelief he was feeling reflected on her face.

"I'm thinking maybe I should have done that a lot sooner," he murmured.

"I'd have been all right with that," Claire whispered. She hesitated, then continued. "You do realize this is going to complicate things. Not just with you and me. But with Lindie."

He nodded. Oh, he knew, and he wondered if his nosy little munchkin had been watching every move they made, all the while her mind was filling with possibilities and promises Sully wasn't sure any of them should be making. "It might be best to distract ourselves. And her."

Claire arched a brow. "Have something in mind?"

"I might." He released her, dropped his hand from her face, but only so far as to cover one of hers and entwine their fingers. "How do you feel about fried clams?"

"Love them. Especially at The Clam—"

"House?" Sully finished her thought. "See? We're on the same track already. Lindie loves their chowder. How about we grab her and go get dinner."

He saw the doubt cross over her like a shadow. Doubt, worry, and hope. All the things he was trying to process himself. It didn't matter that he didn't want to feel this way again, that the idea of falling in love a second time terrified him to the point of paralysis, but it seemed life had other ideas. Perhaps for both him *and* Lindie. "It's just dinner, Claire."

"I know." She nodded and dipped her head. "And a girl's gotta eat. Just dinner."

He unwound their fingers to push himself to his feet, turned and held out both his hands.

When he pulled her up, she stumbled into him, braced her hands on his shoulders and held on. "Sully?"

"I know." He caught a strand of her hair, moved it behind her ear and pressed his lips gently against hers. He was scared, too. But for now?

He didn't care. He was done with overthinking his every move.

4

"*I* am in so much trouble."

"We figured." Jazzy settled into the corner of Claire's sofa with Caleb kicking in his carrier. The little guy was fighting exhaustion, his big dark eyes drooping against the pull of night. Claire knew exactly how the three-month-old felt. She hadn't slept a wink last night; how could she when Sully was the only thing spinning in her head.

Sully and his magic mouth. Sully and his soft touch. Sully and his wide-open heart of understanding and.... Claire groaned and dropped onto the arm of the sofa, pinching the bridge of her nose. "What am I doing? I can't get involved with him!"

"See, this is where you lose me." Leah, sitting on the floor on the other side of the coffee table, moved to refill their wine glasses. Jazzy held up her hand to refuse. Instead, she rubbed her stomach for a short moment, then plucked up a handful of chocolate-covered espresso beans—one of Leah's staples for their "bookclub" meetings—and tossed them into her mouth. "Why can't you get involved with Sully, exactly?"

"That would be my question." Paige leaned back and stretched out her legs. "Seems like a perfect match from where we're sitting, Claire."

"What she said," Jazzy added.

Caleb let out a grunt that was in clear agreement as well.

"What if it doesn't work out? We're so different. He's so…and I'm so…" She tossed up her hands. "And then there's Lindie. I don't want her getting hurt if Sully and I don't—"

"Okay, stop." Leah picked up a bread stick and used it as a pointer. "First of all, you two aren't so different. He's dedicated to the welfare of children, like you, even if he's only in charge of one child." The others nodded.

"And Lindie's crazy about both of you," Jazzy tossed in. "Aren't you the one who's always telling us we should take risks?"

"It's a lot easier to say when it's about someone else." She looked pointedly at Caleb. "And I wouldn't exactly call him a risk."

"Nor would I," Jazzy agreed. "We've got your back in this, Claire. Just like you've always had ours. We aren't going anywhere. But if you're waiting for us to agree with you and say you should walk away from even the possibility of being happy—"

"What if he wants more kids?"

"Shouldn't you two maybe go on a real date before you start worrying about filling up the empty bedrooms?" Leah asked. "Seriously, why are you getting ahead of yourself? You always do this—look for the problems before they appear. And you always assume someone won't take you as you are."

Claire bristled. Leah wasn't wrong. Over the years, she had found excuse after excuse not to explore potential relationships with men; it was just easier to stave off heartbreak before the possibility even presented itself. Only with Sully…her heart had been invested long before last night on the beach.

"If you ask me," Paige added, "and, for the record you did because we're all here, and for 'bookclub,' research purposes," she air-quoted their code for Defcon Five girlfriend emergencies, "you do owe it to us to confirm, once and for all, just how good a kisser Sully Vaughn really is."

"Lord." Claire rolled her eyes and slid to the floor behind Caleb. "Really?"

Leah snort-laughed then sipped her wine. "Oh, yeah. Vicarious existence is the only thing getting me through at this point. Spill, Claire. Was it as good as you'd imagined?"

There wasn't anything about Sully Vaughn Claire wouldn't qualify as good. From his abilities and devotion as a father, to his talent as a salesman and negotiator, right down to his melt-her-into-her-toes kissing.

"Sadly? He's better." Claire's cheeks went hot as her friends giggled and cheered. "But that doesn't mean anything!"

"Oh, honey." Paige scooted closer and grabbed hold of Claire's trembling hand. "I'm sorry to break it to you, but it pretty much means everything." She let go and shoved to her feet, brushed off the back of her jeans. "Something tells me tonight is just getting started. Who's turn is it to order pizza?"

"Mine," Claire grumbled and leaned over for her phone. "I guess I get to pay for the privilege of your support this evening."

Leah toasted them all with her wine. "Works for me. Now hurry up and order." She slapped her hand on the table and made Caleb jump. "We need details."

"And then, do you know what, Daddy.... Daddy?.... Daddy, are you listening to me?" Lindie jumped in front of Sully and waved her hands in front of his face. "Dad-dyyyyy."

"Right here." He shifted her to the side so he could look at his laptop. "I'm listening. What happened next?"

Lindie huffed out a breath and dropped onto the edge of the coffee table.

"No sitting on the table, you know better." He patted the seat of the sofa next to him. "You'd better tell me what happened next so I'm not in suspense."

"It's not funny anymore." Lindie wedged herself into the corner of the sofa, her too-small pink pajamas clashing against the turquoise fabric of the furniture. "What are you doing?"

"Research for a new job." If he took it, he'd have to be gone overnight, but if he pulled it off, he'd have more than enough money in the bank to give them options. Options he needed to seriously consider moving forward.

"Daddy?"

"Hmmmm?"

35

"Remember how you always said I should talk to Mama if I wanted to?"

Lindie's question broke through his focus. "I do." He looked at his daughter. "I know your mother would always be there to listen when I couldn't be." He'd been home the last day and a half. What had he missed? "Something bothering you?"

Her mouth twisted and she plucked at a thread on her pajama pants. "I asked Mama if she'd be mad that I wanted a new Mama."

Well. Sully closed his laptop. That hadn't taken long. "Is this about Miss Claire?"

"Maybe." Lindie continued to look uncertain. "I didn't tell Miss Claire the truth the other day."

"About what?" Sully sat back, put all his attention on Lindie.

"When I said I wanted to hire her to take care of me." She lifted her big eyes to Sully's. "I really wanted to hire her to be my Mama. So I could go to the carnival for real. All my friends go with their Moms, and Cindy Callington and Jenny Fuller…they each get *two* mamas! So I thought maybe I could go with Miss Claire and that she'd be my Mama after."

The inner workings of his child's mind should not surprise him. "But you didn't tell Miss Claire that that's what you wanted."

"Uh-uh. That was bad, wasn't it?"

"It wasn't good," Sully said, his mind racing to find the right words. "You know, it's not nice to put your expectations on others without telling them what they are. It's not fair."

"I know." If she stuck her lower lip out any further, he'd be able to step on it. "But the carnival is so far away and I wanted to make sure I found one. I think Mama would be okay with me having another mama, wouldn't she? She'd still love me from heaven, right?"

"Your mother will always love you." Sully slipped his arm out and around her, pulled her in close. "But you know what? I don't think we should count on Claire being your Mama, Lindie. You know she has a pretty full life, being a teacher and everything."

"But she's helped take care of me this week. And she said she liked spending time with me."

"I know." That fear he'd been pushing aside bubbled up to full percolation. "I know, Lindie, and I've liked spending time with her, too."

"Is that why you kissed her?"

Yeah, he'd figured she'd seen. "Adults who like each other sometimes kiss each other."

"So you like Miss Claire?"

"I like her very much." Too much for his own comfort. Too much for any of their own good. "But I don't think either of us should be making plans for her. I think we all need to be honest with each other." He needed to decide, once and for all, where his and Lindie's future would be.

"So I need to tell Miss Claire I really meant to hire her to be my Mama?"

"What do you think?"

"I don't think she'd mind." Lindie beamed. "I think she would *like* to be my mama."

Sully didn't disagree. And that was part of the problem. There wasn't any doubt Claire loved his daughter, but he did doubt his own feelings. He wasn't sure he was capable of giving her what she needed—his heart. He wasn't sure he had one to give anymore. And that wouldn't be fair to any of them.

He still loved Sarah. How could he not when he had a physical manifestation of that love staring him in the eyes at this very minute?

No. His original instincts had been right. At some point, Lindie would be grown and gone and then what would Claire have but an empty shell of a man who couldn't move beyond the past?

"I think maybe we each need to have a talk with Miss Claire." The very thought made him anxious. But it had to be done. "An honest one, all right?"

"I guess. And then can we get a puppy?"

She was nothing if not tenacious. "Let's see how things go with Miss Claire first."

"Sully, hi."

Finding Sully standing by her car in the school parking lot Friday afternoon brought a smile to Claire's face and a lightness to her heart she'd been missing. They hadn't seen each other very much since dinner the other evening, and had only passed pleasantries when he picked Lindie up later than usual in the nights following. She'd wondered if he'd been avoiding her—worried about it even—especially after her confab with her friends had left her deciding to throw all her reservations aside and embrace the possibilities where Sully and his daughter were concerned. She'd been so afraid of the chance of being burned, she'd never even lit the candle. That was about to change.

Right now.

"I was hoping to see you." As she approached, he straightened, uncrossed his arms and stepped back so she could access her car. "What brings you by?"

"Did Lindie talk to you today?"

"No, not yet. I left her in the playground for a bit so I could do some catch-up work. I was about to go back and..." She hesitated. "Is something wrong?"

"No. Yes. Maybe." He let out a harsh breath. "I think we need to talk."

"All right." Dread pooled in her stomach as she set her bags in her car. "Do you want to talk here or back at my house?" She had a new cookie recipe she thought Lindie would enjoy making as an after-school treat. "You want to meet me there?"

"No, here's good. It's about the other night. On the beach. You know...." He shoved his hands into his pockets. "The kiss."

"Okay." Whoever this man was, the self-assured, happy-go-lucky charmer she'd come to know and like—a lot—didn't seem to be around today.

"I don't know how quite else to say this, so I'm just going to say it. It shouldn't have happened."

"Oh." The dread dropped to her toes, then wafted back up and circled in her throat. "Oh, sure, yeah, I understand." She gave him a quick smile even as regret and hurt mingled inside her.

"You do?"

"Of course," she replied. "You're not ready." The relief that shone in his eyes had her swallowing tears. How could she fault a man for not being able to move beyond the past, when for years she'd been incapable of embracing her own future? "It's all right, Sully." Because he seemed to need it, she reached out and brushed her fingers over the back of his hand. "You lost a lot when you lost Sarah. I can't push you into something you aren't ready for." No matter how much she might want it for herself.

It hadn't struck her, not until this moment, just how much she cared for him. How much she…. Her breath shuddered. How much she loved him.

"I thought maybe I could do this, that I could somehow try again. I know it sounds stupid. She isn't coming back. That's not what this is about. It's—"

"You're scared." Claire moved in, lifted her hand to his face. "You don't have to be, but that doesn't make it so. I can't make this decision for you, Sully. You have to do what you think is best for yourself and for Lindie."

"You're not angry?"

"No." And because he needed her to, she opened her heart enough to let him go. "No, I'm not angry. But it sounds as if maybe Lindie and I need to have a talk." She swallowed hard. "Would you mind if I drove her home?"

"No, that would be fine. I'm sorry, Claire. I wish—"

She pressed her mouth to his, stopping his words. Instead, she took the moment for what it was: a goodbye. Claire tangled her fingers in the soft hair at the base of his neck, memorizing every moment she spent in his arms; knowing it would have to sustain her for a while to come.

Claire was the one who turned away; the one who walked away toward the playground where she'd find his daughter. So she could say one more goodbye.

"How about we stop for ice cream?" Claire glanced up at Lindie in her rearview mirror, more than a little uneasy at how quiet the little girl had been since they'd left the playground. "I hear they got strawberry today."

"I guess." Lindie shrugged as if the entire world sat on her shoulders. "I talked to my Mama the other night."

"Did you?" Claire wasn't sure she'd ever heard anything so sweet. Or so sad. "What did you tell her?"

"I told her that I'd played a trick on you and that I was sorry."

"A trick?" Claire's fingers tightened around the steering wheel as she turned onto the main road into town. "What kind of trick?"

"It wasn't a mean trick. It was…." She bit her lip. "When I asked you to take care of me, I really wanted you to be my new mama. So I could go to the carnival with you like my friends do. With their Moms. I'm sorry." She blinked and two big tears plopped onto her cheeks. "Please don't be mad at me. Daddy said I had to tell you the truth."

"Lindie." It was all Claire could do not to reach back and offer her hand. "Lindie, it's okay. I'm not mad. What did your Mama say when you told her?"

"Nothing." Lindie looked confused. "She's not here."

"Right." Claire bit the inside of her cheek. Smart little Lindie didn't need anyone humoring her. "You want to know a secret?"

"What?"

"I kind of knew what you were really asking me to do. And I was okay with it."

"You want to be my Mama?"

"I would love to be your mama, Lindie." Tears blurred her vision. "But that isn't something that's going to be possible. Your daddy and I talked about it and for now he's going to be staying closer to home, so you won't need me so much."

"You are mad," Lindie sniffled. "You don't want to see me anymore."

"No, Lindie," Claire swiveled in her seat, looked back at Lindie for a moment. "No, I promise, that's not—"

Lindie screamed.

The world dropped into slow motion.

Claire pivoted back to the windshield just as another car in on-coming traffic swerved out of their own lane and straight into hers. Claire wrenched the wheel to the side, but not in time to avoid clipping the other car. The sound of metal scraping and glass shattering registered the instant before she felt the tires lift off the ground.

5

*S*ully wasn't a drinker by nature. Having a six-year-old to look after tended to have that effect, but with Claire driving Lindie home and needing time to tell her of their decision, and Sully feeling lower than the dirt on his work boot, he figured he'd earned himself at least one wallowing beer.

Tank's Bar & Grill was just that—a great place for a beer, a burger, and a chance to lose himself for a while at least. Hank DeLeon, the bar's owner and main bartender—he ran it with his four brothers—wasn't one to pry, but was always there to lend an ear should it be necessary.

Sully was not, however, in a chatty mood. Breaking things off with Claire before they could even get going was supposed to be the right decision. He was supposed to feel better now, lighter. As if he'd stepped back onto the path his life was meant to take.

Instead, he couldn't help but think he'd lost something just as precious as when he'd lost Sarah all those years ago.

"Where's that Sully smile we're all so fond of?" Marisol, Hank's mother and resident do-everything, know-everyone, get-to-the-bottom-of-things woman, stopped beside him and rested a comforting hand on his shoulder. "Never known you not to be flashing it around here at all the ladies."

"Leave him alone, Ma," Hank said and poured two beers for one of his servers to deliver. "Let the man wallow."

Sully arched a brow. Hank recognized wallowing?

"Never known you to wallow, either," Marisol said as if her son hadn't spoken. "I'm thinking it's a girl that has you down. Let me see. Who could it be? Word is your little Lindie's spending her after-school hours with our lovely art teacher, Claire."

"She's good," Sully said and toasted Hank. "Irritatingly good."

"I'm a mother," Marisol reminded him. "We're *all* good. Turned your head, has she? Just spun you around like a top and set you to whirling. You don't look so happy about it."

"Probably because he's not. Ma, really, come on." Hank's plea fell on deaf ears.

"Don't know what it is with men your age. You included," she added, poking a finger at her son. "None of you can see possibilities when they're dangling right in front of your eyes. That Claire, she's a lovely girl. And she loves your daughter. I see that clear as anything—except maybe that front window. Hand me the cleaner." She leaned over and motioned toward the paper towels behind the counter.

"I've got people to do that, Ma." Still, Hank did as he was told.

"You know what man's greatest enemy is? And by man, I mean actual men," Marisol told them. "Fear. You might not want to admit to it, but it's there and there's nothing that scares you men more than change. If you ask me, it's a darn shame. Letting something like that get in the way of something potentially special."

"Ma, no one said he's walked away from anything like that."

"Please." Marisol rolled her eyes. "His entire face says that." She patted Sully's shoulder. "You'll come around. Might take you some time, but you'll see. There's nothing scarier in this world than loving someone."

"Yes, there is," Sully said. "Losing them."

"Ah." Marisol offered that sympathetic head tilt that always grated on him. "Yes, well. I suppose that's true." She moved off to tackle what she determined to be a dirty front window.

"You aren't obligated to listen to a word she says," Hank pointed out. "I'd say she comes compliments of the house but, what can I do? She's my mother."

"The problem is, she isn't wrong." Hank DeLeon was not an un-burden-your-heart-to-him kind of guy, but his mother was clearly a woman who knew what she saw and wasn't afraid to call it out. And she'd only confirmed what Sully already knew.

Walking away from Claire, even at this early stage, hadn't done him or his heart any good. If anything, it had shown him exactly what he had to lose. And her parting kiss—he groaned. It, and her vulner-ability, had warmed the most grief-stricken depths of his heart. "I need to get home." He could walk the four blocks and hopefully beat Claire and Lindie home, or...

Knowing Claire, she probably took Lindie for ice cream on their way home. He checked his watch. If he was quick, he could probably meet them there and undo the damage he'd inflicted in the school parking lot. The second he made the decision, the heaviness around his heart lifted.

Even if he wasn't ready for forever, he was ready for now. With Claire and Lindie by his side, that might just be enough.

Sirens blared the instant he stepped outside. Lights spinning, a sheriff's patrol car, followed by an EMT vehicle, sped past, ripping down the main street like a tornado. He trailed far behind, keeping an eye on the lights as he made his way to the ice cream parlor.

People poked their heads out of stores, cars slowed to a stop as black smoke circled up and threaded into the sky in the near distance. SeaSweets & Treats was empty save for the server behind the counter. No sign of Claire of Lindie. In fact...

Sully went back outside and searched the street. He didn't see Claire's car.

Something uneasy—something greasy, slick, and all too famil-iar—snaked through him as he lifted his gaze to the smoke. He'd only felt this way once before. It was a feeling he'd prayed he'd never feel again and yet would recognize in an instant.

"Lindie." The instant he said his daughter's name, he lost his air. "Claire." Before he could inhale, before he could think, he started to run.

Claire could not stop shaking. Even with Lindie huddled close at her side and knowing the little girl was all right, she couldn't stop.

"That was scary," Lindie whispered, burrowing into Claire's torso. The first responders on scene had arrived just as Claire had shoved her way out of her car, stumbled around to yank Lindie's door open to haul her into her arms. Now, minutes, hours, what felt almost like days later, the two of them sat on the curb on the side of the road, clinging to one another as onlookers milled about, offering words of comfort. Someone, one of the EMTs, draped a thermal blanket around them.

"My phone," Claire croaked as her mind seemed to snap back to focus. "Lindie, I need you to stay here for just a second, okay? I need to get my purse so I can call your father." She shoved to her feet, ignoring the way her knees wobbled.

She hurried as quickly as she could, keeping an eye on Lindie the entire time. She yanked her purse out of the shattered passenger side window and turned, digging inside for her cell even as she saw the familiar head bobbing over the top of the crowd. "Sully."

"Lindie?" Sully called, shoving through the growing crowd. "Lindie? Claire?"

"It's all right. We're okay. She's okay," she whispered. Sully came to a screeching halt, looked first to Claire, then, when she pointed, to his daughter sitting on the curb. Tears swam into her eyes, blurred her vision as she watched Sully scoop Lindie up off the ground and hold her so tight the little girl cried out.

"Daddy, I'm okay. Claire is hurt."

"I've got you," he murmured as Claire approached. Sully looked at her over Lindie's head, his eyes questioning, and, to her horror, accusing. "What happened?"

"I—" Claire shook her head, let her bag drop to the street. "I don't know. I took my eyes off the road for just a second. I didn't—" she could feel the tears threaten to fall. "I'm so sorry." She glanced back at her car, which was a total write-off, and wondered how on earth either of them had walked away. Nausea rolled in her stomach.

"Ms. Bishop?" One of the EMTs approached her as she swayed. "Ma'am, we want to get you checked out in the ER."

"No, check Lindie, please," she protested.

"We already have, ma'am. Remember? Ms. Bishop, please. You're bleeding."

"I am?" She lifted a hand to her head, to where it throbbed. "Oh. You're right." She frowned. That didn't seem right. Not at all. "Lindie's all right?"

"Just suffering from shock. Like you are. Please." The EMT, who looked as if he'd just graduated from grammar school, took her arm and led her to the back of an ambulance. Sully followed at a distance, still holding Lindie in his arms.

"I just looked away for a second." She couldn't understand it. Lindie had been so upset. She should have pulled the car over, taken the time— "I don't feel very well," she murmured as that rolling got worse. "I think I'm going to be sick." No sooner did she speak the words than she doubled over and threw up.

The next few minutes were a blur. She was poked and prodded and strapped onto a stretcher for transport.

"I want to go with her!" Lindie cried over and over. "Miss Claire. Miss Claire. Daddy, I want to go with her. Mama! Mama!"

Claire sobbed, the combination of fear, adrenaline, and dizziness knocking the sense out of her.

"You're showing classic signs of a concussion, Miss Bishop." The EMT told her as they hefted the stretcher into the ambulance. "We're going to take you in for evaluation."

She didn't have the wherewithal to answer. Even as they closed the doors and locked her in the vehicle, she could still hear Lindie screaming.

Sully struggled to keep a desperate Lindie in his arms. "Daddy, let me go. I want to go with her, Daddy, *please!*"

"We'll go see her at the hospital." Sully struggled to keep his voice calm. Between the mangled wreck that only minutes before his daughter had been in, and the sight of Claire being driven off in an ambulance, he felt as if every connection in his brain had been short-circuited.

"Daddy, I'm sorry. I'm so sorry." Lindie's sobs had him rubbing her back even as she clung to him. "I didn't mean to do it. I'm sorry I hurt Miss Claire."

"Hush, Lin. It's all right." He paced back and forth, keeping his eye on the ambulance as it sped out of sight. "Whatever happened, I'm sure it wasn't your fault."

One of the sheriff's deputies passing him stopped at Sully's comments. "She's okay, right?" A middle-aged woman with short, cropped hair and a steely gaze, her voice carried familiar maternal concern.

"I think so." He was going to take her into the ER just to be sure. "Just scared."

"It was my fault," Lindie cried. "I made her look. I was upset and she looked back and didn't see—"

"Lindie, I'm sure that's not true," Sully said again.

"Lindie? That's a pretty name," the deputy said. "Lindie, I'm Deputy Lydia Fairfield. Is it okay if I tell you something really important?"

Lindie tucked her head under Sully's chin and gave the deputy a slow nod.

"The only person at fault is the other driver, Lindie. He was texting on his phone and wasn't paying attention to his driving."

Sully bit the inside of his cheek to stop from swearing. "See, Lin? This wasn't your fault. You didn't hurt Claire."

"You mean it?" Lindie asked, her lashes spiked with tears. "It wasn't me?"

"It definitely was not you," Deputy Fairfield assured her. "How about you and your dad head to the hospital now to see for yourself. I'm sure they're both going to be fine. Get her checked out, just to be safe," she added to Sully.

"Thanks, deputy," Sully said, wishing he felt more relieved than he did. The truth was, right now he felt as if he'd been thrown in the nightmare of his past. Only this time...

He hugged Lindie tighter.

This time, his future had survived.

"Please tell me I can go home," Claire said to the nurse when she pulled back the curtain to her bed in the ER. "I'm feeling perfectly all right now."

"You're lucky, is what you are," Tammy, who had been watching over her the past few hours, chided gently as she disconnected the IV

46

going into Claire's arm. "Scrapes and bruises and one big gash on the head. I heard that crash was pretty intense."

"You should have been there," Claire tried to joke. All she wanted, all she needed, was to get out of this hospital bed and call Sully, to beg his forgiveness and hope he'd at least let her see Lindie so she could know for certain the little girl was okay. "Honestly, I just want to go home."

"So I should tell your visitors to go away?"

"Visitors?" Claire's heart skipped a beat. Had Leah or Paige or Jazzy—

"Miss Claire!" Lindie exploded into the space in front of her, and she would have pounced right up onto the bed if Sully hadn't caught his daughter midair. "Miss Claire, we've been waiting forever and ever to see you." She leaned over and nearly fell out of Sully's arms. "Are you all right? They took you away so fast!"

Had she been standing, her legs wouldn't have held her. She reached out her arms, sent a questioning look to Sully who immediately moved in so Lindie could wrap around Claire like a barnacle. The instant she held her in her arms, her entire body reset. The trembling set in again, and she couldn't stop the tears. How could she have been so careless? She'd almost gotten her killed!

"I'm so sorry," she whispered as she stroked Lindie's hair. "Sully, I'm…" her voice broke. "I didn't—"

"It wasn't your fault," Sully said. At her dubious expression, he continued, "I heard it from the deputy myself. The other driver was texting. Lost control of the car. He's fine, by the way. Of course."

That didn't make her cling to Lindie any less fiercely.

"I think you can go home with your family now," Tammy said as she gathered Claire's belongings. "Something tells me you'll be in good hands."

"Oh, no, it's not like that betw—"

"Yes, she will," Sully interrupted. "Come on, Lin. Let's get Claire out to the car and home, all right?"

It wasn't until they pulled into Sully and Lindie's driveway that Claire realized where they'd been headed. "I called Leah," Sully explained. "Told her what happened. She's going to stop by your house and pick up a few things so you can stay here."

She blinked at the simple little bungalow with a big white rocking chair on the front porch and sea glass windchimes hanging from the eaves.

"We have a small guest room," Sully said. "The doctor suggested having someone check on you through the night, just to be safe. Since I don't think Friday is up to the job, we'll take it on—right, Lindie?"

"Right. I have to clean my room so you can see it!" Lindie announced and bounded out of the car.

"Resilience belongs to the young," Claire murmured.

"It's definitely going to take me some time to get the image of your car out of my head."

"I just looked away for a second. Lindie was so upset. She thought I was mad at her for not telling me she wanted me to be her mom." Tears burned again. "I would have never forgiven myself if something had happened to her."

"But nothing did. She's fine," Sully said and reached over to take her hand. "And so are you. Something I am very, very grateful for. Wait—I'll come around."

It was on the tip of her tongue to tell him she was fine, that she could get out of the car all by herself, but in the blink of an eye her door was open and he was helping her out, picking her up, and nestling her into his arms. She tried not to gasp at the thrill their closeness gave her. The warmth that coursed through her body. Their little house was fitting, she thought as she tried to settle a whirlwind of emotions, with its simple décor and practical furnishings. She saw endless pictures of father and daughter together, as well as numerous framed photos of Lindie and Sully with a woman who had to be Sarah.

Sarah Vaughn, who was the spitting image of her daughter.

Sully got her settled on the sofa, and even draped a blanket over her lap as if tucking her into bed for the night.

"Sully, you don't have to fuss. And honestly, I'll be just fine on my own."

"Humor me. It gives me a chance to figure out how to tell you I was wrong." He stood over her, his handsome face somewhat strained beneath the lamplight. When he spoke again, he sat on the edge of the coffee table and reached for her hands. "You scared me, Claire."

"I know." She bit her lip. "I was stupid and careless—"

"Not that—and no, you weren't. It was an accident. On your part, anyway," he added as he squeezed her hands. "You scared me because I realized that in a few short minutes you could have been gone forever. I don't want to lose you, not while I have the choice." His gaze devoured her, shone with the stirrings of love. "None of us can say what'll happen tomorrow, but all I know right now is that I care about you. A lot. And I'd really, really like to see where this goes.... If you'll give me another chance?" The hope in his voice, in his eyes, had her blinking back a new rush of tears.

"Stupid emotions are all over the place," Claire said on a laugh as she swiped at her damp cheeks. "I care about you, too, Sully." It was too early, she knew, to say the words she already felt in her soul. But soon he'd be ready to hear them and she'd be shouting them from the tallest spire in Sea Glass Bay. "I'd love to see where this goes."

"Daddy! You're not supposed to sit on the coffee table, remember?" Lindie stood in the doorway, hands planted on her hips, that determined, irritated look on her face that lightened Claire's heart. "Can I show Miss Claire my room now?"

"How about later?" Sully suggested. "Instead, why don't you go grab one of your favorite books and you two can read while I get dinner together."

"You cook?" Claire didn't know why she was surprised, but she was.

"Daddy is the best cook in the world!" Lindie declared as she raced back to her room. "He can make anything and he hardly ever burns it."

"Do tell," Claire laughed. "What's on the menu for tonight?"

"Friday is pizza night in our house. It's kind of a family tradition." He bent down and brushed his mouth against hers. "That okay with you?"

Traditions...

Family.

She reached up and caught his face between her hands, held his mouth to hers for a breath of a moment. "That sounds absolutely perfect."

Father Wanted

by Kayla Perrin

1

*J*azzy Dunbar noticed the sparkle in her friend's eyes as Paige gently rocked three-month-old Caleb, who was sleeping, oblivious to all the excited attention around him. Babies tended to bring out every woman's mothering instinct, whether they knew they had it, or not—and Jazzy was pretty sure that she recognized in Paige's expression the same longing she'd begun feeling a year and a half earlier. That urge to have a child. Though, she doubted Paige would take the path that Jazzy had chosen.

"Isn't he just an angel?" Paige asked, her short auburn hair kissing her cheeks as she looked down at Caleb. "He must be having a happy dream. Look at that little smile, and those dimples!"

"Not that I'm biased or anything, but of course I agree," Jazzy said, watching her son's face twitch with a tiny grin. "The first time he smiled and I caught sight of those dimples…my heart melted."

"He really is the cutest," Claire chimed in, peering at the baby over Paige's shoulder.

"And he has so much hair," Leah commented. Standing beside Paige, she gently stroked some of Caleb's black curly strands. "I can't get over all that thick, dark hair."

Jazzy's three dear friends, Paige, Claire, and Leah, were in her market booth this Saturday morning, cooing and fussing over the baby before they started their own work at their respective booths.

Some people brought their various goods and products to the market to set up for weekend business, but Jazzy was one of the vendors who had an actual storefront downtown in the historic district, so she simply set up her booth in front of her store. Jazz It Up—a play on her name—was a popular spot for her to sell arts and crafts, as well as her handmade bracelets, necklaces, earrings, headpieces and an array of other bedazzled trinkets that women tended to love. She also ran an online business, which had really started to pick up in the last couple of years because people loved the beautiful and colorful sea glass she used in her pieces. All of those unique ocean-tumbled pieces of glass were the reason why the town was called Sea Glass Bay, and a hot tourist attraction in Northern California.

"They grow so quickly," Leah said, throwing a glance toward her son, Owen, who was chasing Lindie in circles around the front of her stall. The two young children would soon be joining Claire at her tent, ArtSea Classes and Creations, which offered hands-on crafts for kids. Owen and Lindie spent much of the day getting their hands dirty completing art projects while their parents worked their booths at the market.

"Impossibly," Jazzy said. "I still remember when Owen was a baby. And now he's four."

"How's the breastfeeding going?" Claire asked.

"Great," Jazzy said. "Honestly, he sleeps like a dream, feeds well, and I'm not having any complications with him nursing. It's like the gods have smiled down on me, knowing that I don't need any extra challenges since I'm already a single mother. And I have the flexibility of bringing him to work with me, at least at this stage, because he's so well-behaved."

"Ah, I remember this stage," Leah said. "Before they can climb out of their playpens and cribs and car seats. Treasure it while it lasts."

"And then they become charming and well-behaved little men, like Owen," Jazzy said, smiling at her friend sweetly. "As long as they have great mothers." She knew that Leah sometimes doubted she was giving Owen all that he needed, being a single mother, too, but Owen was such a great kid—even with the divorce—that obviously she was doing something right. Especially considering his father was way too absorbed with his new high-maintenance girlfriend.

"You're going to be a little heartbreaker, aren't you?" Paige asked Caleb. "Especially with those dimples."

Jazzy exhaled contentedly as she watched Paige hold her son, looking at the life she had created with a sense of awe. She wondered if that awe would ever leave her. Maybe when Caleb was two and had his first temper tantrum, but for now, Jazzy was firmly on cloud nine. Every day since Caleb had been born three months ago, she could hardly believe that he was hers. That she had made this little life.

"You're a natural, Paige," Jazzy commented, noting that she didn't seem to want to let him go this morning.

"Come on, Paige. Let me hold him," Claire urged.

"You sure you are up to it?" Jazzy asked, taking in the half-healed scrapes and bruises on her arms from her recent car accident, and the more concerning gash across her forehead.

Claire's green eyes sparkled with warmth. "I'm fine. Nothing a cuddle with a cute baby can't heal." She turned to Paige, raising her arms and flexing her fingers. "Gimmie!"

"I just get so clucky whenever you are around," Paige said to Caleb. But she turned the baby toward Claire and passed him off.

Claire's eyes widened as a huge grin spread on her face. But Jazzy could also see the wistfulness in her eyes, and she knew that came from Claire's lack of ability to bear children. At least now that she was dating Sully, who'd *finally* declared his feelings after almost losing Claire and his daughter in a head-on collision with an irresponsible driver, she had become a surrogate mom to the adorable Lindie. Sometimes motherhood didn't pan out exactly as you planned. Something Jazzy knew all too well.

Claire touched Caleb's enclosed fist, and he opened up his hand and wrapped it around her finger. "Awwww! If he isn't the most precious little thing *ever!* And you know what I really love?"

"What?" Jazzy asked.

"He has that new baby smell."

"Ah, yes," Jazzy agreed, sighing happily. Caleb was perfect. And he was hers.

Leah crossed her arms over her chest and met Jazzy's gaze head on. Jazzy knew that a serious question was about to follow. "How are things with Jeremiah?"

"Actually, he's been great," Jazzy said. "I told you guys not to worry, didn't I? And I was right. He's a good guy. Totally okay with doing this on my terms."

"Just because a guy seems nice and agreeable doesn't mean things will go smoothly when you make an arrangement like…like this," Leah said, gesturing to baby Caleb.

Jazzy knew that her friends thought she'd been crazy when she'd first considered the idea of becoming a single mother. A *planned* single mother. It was a longing that had started after the death of her own mother a year and a half earlier, and the strong woman who had raised Jasmine Alexis Dunbar without a man and loads of love had proven to Jazzy that men weren't required to raise happy children. And without any viable prospects at all, Jazzy had had to find a way to reconcile her biological clock, which had been ticking on steroids. It was the sperm bank, or find a friend who'd be happy to father a child with her—on her terms.

Leah had tried to tell her that being a single mother wasn't as easy as it might seem, but obviously Leah was speaking as someone who'd had her life pulled out from under her when her husband Charlie had decided to trade her in for a new model. The scoundrel.

Jazzy's plan had been to avoid all of that drama by finding just the right friend, making an agreement, and moving forward without hot-headed emotions.

That man had been Jeremiah. Hard-working, dependable—and uninterested in a relationship.

"He answers all my calls, takes Caleb when I need a break, and sometimes he'll bring me lunch when he knows I'm here with Caleb, so I don't have to leave the shop. Can you imagine him doing that if he were my ex?" Jazzy asked.

"Nope," Leah agreed.

"You're forgetting an option," Paige said.

"Oh?" Jazzy asked.

"Who's to say he'd be your ex? He could be doing all that as your *partner*. There are many happy relationships."

"I know there are many people who fall in love and have fairy-tale relationships," Jazzy said. "But I've just never been lucky in love. And when the love dies, there's often so much ugliness. I don't want Caleb caught up in any of that drama. I figured a civilized agreement makes much more sense."

Leah shrugged, clearly wanting to say more but biting her tongue.

It was just as well. Jazzy had already made her decision. This was the way she wanted things. She had never known her father because he had left for greener pastures when she'd been a baby. Over the years they'd had a few conversations, but nothing significant. Then there was the man she'd been dumb enough to marry in her twenties—he'd expected her to be faithful while he had continued to play the field. And while her mother hadn't dated often over the years, there were times she had heard the arguments between her mother and various boyfriends, heard the tears when neglect or cheating or other bad behavior sent the relationship into a tailspin.

No, the examples in her life of men who stuck around and did the right thing were pretty much nonexistent.

Jazzy wanted none of that in her life. She was thirty-one, had her business, and now she had her baby.

"No matter the circumstances of how he came to be," Paige began, "we're all glad that Caleb is here. You wanted a baby, and now you have one. I just think that…maybe you could have it all."

"Has Jeremiah signed the paperwork you asked him to?" Leah asked.

Leah—once again injecting that realism. Jazzy's stomach twisted, thinking of how this was a conversation she did *not* want to have with Jeremiah.

"He said he will," Jazzy told her, but the truth was, she hadn't fully explained to him all she wanted. Just that she'd like them to have a sit down and go over some details in terms of raising Caleb.

She wanted to officially be the parent with sole custody, legally— but she worried this might be a sticky issue. She would never keep Caleb from his father, but she wanted to be the one to make the final decisions if they had a disagreement over an issue.

Leah shrugged. "It's kind of a catch-22, isn't it? If he happily signs over his parental rights, that would kind of worry me. And yet, you want control. Trust me, there are days I wish I had total control and didn't have to hear Charlie's opinions on how I'm raising Owen." Leah forced a smile. "It's complicated."

Caleb started to fuss, and Jazzy shot toward him the way she did every time her baby cried. She knew that some women felt helpless at the sound of that pained little cry, but she felt like a superhero heading in to save the day. She especially loved the sense of satisfaction that came when she took her baby in her arms, his eyes settled on her face, and his cries began to subside because he knew he was with his mommy.

She took him from Claire and began to gently sway him. "You're okay, sweetie," Jazzy cooed. "Mommy's here." As Caleb's fussing waned, Jazzy's heart filled with warmth. "That's my boy."

Leah beamed at her. "The mother's magic touch. It never fails."

"As much as I'd love to stay here and marvel at Caleb's cuteness all day, I'd better get to my booth," Paige said.

"Me too," Leah and Claire echoed in unison.

"If you need a break for a moment, just bring Caleb over," Claire said. "I've noticed that babies are good for business."

"I've noticed that, too," Jazzy said.

As the women began to exit the door at the back of her booth, a male voice said, "Delivery for Jazzy Dunbar."

Slowly, Jazzy turned. It was Jeremiah, making his presence known. Jazzy's eyes lit up when she saw his handsome face, which had grown a sheen of stubble since she'd seen him last two days ago. It matched his low-cropped hair. She let her eyes wander over his body, with his faded blue jeans and steel-toed boots. He was hunched into his light black jacket against the morning chill.

"Good morning." Jeremiah grinned at her, then placed a tray with two coffee cups and a brown paper bag onto the counter.

"Jeremiah!" she enthused, walking toward the front of the booth, holding their son.

The other women rounded the front of the stall from the back, all of them instantly smiling when they saw Jeremiah.

"Good to see you again, Jeremiah,"

"Back working on the pier today, I see."

"Your son is just the cutest."

The women talked over each other, and after they settled, Jeremiah said, "Good to see you, ladies. Yes, I'm back at the pier. I'll be busy here over the spring and summer. And as for my son, I agree—absolutely the cutest boy in the world."

"You have a good day now," Claire said.

"You too," Jeremiah echoed. Then the rest of the women said their goodbyes and they went off in the direction of their own booths.

Paige, however, turned and gave Jazzy a look over her shoulder before walking away. Jazzy understood the look fully. Paige thought Jeremiah was a good catch, and believed the two of them could have a happy relationship.

And there's the rub. Jeremiah *was* a good catch. That was never in doubt and, in fact, was the whole reason she'd chosen him as father material. They'd both been burned badly before and they had a solid friendship that was at the root of their joint parenthood. Neither wanted to ruin a good thing by getting romantically involved.

"How are you?" Jazzy asked, turning her attention to Jeremiah once the women were gone. "I didn't see you yesterday."

"There was an emergency," he explained. "I had to go to a customer's house to address an issue with their recently installed boat lift."

"Nothing too serious, I hope," Jazzy said.

"Nothing a day's work couldn't solve." He paused. "Did you miss me?"

"You know I always like seeing you," Jazzy told him.

"I hope you haven't eaten yet. I brought you a coffee and an egg and cheese English muffin."

"You know that wasn't necessary," she told him.

Jeremiah waved a dismissive hand. "It was also no problem. I figure you were probably busy getting ready to head here with Caleb. You say you rarely stop to eat."

He remembered. She'd noticed that about him. He remembered some of the little things she told him. "Do you want to hold your son?"

"You know I do."

"Let me come around to you," Jazzy said. She headed to the door at the back of her booth and exited. Jeremiah met her halfway, already having lowered his bag of supplies to the ground.

As she handed their son to him, his face lit up in a smile. Everyone's did when they held babies, but there was something special about seeing a big, strong man like Jeremiah become all gushy and smiles as he secured his baby in his arms. It was exactly what she wanted in a father, a man who was excited to be a dad.

Her hands brushed against his before she pulled her arms away from their son, and not for the first time, Jazzy felt a spark of something. Not that she should be surprised—of course she found Jeremiah sexy. It had made sleeping with him to get pregnant so easy. But more than just being sexy, he was a decent guy with a strong moral base. The kind of qualities she wanted in their child. So yes, in so many ways Jeremiah was the perfect partner as well as role model. But they had both agreed that they would be just friends who parented together.

After achieving her goal—which was to get pregnant and deliver a healthy baby—Jazzy figured that she would be so focused on being a mom and busy with all that entailed, that any feelings of desire for Jeremiah would subside back to friendship.

Instead, as she looked at him with his aviator sunglasses and low-cropped hair and that new sheen of stubble that was perfectly groomed, she saw a man who could go from rugged to Hollywood handsome at the snap of a finger. How was that possible?

"Who's my big boy?" Jeremiah asked. At the sound of his father's voice, Caleb's eyelids fluttered open. He stared up at Jeremiah, and then he yawned. He didn't fuss, just looked up at his daddy as he held him.

Jazzy couldn't help it, her heart melted a little. "That's the first time he's opened his eyes for anyone other than me, and everyone was fussing over him not too long ago."

"I guess he knows his father's voice," Jeremiah said with a sense of pride.

As Jazzy let them have their moment, her mind wandered back to the five weeks of unbridled sex she'd had with Jeremiah. When she had made the decision to become a single mother and had resolved that he would be the father, she had invited him over for a friendly dinner, served a bottle of wine of which she'd drank too much, and then she'd boldly blurted out the fact that she wanted to have a baby and wanted him to be the father. Jeremiah's eyes had widened—and then he'd started to laugh, clearly assuming that she had been joking.

Or crazy.

Jazzy then went on to explain that she thought he would be a perfect dad, that they could parent together as friends without any emotional drama. When Jeremiah had started to realize that she wasn't joking, Jazzy had slipped onto his lap and started kissing him, her courage fueled by her intake of wine.

It had been a pathetic way to broach the subject, and of course they didn't have sex that night because Jeremiah was too much of a gentleman to take advantage of a tipsy Jazzy. And no doubt he had been completely floored by her suggestion. But Jazzy had continued to press the idea over the next few weeks, and ultimately Jeremiah had acquiesced. Maybe it was the offer of no-strings-attached sex, but ultimately he had agreed with her. That they could do this because they liked and respected each other, got along well, and neither had any romantic prospects. As long as they could keep the arrangement civil, Jeremiah was game.

The sex had been better than Jazzy had expected, and even though she had planned to only engage in sex with him when the ovulation predictor said it was time, she had shamelessly invited him over more often, telling him that they may as well try as hard as they could for the time being. It had been a long time since Jazzy had been intimate with a man, so why settle for once or twice? It took six times before the pregnancy tests, all seven of them, showed that she was with child. One of the happiest moments in her life.

"Remember, my mom's coming to town on Monday through the weekend," Jeremiah said, interrupting her thoughts.

"I remember," Jazzy said, already feeling a little wistful at the idea of being separated from Caleb for a night. But she had a Wednesday night event with her friend Lauren, and it was perfect timing that Caleb could stay with his father and grandmother. She would look forward to coming home and slipping off her sexy shoes and sinking into her mattress to sleep through the night with no interruptions.

"My mom was hoping we could all have dinner Wednesday night."

"All of us?" Jazzy asked, her eyes shooting upward to meet his.

"Yeah."

"That's the night of my friend's event," Jazzy said. "The one on Gavin's boat."

61

"Oh, that's right. Then we can do it on Tuesday. My mom has plans for later in the week, so if Tuesday works for you, that'd be great for us."

"Sure," Jazzy said. "Tuesday will work."

Jeremiah eased toward Jazzy, offering her Caleb, who was happily sucking on his pacifier. "Time for you to go back to your mother, big guy."

Jazzy smirked as she took Caleb into her arms. "Big guy? He's only three months old."

"I know, but remember when he was just born? How tiny he was? He's grown so much. In the face. His cheeks. He's the spitting image of me when I was a baby."

Jazzy had seen the pictures and knew that to be true. "Well, he's going to grow up to be a very good-looking man."

Jeremiah's eyes flitted to hers, and realizing she may have sounded like she was flirting, Jazzy quickly glanced away. Then she said, "Your mother…. She knows that this is an arrangement, right? I mean, I know she knows, but a lot of people hope…"

"She knows this is an arrangement," Jeremiah agreed. "You're Caleb's mother, which makes us a family, whether or not it's a traditional family. So she'd like to see you as well since you're part of the family."

Jazzy nodded. It wasn't too much to ask. She could get together with Jeremiah and his mother, have a nice dinner. She wanted Caleb to have a good relationship with his only grandmother.

"Sounds good," Jazzy said. "I can close up my shop an hour earlier, at five, so realistically by the time I head home and get ready, six-thirty should be a good time for dinner. A bit late, but—"

"Six-thirty works for me. It's just a casual family dinner. Any time we get together, my mom will be happy."

Jazzy nodded. "I'm looking forward to it."

Caleb made a little cooing sound as he spit out his pacifier, and Jeremiah softly stroked his son's cheek. There was a look of awe in Jeremiah's eyes, and Jazzy knew that he was marveling at the fact that the two of them had created this absolute little treasure.

She couldn't ask for anything more. Her life was complete.

2

"And he's started this little thing with his tongue, where he kind of flicks it against his bottom lip, making the cutest little sound. And he's definitely trying to start turning over. He's not quite there yet, but he's starting to rock his body back and forth." Jazzy flattened the napkin she'd been playing with onto the table. "Listen to me, going on and on about Caleb."

"It's fine," Lauren said. "I like hearing about my godson. In fact, I thought you were going to bring him."

"Jeremiah wanted to take him for an evening walk in the park," Jazzy explained. "And that worked for me so we could have an adult dinner." She snagged one of the cauliflower wings with a fork and popped it into her mouth.

"But you still miss him, if the way you keep checking your phone is any indication." Lauren smiled sweetly as she lifted her glass of white wine.

It was Sunday evening, and Lauren, one of Jazzy's best friends from high school, was back in town after a recent trip, so Jazzy had regretfully bowed out of her usual wine and whine post-market get-together with Paige, Claire, and Leah at The Tipsy Table, to catch up with her longtime pal. Tall, thin, with flawless caramel-colored skin, Lauren worked as a model. Her photos graced the pages of many magazines, and she traveled for commercials and photoshoots all around the world.

Lauren had been there for Jazzy through most of the major events in her life, including her whirlwind romance with Chris that had ended in disaster and divorce, her struggles getting her business up and running, and losing her mother. So of course Lauren had also been there for her when Jazzy had made the seemingly crazy decision to become a single mother.

"Tell me about your recent trip," Jazzy said. "Those photos from Greece blew my mind. That red dress on you in that photo shoot was *stunning*."

Lauren and two other models had been perched atop a yacht in colorful dresses that were incredibly long and flowed in voluminous waves as the wind hit them. The photos had been sexy and sensual and absolutely gorgeous.

"And it was so much fun, Jazzy. I wish you were with me."

"I live vicariously through all of your fabulous pics on social media."

"We should plan a trip somewhere," Lauren said. "I'd happily go back to Santorini. We could tour the Greek isles. Or we could do Italy. Rome, Milan, Tuscany…"

Lauren had such an exciting life. "You wouldn't want me travelling with a baby."

"You can leave him with his father, can't you? I'm sure Jeremiah would be happy to take care of him."

"I…I suppose I could." Jazzy fiddled with the food on her plate. She'd barely eaten a few bites of the spicy cauliflower wings, her stomach feeling a bit unsettled. "But that might be a lot to ask. He's never taken care of Caleb for more than a couple of days."

"Caleb will be fine with his daddy," Lauren said, and Jazzy knew that her friend was right. She also knew that Lauren didn't understand the pull of the maternal connection, not with the glamorous and jet-setting life she led. The very idea of leaving Caleb for more than a couple of days made Jazzy anxious. How could she possibly enjoy any trip when she'd be worrying about Caleb every minute of the day?

"We can think about it for some time down the road," Jazzy told her friend, not sure if "down the road" would be anytime soon. "Maybe early next year, when Caleb will be a little bigger and business here is slow. And I should be done with breastfeeding, so I can enjoy lots of wine."

Lauren, who had just put a forkful of her chicken Caesar salad into her mouth, nodded enthusiastically and raised her glass of wine in agreement.

Jazzy raised the glass of lemonade she was drinking. She did miss wine. She couldn't wait until she could pour herself a large glass of Riesling.

"At least we'll have fun on the yacht Wednesday night," Lauren said, her eyes lighting up. "Thank you for agreeing to be my plus one."

"Of course! How often do I get the chance to be part of a designer's fashion cruise? I'm excited."

Suddenly, Lauren produced a decorative gift bag from beneath the table. "Here," she said, passing it to Jazzy.

"What's this?"

"Two dresses. I brought them home from my recent trip. Personally, I think the black one will look amazing on you for the fashion cruise."

Jazzy glanced into the bag, seeing red and black. "You're so sweet, Lauren. You didn't have to do that."

Lauren shrugged. "One of these days, we'll head to Milan and do some shopping together. There are a couple of outfits for Caleb in there too."

Jazzy's cell made a short musical sound, indicating that she'd received a text. Seeing that the notification was from Jeremiah, she abandoned the gift bag quickly opened up her phone. A moment later, she saw that Jeremiah had sent a photo of himself and Caleb in the park. Caleb's back pressed to his father's chest in the body carrier, both were facing the camera for a selfie. Jeremiah was leaning his head down toward his son's, and Caleb was wide awake and looking perfectly at the camera lens, just like his daddy was.

"Oh, this is such a cute picture," Jazzy exclaimed. "And Caleb's doing that thing with his tongue I was telling you about." Jazzy held up her phone and extended it to Lauren. "See how he sticks his tongue out like that."

"He's adorable," Lauren stated. "And his father is looking quite adorable as well! I like that look on him, that lowly-shaved beard."

Lauren quickly met Jazzy's eyes. "You two are remaining strictly platonic?"

"There's been no sex since I got pregnant," Jazzy said, the words sounding like an accomplishment. When Lauren's face twisted with skepticism, Jazzy continued. "You know I would have told you if there was anything going on. There isn't—but that was the whole point. No relationship, no drama. Just the two of us doing our best to raise Caleb as friends."

One of Lauren's perfectly sculpted eyebrows shot up. "You're not tempted? I mean, look at him."

Jazzy's face flushed. She had been looking at Jeremiah a lot lately—seeing him as attractive and desirable. Strong and dependable. And she'd had the *what if* thoughts. There were times she craved a man's touch, and it would be so easy to go there with him again.

"I didn't say that I wasn't tempted," Jazzy admitted. "But we know the boundaries of our relationship and there's a line I'm not going to cross. Imagine he starts scratching that itch for me, and then things fall apart between us. Seeing each other when we have to deal with Caleb will be completely awkward, or even worse." Jazzy reached for another cauliflower wing, but thought better of it and instead picked up her glass of lemonade and took a large sip.

"You're barely eating," Lauren commented.

"I know. I'm not so hungry." Her appetite had been a bit off over the last week or so. "But these are so good, I'm going to have the waitress pack them up for me to go."

"Send me that picture of Caleb and Jeremiah," Lauren said.

"Of course." Jazzy opened up her phone, and moments later sent off the photo.

As Lauren opened up the text and accessed the photo, she said, "I don't know how you restrain yourself. If I had a guy like that in my life on a regular basis, I wouldn't be single."

"You're all talk and you know it," Jazzy said, chuckling. Lauren didn't allot any time for serious dating, not with her busy schedule. "Trust me, no matter how tempted I might be at times, I'm not going to cross that line. Jeremiah and I have an arrangement that works, and I'm not going to ruin it."

3

"*You*'re going to love my dress," Jazzy said into the phone, speaking to Paige who was on the other line. "My friend Lauren came back from one of her modeling trips a couple of days ago and she brought me two gorgeous dresses that she got from some designer in Italy. She *gave* them to me last night. I think she wanted to make sure I had something decent to wear for the fashion cruise," she added with a hint of humor.

"Ahhh, so that is why you bailed on us at The Tipsy Table," Paige teased. "You know you always look great, Jazzy."

"Thank you, but I'm no model. I think I'll wear the black one for the fashion cruise, and the red one for your Aunt Trudy's birthday bash." Paige's aunt was turning seventy, and the weekend before Mother's Day they were going to have a sunset cruise on Gavin's yacht to celebrate her milestone birthday.

"Ooh, red. Sexy! Send me a pic?"

"Actually, I think I'll reveal it to everyone at the party," Jazzy said. "Make a grand entrance. Pretend for a moment that I'm a model."

"I don't want to wait two weeks to see your dress!" Paige complained. "I'll drop by your townhouse…"

"I'll send you a picture," Jazzy said, and chuckled. "You can tell me which of my jewelry pieces are best to accessorize it. I have some beautiful red sea glass I just collected. Maybe I'll make something new." Jazzy was looking forward to Aunt Trudy's party and the fashion cruise. She hadn't had a glamourous night out in so long, and now she had two events in one month where she would get to play dress up.

"Hey, gotta go," Paige said. "Aunt Trudy's ears must have been burning. She's calling."

"Ok, talk to you later," Jazzy said. She ended the call, then wandered to her shop's front window and looked out at the street. There wasn't much foot traffic, but that wasn't unusual for a Monday. The downtime gave her the opportunity to package up her online sales.

She wondered if Jeremiah's mother had already landed.

Jeremiah had told her that the dinner would be at his home, and that his mother would be doing the cooking. Jazzy wanted to contribute to the meal by baking something for the occasion, and the one thing she knew how to master was an apple crumble. If she got all of the ingredients together and put the dish in the fridge tonight, she could pop the crumble into the oven when she got home from work tomorrow evening so that it would be freshly baked.

When Jazzy saw the familiar head of pink hair heading down the street, and then the stroller, her eyes lit up. Raelyn had arrived with Caleb. Jazzy waved enthusiastically through the window.

With business being slower today, Jazzy had texted Raelyn and asked her to come by with Caleb. Raelyn could use a lunch break, and Jazzy would take Caleb for a walk along the pier and visit Jeremiah. Not only was Raelyn a great sitter, but she was also happy to fill in at the shop or booth when necessary. She was going to eat her lunch in the store and take care of any sales while Jazzy took Caleb on the walk.

"My baby," Jazzy said, looking down at her son as she held the door open for Raelyn to push the stroller into the shop. Seeing his mom, Caleb smiled and warmth filled Jazzy's chest.

Raelyn placed a chocolate bar and a bottle of water on the counter. "Is that your lunch?" Jazzy asked her. "Please let me buy you something more substantial."

"I had a grilled cheese and soup back at your place. This is my dessert."

"Still, if you want something else, take some money from the till. Just let me know how much."

"Enjoy your break," Raelyn said, waving her away. "Don't worry about me."

Jazzy didn't know what she'd do come the end of summer when Raelyn was planning to head out of state for college. Yes, she'd been able to rely on Paige, Leah, and Claire for babysitting in a pinch, but they had their own jobs and obligations. It was great having a full-time babysitter.

Leah was in the window of her shop, The Flower Girl, and waved at Jazzy as she walked by. Jazzy returned the wave, smiling.

It was a warm day with a slight breeze and the sun was high in the sky. The trees had come alive with leaves and buds. Jazzy loved this time of year. It was a time of renewal, rebirth. Spring always made her think of putting any disappointments behind her and starting fresh.

She glanced down at Caleb, noted that he was still awake. Some babies would instantly fall asleep while being pushed in their strollers, but Caleb was curious. He liked to see the world around him.

Jazzy made her way to Roy's Fish Shack, where she bought a meal of fish and chips for Jeremiah. He'd been so good to her over the past week, bringing her coffee every day, and either a breakfast sandwich or muffin as well. It was time she returned the favor.

"Oh, he's getting big!" Sally said. She was Roy Croydon's wife, and the two of them had been running Roy's Fish Shack for over thirty years. Every day from morning until evening, Roy and Sally were there, serving meals to eager customers. Roy's Fish Shack was one of the most popular eateries along the boardwalk.

"Everyone keeps saying he's getting big," Jazzy commented. "But it's so weird, you don't notice the growth spurt until one day you're like, hey, when did you grow so much?"

"That's the truth. Our Molly is twenty-seven now. James is twenty-two. I swear, I blinked and they went from babies to adults. It all goes so fast."

That's what Jazzy was afraid of. That time would fly by, and these precious moments now would soon be a distant memory. It seemed illogical, and yet people said it all the time. That their babies turned into adults before they knew it. Jazzy was going to treasure every moment she could with Caleb.

"Here you go, sweetie," Sally said, presenting Jazzy with her order in a brown paper bag.

"Thanks, Sally." Then Jazzy made her way down the boardwalk and turned left to the area where there the boats were docked. Caleb was still awake, sucking on his soother and taking in the sights and sounds of the squawking seagulls.

"There's your daddy," Jazzy said softly.

Jeremiah's back was to her, and he was hunched over a miter saw. His white T-shirt clung to his strong muscles, and so did his jeans. Jazzy allowed herself a moment to drink in the sight of him. Strong and sexy. Hardworking and dependable.

The saw's blade seared into the plank of wood he was cutting. The sound startled Caleb and he began to cry.

Roberto, the other man working on the dock, gestured to Jeremiah to stop. Jeremiah whipped his gaze over his shoulder and seeing Jazzy, he then put down the plank of wood, turned off the saw, then pushed his safety glasses up. His face lit up.

"Hey," he said, wiping dust and debris from his jeans before starting toward her.

Jazzy pushed the stroller back and forth, hoping that the motion would calm Caleb. "The sound of the saw scared him."

"Did Daddy scare you, big guy?" Jeremiah bent onto his haunches. "I didn't mean to."

Caleb began to settle, and Jeremiah stood upright. He moved a few feet away, making sure to fully brush any possible debris from his clothes. "This is a nice surprise."

"I figured I'd bring *you* something to eat for a change," Jazzy told him. "I hope you haven't had lunch yet."

"I haven't." Jeremiah deeply inhaled the aroma of the food. "Is this from Roy's?" he asked, his voice rising with anticipation.

"It is," Jazzy confirmed. "Halibut. I know how much you love fish and chips, so I thought I'd pick you something up. You've been so good to me this week."

"This is perfect, Jazzy. Thank you so much."

Roberto wandered closer and wiggled his fingers at Caleb. "Hey little man. Come to see your dad?"

Caleb stared up at the new face, sucking contentedly on his pacifier.

"You're a lucky guy," Roberto said to Jeremiah, clamping a hand on his shoulder. "I wish my girl would bring me lunch when I'm out here working. She's just happy to take the check I bring home and head to the mall."

Jazzy's lips parted, and she was about to say that she wasn't Jeremiah's girl, but then she thought better of it. She couldn't correct everyone who misconstrued their relationship. "I didn't realize that you were working with Jeremiah today," she said. "Otherwise I would have brought you some food as well."

Roberto waved off the suggestion. "Don't worry about it. I'm just glad to see someone taking care of my man here. It's a nice change."

Jeremiah shook his head. "You're making me sound like some kind of invalid."

Jazzy ignored the playful banter between the two men and passed Jeremiah the bag of food. "I hope you can eat it before it gets cold."

"Where's yours?" Jeremiah asked her.

"I didn't get one for me. I've got some snacks at the shop. I'm just gonna nibble on that."

"Are you sure?" Jeremiah looked surprised. "If you want, we can take a break together and have lunch. I can share this with you."

Jazzy had considered bringing up the topic of the document she wanted him to sign when she brought him this lunch—lower his guard so he'd be more agreeable when she broached the serious subject. But suddenly the timing felt wrong. Besides, Roberto was here, and she'd prefer to have this talk when no one was within earshot. "No, you're working hard. You need the calories."

"You sure?"

"I am," Jazzy stressed. She paused, wondering if she should at least give him the agreement she'd drafted. It had been burning a hole in her purse for days. Maybe he could look it over on his own time, then they could discuss it.

"Um," she began. "There's something I'd like to show you." Her hand slipped into her purse where she'd put the envelope with the agreement. But then she pulled her hand back. She couldn't very well just give him the agreement and leave, with no discussion over it.

No, this wasn't the right time, but she wanted to deal with this issue soon.

Jeremiah gave her a curious look. "Everything okay?"

"Yeah. I just want to…go over a few things," Jazzy said. "But we can talk about it later."

"Hey, guess what? I'll be seeing you Wednesday night on your fashion show cruise."

Jazzy blinked, surprised. "What? You were invited?"

"Gavin asked me to stand in as a crew member." Jeremiah shrugged. "I figure why not."

"Ah, I see. So we'll both be at the party. And Caleb—"

"Will be fine with my mother for the night. In fact, she'll be thrilled to spend that much time with her grandson."

Slowly, Jazzy nodded. "Of course. That makes…sense…" The words barely made it from her lips before a stabbing pain sensation filled her belly. She gripped her stomach as a moan bubbled up in her throat.

"Jazzy?"

She heard Jeremiah's voice as if through a fog, rocking unsteadily on her feet. Moments later, the sharp pain subsided but the discomfort remained.

Jeremiah wrapped an arm around her waist and gazed down at her with concern. "Are you okay?"

"I'm fine. Just a bit of a stomachache."

"You looked like you were in a lot of pain."

"Probably just hunger pangs."

"That's why you need to eat," Jeremiah told her.

"I'll grab something before I go back to the shop," she promised. The discomfort fully ebbing away now, she took a deep breath. "Don't worry about me. I'll get some food and I'll be fine."

Jeremiah didn't seem convinced, but he bent down onto his haunches to talk directly to Caleb. Caleb began to punch his little hands and kick his feet with excitement. He recognized his daddy, and seeing that made Jazzy smile.

"You take care of your mommy now," Jeremiah said to Caleb. "Make sure she's taking care of herself, because you need her. And always remember daddy loves you."

Jeremiah touched the outside of Caleb's hand, then got back up. "I'm sweaty, dirty. I shouldn't hold him right now."

"I fully understand," Jazzy told him. "I'll let you enjoy your lunch and get back to work. Raelyn was just giving me a little break."

"Make sure you get some food," Jeremiah told her. "Put something decent inside you. You look like you've lost a bit of weight."

"Don't worry. I will."

On Tuesday night, Jazzy pulled into the driveway of Jeremiah's home, a pre-war house that he had fixed up immaculately, both inside and out. The exterior was wood, and painted a royal blue with white trim and highlights. Though he'd painted the house before Caleb's conception, the blue now seemed perfect in terms of his son. Almost like an announcement to the world that he was the father of a boy.

There was silver Chevrolet Cruze in the driveway with California plates, clearly the rental for his mother. It was parked beside Jeremiah's truck, a shiny black Ford F150 with all kinds of tools thrown into the back.

Caleb had slept for the short drive to Jeremiah's place, but now that the car had stopped, he began to fuss. Jazzy unbuckled her seatbelt and quickly went around to the back, unfastening the baby's car seat. "You're okay, sweetie," Jazzy said softly. "We're here to see your dad."

By the time Jazzy was lifting Caleb from the car in his carrier, she heard, "Oooh, is that my grandson?"

Jazzy turned to see Jeremiah's mother rushing toward them, beaming from ear to ear. She had the same full cheeks that Caleb did, including the dimples. She was short, about five-foot-two, and heavyset. She wore the weight well, and looked stylish in a bright yellow dress that accented her curves. A classic strand of pearls graced her neck. The only thing that didn't match the outfit were the fuzzy slippers she'd stuffed her feet into in order to hurry out of the house.

"Oh, look at my little grandbaby!"

"Hello, Mrs. Caldwell," Jazzy greeted her. She felt underdressed in her blue jeans and simple blouse.

"Hello, Jazzy. Please, call me Catherine."

"Catherine, then."

Catherine hovered over Caleb, her eyes alight as she took in the sight of him. "Of course I'm happy to see you as well, but you know how it is. Oh, isn't he the most precious thing?"

"I couldn't agree more," Jazzy said. "He *is* the most precious baby. Ever."

"Oh, what's the matter?" Catherine asked Caleb, who was making soft sounds of distress. "Are you hungry, sweetie?"

"He was sleeping soundly as I was driving, and I think the car stopping kind of startled him."

"Jeremiah used to be the same way. He loved to sleep in cars. I used to have to drive around the block sometimes at two in the morning to make sure he stopped crying." Catherine chuckled. "Oh, I miss those days. But that's why we have grandchildren, isn't it?"

Jazzy smiled. "How was your flight?"

"It was fine. No issues at all." As Caleb began to cry a little more earnestly, Catherine said, "He's probably hungry."

"Possibly. When I get inside, I'll feed him."

"Is there anything you need me to help you get from the car?" Catherine asked.

"If you can grab my purse on the front seat. And I've baked an apple crumble, it's beside the purse."

"So you can bake," Catherine said in a singsong voice. "I'm sure Jeremiah likes that."

Jazzy glanced beyond Catherine to see Jeremiah standing on the wraparound porch. She felt that little twitch inside her chest again. The pull of attraction that seemed to grow stronger every time she saw him.

Why was her mind even going there? Maybe it was completely natural, especially since she liked Jeremiah and they had created a beautiful child together. But she didn't want any fanciful thoughts clouding her mind and ruining the arrangement she had so carefully crafted. The sooner she talked to Jeremiah about the agreement she wanted him to sign, the better.

"I'll keep that in mind," Jazzy told her.

"You know they say the way to a man's heart is through his stomach," Catherine said, then affectionately rubbed Jazzy's forearm.

"Does he have a favorite baked good?" Jazzy asked.

"He loves banana bread. And this apple crumble will go down well with him. It will certainly score you some points."

Clearly, Catherine didn't see her son's relationship with her as simply platonic. As Jazzy followed Catherine toward the house, she couldn't help wondering what the woman's view of their relationship was. Did she think that there was a specific reason other than an arrangement that they weren't together? She almost made it sound as though she thought Jeremiah was the holdout, and Jazzy needed to play the perfect role in order to get him on board to be her man.

Or maybe Jazzy was reading into things.

"Hey, Jeremiah," Jazzy said as she got closer to the porch. Jeremiah began to descend the steps as Jazzy arrived at the foot of them, and he reached for the baby carrier.

"You look nice," he told her.

"Oh, really?" Jazzy asked, sounding surprised. She hadn't even done anything special with her hair, just pulled it all back into a bun. She loved her natural locks, but sometimes they were too much to deal with. Coming straight from her shop and starting the apple crumble, she hadn't had much time to make herself look extra pretty. "It's not like I dressed up or anything, but you know I was working all day."

"You always look nice," Jeremiah said. "You're a natural beauty."

Jazzy's pulse raced at the compliment. Instinctively, she raised her hand to her ponytail and twisted some of the curls. "Thank you."

Jeremiah didn't look too bad himself, though she wasn't sure if she should tell him. He was dressed in denim jeans, and a cream-colored button-down shirt.

Honestly, anything he put on looked good on him. But again, she didn't want to tell him that. Because lately, every time he looked at her, she felt there was something brewing between them. Much like it had all those months ago before they'd first started making love.

"I still can't get over how well the renovations went here," Jazzy said, needing to say something to take the attention away from the two of them. "You preserved the original style while refreshing it and making it better."

You would never know that his house had originally been constructed in the 1940s. Jeremiah had refinished the exterior to match the old look while making it seem newly built. One of the times they'd ended up in his bed had been when Jazzy had come to visit and seen him with his shirt off, a sheen of sweat streaming down his sexy chocolate-colored back as he had been tearing up the old wood planks. The sight of all those hard muscles moving in unison had been her undoing. Her body had reacted of its own will, uncontrollable desire seizing her. And unlike her normal self, she'd walked up to him from behind and placed her hand on his back and trailed her fingers along his moist skin. Startled, Jeremiah had whirled around and looked up at her in shock. But the moment he had recognized the look of lust in her eyes, he had eased up and curled his hand around her neck and pulled her down onto him.

"Jazzy?" Catherine asked.

"Huh?" Jazzy responded, pulled sharply from her erotic thoughts.

"I was asking if you wanted me to change the baby." Catherine was softly stroking Caleb's forehead. "I think he needs a diaper change."

"If you want to change a stinky diaper, go right ahead."

"Let me take him, then," Catherine said, extending her hand to the carrier as she passed Jeremiah the pie. "I love that Caleb has a room here with all the necessary supplies. But I don't know why the two of you need to have two separate places. It would be so much easier—"

"Ma," Jeremiah interjected.

"You young ones and your strange arrangements," Catherine said, more to herself. "What's wrong with the old-fashioned way?" Then she disappeared into the house.

"Sorry about that," Jeremiah said. "She can't help herself. I told her not to make any comments, but…. You know how mothers are."

A wave of sadness suddenly washed over Jazzy. She and her mother had been so close, and the one wish she had now was that her mother was alive to see Caleb. To fuss over him and want to change dirty diapers and hold him while he cried. If only she'd had a child sooner…

Jeremiah placed a gentle hand on her shoulder. "You're thinking about your mother, aren't you?"

Tears springing to her eyes, Jazzy nodded. "Yeah. I just think about how much she would love Caleb."

"You know she loves him. You know she sees him and she's so proud of you. She's his angel."

The words were just what Jazzy needed to hear, and she smiled, then wiped at her eyes. "I know. It's just…. I wish I could see her face as she looks at him. Just once, I wish I could see the love for him in her eyes."

"You feel it though, don't you?" Jeremiah asked. "In your heart."

Jazzy nodded. "I do." Jeremiah's words were no doubt making her feel better. She had many days where she wished she had tried to make this family thing a reality earlier. But she hadn't expected her mother to drop dead of a stroke.

That had been the hardest thing. The sudden loss. One minute everything was fine, and the next her mother was gone.

"There will be times that you will absolutely know she's with you. It was the same after my dad died of a heart attack when I was a teenager. Something would happen, and there'd suddenly be a sign—and I would know."

"You're so kind, Jeremiah. Thank you for making me feel better."

Jeremiah slipped his arm around her waist, and Jazzy couldn't help leaning into him. For this moment at least, she needed his strength and comfort.

"Let's head inside," Jeremiah said. My mother's been cooking nonstop since she arrived. She's prepared quite the feast."

5

To say that his mother had prepared a feast was understatement. Jazzy knew of mothers like this, mothers who slaved over a hot stove and produced magic every time. Mothers who were up early before their children and their husbands making sure to create meals with love so no one went hungry.

Jazzy's mother, however, hadn't quite been the same. Her mother had worked two jobs most of the time to support them, and had turned to microwavable meals more times than Jazzy could count. On Sundays, her mother would usually make a home-cooked meal, Shake and Bake chicken and mac & cheese with some sort of green—and it had been Jazzy's favorite day of the week.

While Jazzy had her moments when she enjoyed getting creative in the kitchen, like her mother, she definitely didn't have all day to slave over a hot stove.

"Your mother went all out," Jazzy said. She perused the various pots. There was roast ham, what appeared to be maple carrots, collard greens, mashed potatoes, a green salad filled with colorful vegetables and even coleslaw. "She made all of this?"

Jeremiah nodded. "Yep. There's also scalloped potatoes in the oven."

"Scalloped potatoes, too?"

"She wasn't sure if the mashed potatoes were a better match or the scalloped potatoes." Jeremiah shrugged. "I guess she figured she had another hour or so, may as well do some more cooking."

"She certainly outdid herself. Let's bring the platters to the table."

All of the food was laid out on the center island in the country-style kitchen Jeremiah had created. It was something he'd added to the house, after taking out one of the walls between the kitchen and the dining room to create one giant open-concept space. She couldn't deny that having a man who knew how to fix things had always held appeal. Maybe because between her and her mother, they'd had to scotch tape peeling wallpaper and put duct tape around leaky pipes until someone could come fix them.

Jeremiah took the ham from the roaster and put it on the serving tray. The smell wafted into Jazzy's nose, and she moaned heavenly. She was looking forward to a home-cooked meal.

Jeremiah carried the steaming-hot meat to the table, which could easily seat ten people. There was more than enough room for all of the food. Jazzy followed with the bowl of salad and the mashed potatoes.

"Oh, you didn't have to do that," Catherine said as she descended the stairs holding Caleb up and patting his freshly changed behind.

Why did babies' butts look so cute in their little diapers? Jazzy wondered.

"We wanted to," she added out loud, turning back toward the island to get the container of collard greens. "Is he okay?"

"He's no longer crying," Catherine said. "If he's hungry, I think he'll be okay for a little bit."

"Probably just needed a diaper change," Jazzy concluded. "Thank you for all of this food. You made so much."

"I love to cook. And the food never goes to waste. Isn't that right, Jeremiah?" she asked, looking toward her son.

Jeremiah chuckled softly. "No, it certainly doesn't, Ma."

Caleb had a mobile swing near the back window facing the large backyard. He enjoyed sitting there and looking outside. Jeremiah went to grab it and brought it closer to the table, putting it between him and Jazzy.

"I hardly want to put you down," Catherine said, but put Caleb into the swing, nonetheless. "There you go. Maybe all the smells of Grandma's cooking are going to have you fussing for some of my food."

"I wouldn't doubt that," Jeremiah said. Turning to Caleb, he added, "You have no clue what you're in for once you get old enough to try your grandmother's food."

And Jeremiah was right. The food was scrumptious. The ham was soft and succulent. The coleslaw had a little something extra to it that made it the best Jazzy had ever tasted. The mashed potatoes were buttery and light. And Jazzy devoured much of it, glad that her appetite had returned. Maybe all she'd needed was some good home-cooking to settle her stomach.

"I wasn't thrilled when Jeremiah said he was leaving Wisconsin," Catherine said. "But he got that great offer with the boating company, and he couldn't very well say no to that."

"I'm just a plane ride away," Jeremiah said. "And more importantly, I'm still a proud Cheesehead," he added, referring to the affectionate name the Green Bay football fans were known as.

"Your brothers would disown you if you rooted for any other team!"

"Graham and Ty don't have to worry about that," Jeremiah said. "In fact, I can't wait to get Caleb some Packers outfits."

Jazzy playfully rolled her eyes. "Oh, goodness. He's too young for all of that."

"There's no such thing," Jeremiah said, and Catherine nodded in agreement.

Jazzy tried to picture Caleb as a toddler, holding a mini football and dressed as a Green Bay Packers' player. Personally, she didn't care for football, but Caleb would probably enjoy learning the game with his father.

"That apple crumble smells delicious, Jazzy," Catherine said. "You'll have to give me the recipe."

"Thanks," Jazzy said. "And absolutely, I'll share the recipe."

"She made it from scratch," Catherine added, looking at Jeremiah, and Jazzy easily read the words in her gaze. *Don't you think she's perfect for you?*

"I forgot to bring ice cream," Jazzy said. "The crumble is so much better with ice cream."

"I have vanilla in the freezer," Jeremiah said.

"Perfect!" Catherine got to her feet. "Am I the only one ready for it?"

Jazzy patted her stomach. "I'm not sure I can eat a bite of it right now. Maybe a bit later."

"Oh, I'm ready," Jeremiah said.

"He's still a growing boy," Catherine mused.

As Catherine headed toward the kitchen, Jeremiah met and held Jazzy's gaze. He smiled softly, then winked.

And Jazzy felt it again, that pull of attraction. That desire to feel his strong arms wrapped around her.

She quickly averted her gaze, instead looking down at Caleb. He was putting his fist into his mouth. "You've been so patient, haven't you? But I think it's time I feed you."

Jazzy removed Caleb from his swing. Then she explained, "I'm gonna take him upstairs and feed him."

As she wound her way through the living room to the staircase along the side wall, she was all too aware that she was using the need to feed Caleb as an opportunity to escape what she was feeling for Jeremiah.

6

*A*n hour later, Caleb was lively and vocal. He was cooing happily and smiling in response to Catherine's interaction with him, much to her delight. As Jazzy regarded them, she once again couldn't help thinking of her own mother and wishing that she could also be playing with Caleb like this.

"I know it's early," Catherine began, facing Jeremiah and Jazzy who were sitting on the sofa across from her. "But I was thinking you both could come to Wisconsin for Christmas. I'd like to have all of the family there. And of course, we need to have Caleb, the newest addition."

Jeremiah looked at Jazzy, shrugging. "What you think?"

"I don't know. That's several months away."

"I know you no longer have your mother," Catherine began, her tone sympathetic. "And of course, I see you as part of our family now. You'd be more than welcome."

"I appreciate that," Jazzy said, and offered Catherine a soft smile. It was true, her mother was gone, but her aunt and uncle were only forty minutes away. They would want to spend time with Caleb over Christmas as well, along with their children who would no doubt be back in town for the occasion. Besides, the more time she spent with Jeremiah and Caleb as a family, the more it might seem that they were a couple.

It was time she talked to Jeremiah about the agreement she wanted him to sign.

"Jeremiah, can we talk for a moment?" Jazzy's eyes darted to Catherine. "Privately."

Catherine, who was holding Caleb, said, "I can go upstairs."

"Or maybe we can go sit out on the porch swing," Jazzy suggested.

"Sure," Jeremiah agreed. "It's a warm evening."

Jazzy had her purse with her, in which she'd placed the envelope with the agreement. She followed Jeremiah outside onto the porch, and looked off at the sun setting over the bay in the distance. It was truly a spectacular view, with the trees and shrubs and the bright orange sun dipping over the horizon. The vista truly inspired a sense of peace and tranquility. And it certainly lent itself to romance.

Feeling Jeremiah's gaze on her, Jazzy looked up at him. He smiled down, his eyes lighting up. Was he thinking what she had been? That this beautiful setting was perfect for intimacy?

He placed a hand on the small of her back. "Lovely evening, isn't it?"

Jazzy nodded. "It really is. You have a beautiful piece of heaven right here."

"It's much better shared with someone by your side," he told her, and there was no mistaking what he was getting at.

Jazzy's eyes widened slightly, both alarm and desire shooting through her. Her stomach began to twist. Ever since dinner, it had been slowly starting to feel upset again. She needed to get this conversation over with—stop in its tracks whatever was brewing between them.

"I'm glad to see you ate something substantial tonight," Jeremiah continued. "I've been worried about you. You've hardly been eating over the past week from what I can gather."

"I guess it's easy when someone's cooking for you," Jazzy said. "Lord knows I'm no Martha Stewart."

"Your apple crumble was fantastic. I look forward to seeing what else you can make. But I'm pretty easy to please."

His smile was effortless and genuine, and it was also unnerving. This was the moment for Jazzy to tell him what she wanted to have sole legal custody. It suddenly made sense why her stomach was so upset over the past couple of weeks. She had started to fear that maybe she was getting an ulcer, but now she knew that she had been dreading *this* moment. She didn't want Jeremiah to take things the wrong way.

"Can we go sit on the swing?" Jazzy suggested.

"Of course," Jeremiah said.

He led the way, his hand still on her back. Lord, it felt good there. She wanted to pull away, but selfishly she didn't. She would enjoy this simple moment of intimacy one last time because things would change after he heard what she had to say.

They sat, and the swing creaked as it adjusted to their weight. Jeremiah faced her. "Okay, what's so important?"

Jazzy slipped her hand into the purse and pulled out the envelope in which she had the agreement. She passed it to him, saying nothing.

"What is this?"

"Maybe you can just read it?" she suggested.

"Okay." Jeremiah sounded wary. He opened the envelope and pulled out the three sheets of folded paper.

Holding her breath, Jazzy watched him. She watched, waiting to see how he might react. If his shoulders tensed. If the pleasant look on his face morphed into something else. His eyes began to move more quickly across the page from left to right, and they went wide with curiosity—then narrowed with confusion. As he flipped to the second page of the agreement, Jazzy thought she saw a flash of anger in his gaze. As she had suspected, he was not happy.

"I just wanted to, you know, get things officially put down on paper—exactly what we discussed *before* I got pregnant, nothing more. So we'd have a legal agreement, you know." She was rambling, not completely making full sense, but she was nervous. "It's not gonna change anything. It's just going to make things easier. You know, if I want to go away, like to Amsterdam, or Greece, or I don't know… anywhere with Caleb…then I can take him. And you can't stand in the way of that."

"Stand in the way of that?" Jeremiah's face contorted with confusion. He stuffed the pages of the letter back into the envelope and placed it on her lap, though Jazzy got the distinct impression that he wanted to throw it to the ground. "Is that what you think? That I'm going to stand in the way of you doing things with Caleb?"

85

She'd said the words wrong, and now he was angry. "I don't mean it like that. I'm just trying to make sure that there are no issues."

"What kind of issues could there be?"

"You might not agree with something I want to do. If I want to go away at a certain point. Lauren was suggesting maybe a trip to Europe, for example."

"You want to traipse around Europe with a baby?" he exclaimed, incredulous.

"See?" Jazzy said. "That's exactly my point. What if I do want to go away with Caleb? And there are other things. You might not want him to do French immersion, and maybe I will. I just want to be able to make the final decisions where he's concerned. This was my idea to have a baby, something you agreed to go along with. We had agreed to this arrangement so I could have a child as a single mother. It was always agreed that this would be my child—the paperwork was just to formalize that."

"*Your* child? As if I have no part in this?"

Why was she saying all the wrong things? "Perhaps I should start over," she said. "I'm nervous, and I'm not expressing myself the right way."

"I saw the agreement that you want me to sign. You went to a lawyer? Had someone draft this up? You couldn't have even spoken to me about it first?"

While the agreement did sound official with all the appropriate legalese, Jazzy hadn't gone to a lawyer. She scoured the Internet and found case files and sample documents and simply drafted her document based on those.

"Essentially you're asking me to sign away my paternal rights," Jeremiah concluded.

"Not exactly. I just want to be the parent who makes all the final decisions. We had discussed this."

"Whatever happened to the idea that we would discuss things as two friends and make the best decision for Caleb? When you proposed the idea of me fathering a child with you, you always said we would both be in his or her life."

"You think I don't want you to be in Caleb's life? Of course I do. Why do you think I'm here right now, tonight? That's what I'm saying, that this agreement isn't really changing anything. It's just… solidifying the plan I had from the beginning. You know you're not the one who wanted a baby. I'm not trying to say that you don't want Caleb now, that you don't love him deeply." She was starting to get exasperated having to explain herself, repeat herself. She was not the bad guy in this situation. She's just clarifying it. Or, trying to. "I'm just saying that this was *my* idea. *My* plan to raise Caleb as a single mother."

"With a halftime father on the side?" Jeremiah supplied.

Jazzy didn't know what to say, so she said nothing.

"No matter how this started, I'm a father now. Caleb is as much mine as he is yours. And this agreement—it hits below the belt. You went to a lawyer without giving me any warning, and now you give me this and just expect me to just sign it?"

"I didn't go to a lawyer," she said, exasperated. "I just went online for some advice and…. Look, maybe I should have talked to you about it first, but we *did* talk. *Before* I got pregnant. I *always* said we should put something down on paper."

"I didn't think you were going to come up with something that said I would no longer have any decision-making power in my son's life."

This wasn't going the way she wanted it to. Not at all. Jazzy quickly stood. "I think I'm going to leave now."

Suddenly she could hear the warnings from Leah, Paige, Claire and Lauren that she'd ignored. *I don't see how this is going to work. What man is going to go along with this? The best laid plans always fall apart….* And, *You can't control emotions, no matter how hard you try.*

Jeremiah hadn't seemed so against this idea when she'd broached the subject initially. Maybe she should have had this agreement fully signed before the baby had been born. Now that Caleb was here, Jeremiah loved his son and no longer wanted to respect the idea that she would be the primary parent. "Just look over the agreement fully, and if you have anything you want to add to it, we can certainly talk about it. We can even go to a lawyer together. We're friends, remember? That was the whole point of this. Two people who like and respect each other coming together to raise a child."

"Except you decided that you need to be the primary parent and I'm just what, extraneous?"

Jazzy tossed the envelope onto the swing beside Caleb. "We can't have a conversation about this right now, and the last thing I want is for your mother to hear us arguing. I hope you won't be upset, but I'm going to take Caleb and head home. I would like for us to talk about this when you've cooled down, and I've cooled down and…. At least I've brought the subject up and you know what I'm thinking of now, so I welcome any suggestions."

Jeremiah picked up the envelope and, for one moment, Jazzy thought he was going to rip it into pieces. Instead, as he stood, he folded it and shoved it into his back pocket. "Fine. We'll talk later."

Jazzy hurried into the house. Catherine was in the living room holding Caleb, who was sleeping now, and there was a concerned look on the woman's face. Had she overheard them?

Jazzy forced a smile. "I'm going to head home with Caleb," she told Catherine. "My stomach has really been unsettled, and I think I just need some tea and some rest. But it was so good to see you. And, of course, I'll see you tomorrow because you'll be watching Caleb for the night."

"Absolutely," Catherine said gently. "I hope everything's okay. With your stomach," she quickly amended, but Jazzy didn't believe it. She was certain that Catherine was talking about things being okay between her and Jeremiah.

Jazzy hoped they were as well. She would let Jeremiah sleep on this conversation. Maybe she'd just chosen the wrong time to bring it up, but she'd put off this discussion for far too long. She'd dilly-dallied and delayed and now hit him with this out of the blue.

He would be okay once he had time to think about everything.

She was sure of it.

7

*J*azzy looked sexier than she ever thought possible. The black dress Lauren had given her, now fully accessorized, made her look like one of the models who had no doubt worn it.

A smile touched her lips. She was determined to have fun tonight and forget about the argument between her and Jeremiah.

She'd felt a little bit of stress earlier when she brought Caleb to Jeremiah's house. The weight of the agreement she had given him to sign was still heavy between them. But to her relief, Jeremiah wasn't there. He had already gone to the boat to help prepare for the party. So Jazzy had only had to interact with Catherine briefly as she dropped the baby off.

Then she had a couple of hours to get herself ready, and now, as she checked out her reflection in her floor-to-ceiling mirror, she was blown away by how good she looked. The black dress was formfitting with a bit of stretch to it, allowing it to easily adjust to one's curves. The fabric felt incredibly luxurious and soft on her skin, but Jazzy would only expect the best from a renowned designer. The black had a shimmery quality to it, and looked different depending on where the light hit it. It had a plunging neckline—far more than Jazzy would normally be comfortable with. But Jazzy had the perfect necklace for it. It was a multistrand silver necklace, one she sold many of because each ended up being one-of-a-kind. The jewels and beads she put onto each strand were never the same. This one had a mix of the rarer black and more common white sea glass, offset by silver metal beads. The color combination went well with the dress, especially the way it shimmered under the light.

She also had the perfect silver shoes to go with the dress. She'd bought them a few years ago, strappy and bedazzled, and she hadn't worn them yet. She knew one day they would be perfect when she had a fancy event to go to where she could totally rock them. They'd stayed in her closet until now.

She'd braided her natural hair today and then let it loose, giving it a curlier look tonight. She added a hairpin on the side that had a jeweled flower, also silver and black. Topping off the look were a few sparkly bangles.

"You've really gone all out," she told herself. She snapped a selfie and sent it to Lauren. She looked like she should be heading out for a night on the town with a man.

The thought made her stomach twist. How would Jeremiah react when he saw her? He hadn't messaged her at all today, and she hadn't messaged him.

Would he still see her as beautiful? As Jazzy applied a coat of burgundy lipstick, she wondered in part if she'd gone all out with her look because of him. Her heart and her brain were conflicted. Her heart wanted him to look at her and see her as beautiful, because her feelings toward him were intensifying. And yet, her brain wanted to make sure they remained strictly friends.

The ugly conversation between them the night before still weighed on her.

"Oh, Jazzy," she said softly as she adjusted the flower pin in her hair. "Let's hope the night goes well."

Jazzy saw Jeremiah the moment she stepped onto the 92-foot yacht they would be sailing on Sea Glass Bay for the evening. And despite the tension between them, her breath caught in her chest. Then came an odd feeling, one that had a sensation of warmth attached to it. Decked out in sailor's gear—white pants, a white top and aviator sunglasses—he looked gorgeous. What was the saying about a man in uniform? Yes, he looked *very* good in a uniform.

"Ooh la la," Lauren crooned. "Jeremiah looks as hot as fire!"

"Mmm-hmm," she agreed. Jazzy hadn't told her about their argument. She hadn't told any of her friends yet.

"The yacht looks amazing," Jazzy said. She gestured to the festive balloons and the table with bottles of champagne chilling and the ice sculpture in the shape of a woman's high heel.

"Are you going to say hello to Jeremiah?" Lauren asked.

"He's working," Jazzy said. "Why don't you introduce me to the designer?"

Jazzy threw another look in Jeremiah's direction before she and Lauren headed off. Despite how sexy he looked in his uniform and those aviator sunglasses, he was a down to earth, hardworking guy. Any woman should be happy to have him on her arm.

So why was she pushing him away?

Jeremiah wanted to be angry when he saw Jazzy. They hadn't spoken since the night before when she dropped her bombshell on him. But when he saw her in that shimmery black dress that hugged her beautiful curves, all he could think about was how much he wanted to pull her into his arms and kiss her until she told him she regretted ever drafting that stupid agreement.

But she'd given him the barest of nods as she'd stepped onto the yacht, forced a smile and then quickly looked away.

Jeremiah swallowed a spate of desire. She looked absolutely incredible. The dress, and those shoes, and that showstopping necklace—all of it looked amazing on her, but he was suddenly remembering what she looked like *without* clothes on, lying in his bed and smiling at him in invitation.

He'd always liked her. That's why her out-of-the-blue agreement was a slap in the face. Yes, she had suggested having a no-strings-attached relationship and creating a child, but she couldn't expect him to just sign off all of his rights so she could happily play single mother.

He thought they'd been growing closer since Caleb's birth. Since before that, really. He'd been there for her. During her pregnancy, and of course at her side as she'd delivered the baby. It had not been traditional, but Jeremiah had always felt in his heart that the two of them were moving toward something. Their relationship hadn't started the way most relationships did, but they'd had a foundation of friendship and trust and that had led them to creating a baby together. Didn't that take the most amount of trust?

He knew she was stuck in her head and scared, and the truth was, so was he. When Jazzy had detailed this whole diatribe about her ex, his ex, and how since they didn't want a relationship they could be perfect parents, he had been on board with it. And at the time, Jeremiah hadn't been thinking about a relationship. But Jazzy wasn't Sharon. She was sweet and thoughtful and hardworking.

And stubborn.

He looked at her, her head thrown back in laughter, and wondered if she really felt this carefree and happy as she was appearing to be. Because he was still hurt by that letter.

Then Jazzy headed further onto the yacht, slipping out of his sight.

Jazzy turned with the plate of fruit she'd just collected, and nearly dropped it when she saw that Jeremiah was standing behind her.

"Oh my, you startled me."

"Cake?" Jeremiah asked, presenting her the tray that had plates of the sliced cake on it.

He sounded matter-of-fact, but was there a hint of anger simmering beneath the tone?

"I already had a small piece, thank you."

"You haven't said a word to me tonight."

"You're working," Jazzy said by way of explanation.

"Is that the real reason? It has nothing to do with that agreement you wanted me to sign last night?"

Jazzy quickly looked around, saw Lauren smiling as she was talking with some of the guests. This wasn't a conversation Jazzy wanted to have right now.

"Can we talk about this later?" she asked.

"I hardly slept," Jeremiah said. "And now you're acting like you're afraid to be around me. Everything was fine before that agreement."

"Outside," she whispered. Then she whirled on her heels and started toward the steps that led up to the exterior. There were a few guests mingling on the far right of the bow, so Jazzy headed toward the left. At least she and Jeremiah could have some privacy to talk, because clearly he wasn't letting this go.

When she got to the yacht's railing, she gazed out at the sparkling lights of the city and the hillside and thought about how magical it looked. Magic that was meant to be shared with someone.

Someone like Jeremiah.

Lord help her, she was in trouble. Maybe it was the setting, and the fact that Jeremiah looked amazing.... But she couldn't forget the big picture, that she and Jeremiah had come together as friends to raise their son. They weren't supposed to cross that friendship line. Because if they did, and things went sour, then what?

Except that things were already sour now, weren't they? Hopefully their friendship hadn't been irrevocably damaged because she had asked him to sign that agreement.

"My intention wasn't to change our agreement," Jazzy said softly, turning to face Jeremiah. "Just to clarify it."

"I don't want to be a part-time dad to Caleb."

"That's not what I want, either." Jazzy glanced around to make sure that no one was approaching. She continued in a calm tone. "This isn't about keeping you from Caleb, just clarifying things legally."

"I would never *not* sign off on anything for Caleb as long as you consulted and respected me about it. Don't you know that?"

In her heart, she did know that. But she was afraid. Afraid that good things didn't last. Life had taught her that. Sometimes it was best to have a rock-solid agreement that could not be disputed in a court of law. "I don't want to be out here discussing this right now. I want to get back to the party."

She began to walk away, lifting a strawberry from her plate and putting it into her mouth. Her stomach was starting to twist again, her nerves getting to her.

"Was this whole thing a bad idea?" Jeremiah asked before she reached the steps.

She halted. Took a deep breath and turned to face him. "You think having Caleb was a mistake?"

"That's not what I'm saying."

She knew it wasn't. He was talking about the two of them believing that they could parent as friends, without any hiccups.

Had their arrangement been a mistake? Had everyone been right to think that a no-strings-attached partnership couldn't fly?

"I love my son," Jeremiah went on. "I think his mother is pretty awesome too, but she's determined to shut me down at every turn."

With the sound of happy laughter retreating behind her, Jazzy made her way back over to Jeremiah. "This is because of your mother, isn't it?" she asked. "It's natural that she wants you, me and Caleb to be a happy family."

"This has nothing to do with my mother," Jeremiah rasped. And then suddenly, he was pulling her into his arms and planting his lips on hers. Jazzy was so startled that she didn't know how to react. She stood there for at least a couple of beats, unable to process what was happening. Then came the rush of emotions. Excitement. Giddiness. Desire. Jeremiah was kissing her.

While she wanted to reach her hands around his neck and hold on and lose herself in this kiss and this man, doubt and confusion marred her thoughts. This was the wrong place, and why was he kissing her anyway?

She pulled back, breaking the kiss. "Jeremiah—"

"Oops," came the sound of Gavin's voice. "So that's where you are."

Jeremiah rubbed a hand over the back of his neck, clearly uncomfortable having been caught in a compromising position with Jazzy. "Sorry, Gavin. I was just chatting with Jazzy for a minute."

He continued to look at her with a dark, heated gaze. Jazzy couldn't stand the intensity. She needed to get away.

She wiped her hand across the back of her mouth and forced a smile. Then she turned. "If you need Jeremiah, he's all yours," she said to Gavin. "I didn't mean to keep him from his work."

And then she darted off, but she couldn't easily flee thoughts of Jeremiah's hot mouth on hers.

8

*J*eremiah had been watching Jazzy keenly throughout the evening, and every instinct inside of him told him that something was wrong. Something not related to her complicated feelings for him. She laughed, sipped juice, but she had barely eaten. She'd nibbled at her cake, nibbled at the fruit. Taken small portions of the food that she didn't finish. That in itself wouldn't be so concerning, but every so often he saw her place a hand on her belly and make a little face. As if she was experiencing discomfort.

A sudden and shocking thought burst into his mind. Hadn't she done the same when she'd been pregnant? During those months where she had experienced morning sickness?

The thought slammed into Jeremiah like a kick to the gut. Pregnant? Could it be? Was that why she had come up with this agreement out of the blue? Was there someone else?

"Thanks again, both of you," Jazzy said, raising a hand in a wave to Lauren and Jared Dumont, the local designer who'd chartered Gavin's boat for the fashion show. She had her parting giftbag and was heading down the yacht's steps, without Lauren.

"You sure you don't want to stay a bit longer?" Lauren asked.

"I've got to be up early in the morning," Jazzy told her. "You stay and enjoy the rest of the night."

Jeremiah lowered the box of discarded plastic champagne flutes he'd been collecting, seeing this as his chance. He could walk Jazzy to her car and find out the truth. Was she seeing someone else—and was she pregnant?

"Holdup, Jazzy," he called and quickly scurried over to the steps. "Let me see you to your car."

"Good idea," Lauren said.

Jazzy looked up at Jeremiah from the dock below as he descended the steps, and he saw the quick flash of panic in her eyes. She didn't want to be alone with him.

Well, too bad. Jeremiah needed answers.

"This isn't necessary," Jazzy told him. "I'm fine to get to my car."

"And I'm going to be a perfect gentleman and make sure you get there safely."

Jazzy fiddled with the gift bag, and then her clutch—anything to ignore him. They walked in silence until they got to the parking lot. Far enough away from the yacht and from anyone else, Jeremiah placed a hand on her arm, forcing her to stop. He asked without preamble, "Are you pregnant?"

She looked at him as though he had sprouted a second head. *"What?* Why on earth would you say that?"

"It would explain that written agreement." Though he spoke matter-of-factly, Jeremiah's palms were suddenly sweaty. "You met someone else. You want to have a way to cut me out of the picture."

"Where is this coming from?"

"I'm trying to make sense of everything. Because one day we were fine, and the next day you want me to sign away my rights as Caleb's father."

"That's not what I'm trying to do." Jazzy sighed. "You are completely overthinking things."

"So you're not seeing anyone?"

"No!"

The word filled him with more relief than he thought possible. But the relief soon turned to concern. Because there it was again, the slight pained look on her face, and her touching her belly.

"Jazzy, what's wrong?"

"I just want to go home."

"You don't seem okay. Stomach issues again?"

She looked up at him, and beneath the rays of light coming off of the pier, he could see that her eyes were moist. "I've been stressed out." Her tone was clipped. "Clearly."

"I know that. And…. Obviously there's a lot we need to discuss. But that can wait. Right now, I'm worried about you."

Suddenly, she doubled over and cried out in pain. "Oh God."

"That's not stress," Jeremiah said. "Something's wrong. I'm going to take you to the hospital."

"No, no! It's not as bad as all that—I just want to go home."

He pursed his lips together, not agreeing but trying to respect her autonomy. "Fine. I'm taking you."

Jazzy didn't protest. When she sat in the passenger seat of Jeremiah's truck, she wondered why her stomach was hurting so much. Maybe she'd worked herself up to the point where she did have an ulcer, all over this stupid agreement she wanted Jeremiah to sign.

This was supposed to be a blissful time in her life. She was a new mother, with a beautiful baby. But suddenly, everything was going wrong.

It seemed like it took forever to get to her house, and when she did, she gathered her strength and climbed out of the vehicle. She strode up to the front steps of her townhouse quickly, but Jeremiah was fast on her heels.

"Hey, slow down," Jeremiah said.

"I'll be fine from here."

"Let me see you inside," Jeremiah insisted. "Maybe make you some soup or something."

"I'm fine. I just…. I just need to rest." But as she said the words, her stomach roiled in pain. The pain was worse than it had been before, twisting and turning her insides. She was starting to get worried now, but didn't want Jeremiah to stick around. Not out of pity.

"I'm not going anywhere."

"All I need is some rest…" The keys tumbled from her hand.

"Like hell," Jeremiah said, and quickly bent to scoop up her keys. He unlocked her door, then put his arm around her waist and guided her inside.

Jazzy whimpered softly, trying to keep in her tears. Surely this couldn't be just stress. "I can take care of myself."

"Dammit," Jeremiah whispered as he looked down at her. "Don't you know that I care about you? You think I'm going to just leave you when you're in pain like this?"

Jazzy said nothing.

"I think maybe you should go to the doctor."

Jazzy's eyes widened in alarm. She was wondering that, too. She'd been experiencing these bothersome symptoms for a couple of weeks now, symptoms she'd been ignoring. Symptoms she had attributed simply to stress. But what if it was something worse? What if it was something serious, like cancer?

She couldn't let her mind go there. She refused.

"I…" She wanted to insist that Jeremiah leave. More pain hit her and she pushed herself out of his arms. "Please, I need to…" She let her voice trail off as she hurried to the bathroom and straight to the toilet.

Several minutes later she exited, feeling embarrassed and out of sorts. But also a bit better. Was this what stress did to you? Caused you gastrointestinal problems?

Jeremiah's eyes were filled with concern. Concern that reached deep into her soul and touched her. He wasn't here just because he was Caleb's father. He was here because he cared. "Can I get you some tea? Some soup?"

"Soup." As she said the words, she felt relief. Instinctively, she felt that hot soup would agree with her.

"Why don't you lie down on the sofa? Or if you want to change out of your dress, I can bring you the soup in bed."

Jazzy felt too weak to even head upstairs. "I'll just lie on the sofa."

She made her way over there, kicked off her shoes, then stretched her body out on the sofa and closed her eyes. Moments later, she felt the warmth of her plush comforter being draped over her body.

"Obviously Caleb will stay at your place tonight," Jazzy said, her eyes closed.

"Caleb was always going to stay at my place tonight. Don't worry about him. He's fine. Right now, we need to worry about you."

98

"Once I have the soup, I'm sure I'll feel better. You don't have to stay."

"Is there a particular soup you'd like?"

"There's a can of chicken noodle. That sounds heavenly."

"One can of chicken noodle soup coming right up."

Jazzy's eyes opened slowly, adjusting to the light in the room. There was a morning glow; it was daylight. She was in her bed, but something wasn't right.

A nanosecond later, it hit her. The sheets were directly against her body—meaning she wasn't wearing her pajamas.

Her heart began to pound. Last night. *Jeremiah.*

She quickly whirled around in the bed, turning in the direction of the bay windows and the rocking chair she used when she was nursing Caleb. And there he was, his sexy frame filling the chair. He was still wearing his outfit from the night before, but it was unbuttoned now, revealing a white undershirt. And he was barefoot. Jazzy had always like the look of his feet. Long and masculine with perfectly aligned toes.

Jazzy held the bed sheet high over her breasts. She wasn't naked, but she was wearing only her strapless bra and her underwear. Even her jewelry had been removed. It shouldn't bother her that Jeremiah had taken off her dress—he had seen her naked a number of times—but still, they hadn't been this close in over a year.

"How are you feeling?" Jeremiah asked without preamble.

Jazzy made a face. "I…I want to say I'm feeling better, but my stomach. Something's wrong."

Jeremiah got to his feet and came over to the bed. "I think you should go to the hospital."

Jazzy nodded. She wanted to say no, that staying in bed for the day would be the solution. But she'd started to get a very bad feeling. People ignored symptoms all the time and ended up creating worse situations for themselves. Had she ignored this stomach issue for too long?

Jeremiah leaned forward and gave her a soft kiss on the forehead. It surprised her, and perhaps the downcast shift of his eyes as he pulled away indicated that it had surprised him, too.

"How's Caleb?"

"My mother said they're having the time of their lives. She also said to tell you she hopes you'll feel better soon."

Jazzy swallowed slightly, nausea filling her gut. "Can you get me a glass of water?"

"Absolutely."

Jeremiah was back in less than two minutes, time in which Jazzy had gotten up and slipped into her robe. "I'm wondering if this is maybe Crohn's disease," she said. "Or diverticulitis, or…"

"Don't self-diagnose."

"Or it could be something worse. Couldn't it? It could be a tumor. It could be…. *Oh God.* What would happen to Caleb?"

"You're getting way ahead of yourself." Jeremiah put the glass of water into her hand and guided it to her lips. "Drink. Then get dressed. I'm taking you to the hospital. We're going to find out what's wrong with you."

9

*J*eremiah could have left and gone home after Jazzy had been admitted to the ER and started undergoing tests, even if just to change, but he didn't want to leave her. He finally saw her again after the various tests—blood tests, x-rays, and ultrasounds. They'd given her something for the pain and taken her off to an ER room, where she'd fallen asleep, according to a nurse. Jeremiah used that opportunity to go to the cafeteria to get himself a sandwich and a coffee.

He garnered lots of looks in his sailor's outfit. Maybe people wondered if there'd been a mishap aboard a boat. But no one approached him to ask questions.

Jeremiah sat with his phone while he waited, passing the time. He wanted to call Jazzy's friends, but she had expressly forbidden him to call anyone until she knew what was going on.

"Jeremiah?"

At the sound of his name, Jeremiah looked up. A young Asian man moved toward him. "That's me," Jeremiah said.

"I'm Dr. Lu. You're waiting on Ms. Dunbar?"

"Yes."

"You're her husband?"

Jeremiah hesitated. Then he said, "Yes. I'm her partner. How's she doing?"

"I'm going to explain to both of you what's going on." The man led him down the hallway back into the ER. He looked far too young to be a doctor, but Jeremiah wasn't going to question it.

Dr. Lu pushed aside the curtain that was giving Jazzy privacy, then entered the small room. Jeremiah's eyes immediately landed on her. She looked frail and scared in the hospital bed. Her arm was hooked up to an IV, and she was getting fluids. There was another bag attached, too. Maybe some kind of medication?

"I wanted to have your husband come in and join us," the doctor said. "So I can tell you both what's going on."

Jazzy's eyes widened with alarm. Was it the word *husband* or the fact that she was fearing the worst—or both?

"Are you feeling better?" Dr. Lu asked. "Have your gastrointestinal problems calmed down a bit?"

Jazzy nodded. "Yes. Thankfully."

Why was the doctor taking his sweet time instead of just telling them what was wrong? Jeremiah didn't know if he was trying to brace them for the worst. His own gut clenched as he allowed that horrifying possibility to penetrate for the first time.

"We ran all sorts of tests, checked for everything. The good news is, you have something that we can treat. You have a parasite. Giardiasis."

"Giardi*what?*" Jazzy exclaimed.

"Giardiasis. It's an intestinal disease that can cause bloating, nausea, stomach cramps, diarrhea. The giardia parasite is a common source of waterborne illness in this country. You can get it from eating contaminated fruits or vegetables that haven't been washed. Or from water in a river or a stream. Or someone may have served you something at a restaurant and infected you that way. There are numerous ways you could have picked this up, but the good news is, we now have a diagnosis and we're treating you with antibiotics. This will clear up for you in no time."

"There's nothing more serious going on?" Jazzy asked. "Not an ulcer, not a tumor...?"

"No. Just a pesky parasite," Dr. Lu said. "That explains all the gastrointestinal cramping and bloating you were experiencing. Some people experience no symptoms and the parasite goes away on its own. Others experience symptoms that can be quite severe." He offered her a small smile. "You're in the right place. We're treating you now, and you'll be fine."

"Thank God," Jeremiah said. Finally he approached Jazzy's bedside, and kissed her on the forehead. She wrapped her fingers around his arm and held onto him tightly, and he knew in that moment she needed him and didn't want him to leave her side.

Why had she come up with that crazy agreement? They didn't need it.

"We'll keep you overnight for observation, but in the morning you'll be able to go home with a prescription and take some oral antibiotics. If anything persists, call your family doctor."

"Thank you, doctor," Jeremiah said.

Dr. Lu turned, ready to leave, but Jazzy suddenly said, "Wait!"

"Yes?" The doctor faced her again.

"I have a baby. I'm breastfeeding. Will this affect him? Oh God, I can't imagine Caleb going through what I went through."

Jazzy's eyes flitted from Jeremiah to the doctor, filled with panic. He could see guilt on her face. The very thought that she might do something to hurt Caleb was causing her distress.

"Rest assured, there's no need to worry about that. This parasite does not affect a mother's breast milk. And there are prescription options that also won't affect your breast milk."

"You sure?" Jazzy asked. "Because my baby's only three months old, and I'm not ready to stop."

"Yes, I'm sure." Dr. Lu nodded reassuringly. "As far as things go, this parasite may be unpleasant, but it's not going to affect you long-term and it's certainly not going to affect your baby one way or the other."

Jeremiah gently stroked his hand over Jazzy's thick hair. "It's okay, you can trust the doctor."

Her body relaxed then, and she lay back on the bed, which had been positioned upright so she was in a reclined sitting position. "I got so scared for a second. I would never want to hurt Caleb."

"Of course you wouldn't. You're a fantastic mother."

"If you have any other questions," Dr. Lu said, "you can ring for a nurse and I'll come back. And I'll be checking up on you before you leave." He smiled politely, then turned and left the room.

Jazzy threw her arms around Jeremiah, her relief seeming to flow from her body to his. She was going to be okay, and he was forever grateful for that.

"I'm going to need my breast pump," she said after a moment. "I'll have to express my milk so that I don't lose it."

"I'll get it for you."

"And obviously I'm going have to ask that you watch Caleb while I'm here," Jazzy said.

Jeremiah took her chin between his finger and thumb. "Jazzy, that's the least of your concerns. You know I will always be there for Caleb. Especially in a situation like this. You can't think that I would ever have it any other way."

"It's just that your mother.... Didn't you say she had other plans? Isn't she supposed to be heading down the coast to visit a friend?"

"She cancelled her other plans for the time being so that I can devote all of my attention to you and she can watch Caleb. I'm here for you, Jazzy. I always will be."

He held her gaze, hoping that she fully got his meaning. She may have wanted this to be a strictly friends relationship, but he was done pretending that he could play that game. He'd always liked her. And the feelings of like had morphed into love. She was thoughtful, beautiful, a good mother. And they'd created a child, the best gift of all. He wasn't going anywhere.

"That agreement... I was wrong to just spring that on you. It wasn't fair of me." She eased back onto the pillow. "Thank you for being here. Honestly, I don't know what I would do without you."

Jeremiah took her hand. "I'm here with you as long as you need me to be."

And as far as Jeremiah was concerned, that would be a lifetime.

For the next few days, Jazzy took it easy. She stayed at Jeremiah's place, at his insistence. And she was in complete agreement with that. She could be close to her son, while Jeremiah took care of both of them.

And Jeremiah was taking extremely good care of her. He knew when she needed to take her antibiotics, made sure that she rested, and he even cooked for her. Jeremiah had practically not left her side the first thirty-six hours, then had gone to work only when she had insisted that he do so.

Catherine had stuck around, helping out with the baby and some meals, but Jeremiah had made sure that he and Caleb spent alone time with Jazzy in his bedroom. For the first time, Jazzy saw them as a real family. A family with a mother and father who loved each other and had created a baby out of love.

Did she love him? She knew she did. Maybe that was why she'd been so afraid and determined to have him sign away his parental rights. She'd wanted to halt the momentum of what was growing between them, fearing that love would only make things complicated.

All of her friends were worried about her and had come bearing gifts of fruit baskets and roasts and desserts. Jeremiah, ever the protector, had made sure that they spent a little time but not too much. He was insistent that she rest and recover.

Sometimes, when he thought she was sleeping, she saw him with Caleb keeping guard. Caleb was completely content with his father. Jeremiah so loving. And he was the ultimate protector.

Right now, as the early morning sunlight filled the room, Jeremiah clearly thought she was sleeping.

"What do you think, buddy?" Jeremiah said softly. "You think your mother would like that for Mother's Day?"

Her ears perked up, but she kept her eyes closed. She'd missed the first part of what he'd said.

"I know, Mother's Day is two weeks from now, but I think that's the perfect time to let her know how I feel about her," Jeremiah went on.

Caleb gurgled.

"What's that? You think I should go for it? Hmmm." Silence ensued. Then Jeremiah said, "You think she loves me, don't you? You do? Yeah, big guy, I hope she does. Because I do love her. And we're a family."

Warmth filled Jazzy from head to toe. Slowly, she sat up in the bed. "You love me?"

Jeremiah's eyes registered shock. "You're awake."

"Yes. And I heard what you said. Do you really mean it?"

Jeremiah rose from the chair where he was sitting, carrying Caleb in his arms. He approached the bed and sank onto the mattress beside her. "It's not obvious?"

He had been there for her throughout this health scare. He'd stepped up as a father without hesitation. He was protecting her, caring for her.

Loving her.

"I guess… I guess it is."

"There's no guessing, Jazzy. I love you. I think I have from the time you came to me and asked me if I would father a baby with you."

"Oh, God." Jazzy planted a palm on her face, embarrassed by the memory. She'd had everything so planned out at the time—or so she'd thought.

Jeremiah gently took her hand and lowered it. "Don't be embarrassed. That started everything in motion. I know at the time I thought I didn't want a relationship because of what happened with Sharon, and you had your own demons. But we're not like the people who have hurt us, are we? We've had a year to see that. We've had a year to grow in love."

Tears sprang to Jazzy's eyes. Suddenly she was thinking of her mother, whom she knew would love Jeremiah. Her mother had often told her that she was too young to give up on love, that the perfect man would come into her life when she least expected it. *"It surely won't be the traditional way,"* her mother had said. *"Not for my Jazzy. But it will be the real thing. Mark my words."*

Jazzy hadn't believed it, determined to plan her life out on her terms.

Yet here she was, with a perfect man and a beautiful baby. What exactly was she running from?

"I love you, too, Jeremiah. And I love our family. And I don't want to be without you. Ever."

Jeremiah's lips spread in a grin from ear to ear, and his happiness flowed straight into Jazzy's soul. This man loved her. He really did.

"Then you're in luck, because you never have to worry about me going anywhere. Know that."

He leaned forward and softly kissed her lips. Jazzy slipped her arms around him and Caleb, holding onto the two people who meant the most to her in the world.

Caleb squealed happily. Both Jazzy and Jeremiah pulled apart, chuckling.

"Looks like our son approves," Jeremiah said.

Jazzy's heart melted as she looked at the two guys she loved. "He's probably wondering what took us so long."

Hero Wanted

by Melinda Curtis

1

I've been invited to my ex-husband's wedding. A week before the wedding, no less.

Leah Martin consolidated bouquets of daffodils in her Sea Glass Bay market stall and considered her options regarding the unexpected invitation.

"Eat a cookie and bring a hot date." Leah glanced at Marisol, her booth companion, and tugged on the waist ties of her work apron. "Did I say that out loud?"

"You did." Marisol, the middle-aged dynamo, waved a cellophane-wrapped, green-frosted seahorse cookie until she caught the attention of a passing family. Her auburn hair was pulled back in a neat bun that showed every smile line on her cheerful face. "You often say what you're thinking. You probably also talk in your sleep."

"Not that anyone is next to me to hear at night." Leah sighed, glancing around the booth set up on the sidewalk, and then the porch in front of her flower shop. Both needed sweeping. She breathed in the soft scent of roses and tried to channel the peace of a rose garden.

Marisol made a sale of the daffodil bouquet and gave the two kids each a cookie. "I can hear you. And while we have a lull, I wanted to thank you for letting me cook in your flower shop kitchen."

"You're good company." Leah meant it.

When Marisol had wandered into The Flower Girl shop several weeks ago, she'd struck up a long conversation. And because Marisol was new to town, and Leah ran the small-town florist shop all by herself, they'd drifted to the back room where Leah could work on some bouquets that had been ordered and watch her four-year-old son Owen play in his corner of the shop. And then, before Leah realized what was happening, Marisol was making cookies in the store's small kitchenette and charming both Leah and Owen. The upbeat widow had been coming back to make cookies every day since.

"I wish my sons agreed with you." Marisol arranged the last of her cookies in a basket. She used those cookies as an excuse to strike up conversation. "They insisted I move here after Paulo died, and yet they don't want to spend any time with me. Those four boys.... They don't want me cramping their style in their kitchen or with the ladies."

Her four sons ran Tank's Bar & Grill, which was located on the other side of the alley behind The Flower Girl. It was a popular hangout with singles, be they locals or tourists.

Marisol harumphed. "Those boys need to settle down and give me some grandbabies."

Those boys were in their thirties and enjoying the bachelor life too much to think about settling down. Everyone in town knew it. Everyone except Marisol.

Leah sold a few more bouquets. Meanwhile, Marisol delighted her customers with free cookies.

The bell in town square began to ring, signaling the close of Sea Glass Bay's market in the historic district, and the start of happy hour at many local restaurants.

"You're welcome to use my little kitchen anytime you want, Marisol." Leah began folding tables and transferring flowers from outside to the refrigerated case inside The Flower Girl.

Around them, other vendors were doing the same. Soon, the street would reopen to traffic. Soon, Leah would join three of her closest friends for a glass of wine at The Tipsy Table. Maybe her friends could tell her what to do about that wedding invite.

"I saved cookies for Owen and his friend Lindie. Think about finding that hot date." Marisol set two orange starfish cookies on the

112

table. And then she carried her basket of cookies out to the street, approaching the smattering of remining shoppers. "See you tomorrow."

A few minutes and a few last-minute sales later, and Leah had locked up The Flower Girl and was heading toward the ArtSea Classes & Creations booth to pick up Owen. The hands-on craft booth for kids was run by her friend Claire Bishop, who had a seemingly endless supply of energy when it came to kids.

There were only two kids left in the booth—her Owen and Lindie—the later belonging to another hard-working parent: Claire's boyfriend, Sully Vaughn. Both kids wore full-length craft aprons and happy smiles.

Leah carried three daffodil and daisy bouquets. She set one on a table for Claire. "What a busy day."

"You're not kidding." Claire was cleaning Owen's hands and face with a wet-wipe. Her strawberry-blonde hair lifted in the light ocean breeze. She smiled when she saw Leah. "We just finished finger-painting."

"Mommy, I made a rainbow for you." Owen grinned. There was green paint streaked through his dark blond hair and a smudge of red that Claire had missed on his cheek. His apron looked as if he'd wiped his paint-covered hands on it at some point. All the colors had blended into a murky black. "And tomorrow we're gonna make sparkle flowers."

"Glitter on paper cups with pipe cleaner stems." Claire informed Leah. "I'm sure the glue monster will make an appearance." She raised her hands on either side of her face and curled her fingers in and out like flexing claws. "Who likes the glue monster?"

"Oh-oh. Me!" Lindie's little hand shot up.

"And me." Owen's followed.

"Is the glue monster single?" Leah teased. "Maybe I can take him to Charlie's wedding."

"Mommy, the glue monster is our sticky hands." Owen mimicked Claire's finger curls. And then he ran to one of her supply tubs. "I'll show you."

"Nooooo—not today." Claire laughed, cutting Owen off at the pass. "We're closing up and cleaning up now, remember?"

Owen nodded, hand caressing the plastic tub as if he couldn't quite let go of the idea of the glue monster.

"I helped clean up," Lindie said brightly, hovering near Claire, who she adored. She was two years older than Owen and a big help with the little ones, according to Claire, who'd only recently begun dating Lindie's father.

"It's always good to have helpers." Leah gave Owen and Lindie their starfish cookies, in response to which they whooped. "These are for *after* dinner."

That statement dulled their excitement somewhat.

"Can I have my rainbow picture, Miss Claire?" Owen pointed to where a colorful fingerpainting was hanging on the drying board. "I want to give it to Mommy."

"Sure." Claire went to unclip it. "Just be careful. It's not quite dry."

And neither, it seemed, was Owen's craft apron. While watching Claire, he'd ran his hands up and down his apron-front, and now his hands were paint-stained once more.

"Hey, buddy." Charlie approached the booth. He wore black khakis, a black polo, a disapproving frown, and his fiancée's manicured hand possessively on his arm. "Why don't you give your rainbow picture to Mommy Ashley?"

A small voice inside Leah cried out in protest.

"I love rainbows." Ashley smiled. Her lipstick was perfect. It hadn't been chewed off after a long day of work. Her bright yellow dress hung perfectly over her slender Pilates instructor frame. She had a pedicure and a manicure and a man.

None of which Leah had time for. And if she was being honest with herself, she didn't begrudge her Charlie either. He'd never been happy to let Leah shine.

Owen frowned at his father. "I don't want Mommy Ashley to have my rainbow. Mommy puts my pictures on the 'frigerator. Mommy Ashley puts them in the trash."

Leah stifled a laugh.

I owe that boy an ice cream!

Charlie frowned.

"Oh, Baby Bear." Ashley looked aghast, running forward in her impractical heels and her too-short yellow dress, bending her knees to embrace Owen, who was still wearing his stained crafting apron. Before Leah or Claire could warn her, Ashley had swept Owen into her arms and stood. "I *adore* rainbows. And I adore you."

"Oh," Leah and Claire said at the same time, spotting the damage to Ashley's dress before she did. Dark handprints on her shoulders and a black stain to her bodice.

Ashley glanced down and gasped, practically dropping Owen to the ground, which was the wrong move to make since it caused a black paint streak from her ribcage to her hem. "My dress!"

"Mommy Ashley, you look like a bee." Owen smiled, and then made a buzzing sound.

While Ashley assessed the damage and Charlie made sympathetic noises, Claire and Leah burst into action. Claire wiped Owen's hands clean again. And then Leah carefully removed his apron, stuffing it into a plastic bag Claire gave her.

"Mommy Ashley is a pretty bee." Owen buzzed some more.

"This is Italian silk," Ashley whispered mournfully, staring down at her ruined dress.

"It's okay, babe. I'll get you a new dress." Charlie frowned at Leah. "Come along, Owen."

"Oh." Leah glanced down at her little one. "I thought you were picking him up at six tonight at my place."

"Ashley wanted to pick Owen up early to try on his tuxedo for the wedding and then we're having dinner with the caterer," Charlie said in that superior tone of his. "You should be able to keep him clean, you know."

Leah wanted to say: *He's a boy!* But that sounded sexist.

She considered saying: *Dirt has a way of finding him!* But that seemed inappropriate.

Instead, Leah smiled and took Owen's hand, giving it a squeeze. "Good explorers show it at the end of the day, don't they, buddy?" It was what she told him every night when he shed his smudged and stained clothing.

"Yup." Owen beamed up at her.

"Explorers don't get dirty sticking flowers in water for their mother's hobby," Charlie muttered.

"But crafty explorers do," Claire said staunchly. "Who's doing the flowers for your wedding?"

"A professional we found elsewhere." Charlie smirked.

"Leah, do you have a date for the wedding?" Ashley had snuck up behind Leah, the same way she'd snuck up on her ex-husband during their marriage—quietly and with her cleavage on display. "I need to let the caterer know the final headcount."

"Uh…"

"Of course, Leah has a date." Claire jumped into Leah's rescue, despite Leah not having dated in the two years since her divorce. "He's hot."

"Is he on fire?" Owen asked, wide-eyed. "Mommy shouldn't touch him if he's hot."

"Somehow, I don't think your mom's at risk of being burned," Charlie said in a haughty voice.

And Leah wanted to slug him. She'd been raised with three brothers, who'd taught her to fight her own battles. But her mother had always counseled her to use her words instead of her fists. And with Charlie, Leah found it hard to jab back in any way.

Why did he have to be such a jerk? Wasn't it enough that he'd lied when he'd promised to love her forever? Did he have to take every opportunity to make her feel small?

"Oh, Leah's date is hot." Claire kept on championing Leah's cause. "And Leah's touching him. Wait until you see them together. They sizzle." Claire licked her finger and then touched her hip with it, making a sizzling noise.

Charlie and Ashley turned their gazes toward Leah.

Leah's cheeks were heating. She should have told them that Claire was joking. But they stared at her as if the idea of Leah dating a hot guy was impossible. Ashley even rested her hand on one hip, as if she were incredulous.

And suddenly, Leah wasn't embarrassed. She was mad. How dare they think she wasn't woman enough to date a hot guy! "He's smokin' hot."

Ohmigod. What is wrong with me?

"I'll be careful not to get burned, Owen," Leah added quickly before her son could express his concern. She collected the rest of his artwork from his bin beneath the back table and then his rainbow painting from Claire. "You guys probably need to leave if Ashley's going to change. Otherwise, you won't keep to your schedule." And Ashley loved her schedules.

"She's right," Ashley said, holding her dress away from her. "I saw a cute little dress in the window of Splendiforous. Let's just run in there and see if they have it in my size."

"All right, baby." Charlie lifted Owen into his arms, and then the couple walked off without so much as a goodbye.

"Bye, honey!" Leah called after Owen, waving.

"Bye, Mommy!" Owen tilted his body away from Charlie, waving both hands.

"I don't know how you can be so nice to them." Claire commenced packing up her art supplies with the help of Lindie, who was softly singing a song about a bumblebee while stacking yarn skeins in a plastic tub.

"I have to be nice for Owen's sake." But that didn't mean their snobbery didn't hurt. "I shouldn't have told them I had a hot date."

"Oh, yes, you should have." Claire snapped a lid on a storage bin. "They only gave you an invitation last week! And only because Owen is the ring bearer, and they want you to keep him out of trouble so they can pretend to be the perfect couple on their perfect day."

"Well, there is that." Leah folded an easel. "But I want Owen to have a good time."

"You deserve a good time, too. You need a hot date," Claire said in low tones, in case little Lindie was paying more attention to their conversation than the sorting of yarn skeins.

"Can you find me someone hot enough to impress Ashley but who's not my type?" Leah's cheeks were heating again. "I'm too busy for romance."

"I know someone hot." Claire waggled her brows suggestively. "Someone sure to make Ashley respect you and Charlie to see you with new eyes."

"Hey, ladies." Sully, Lindie's father, arrived with a large wagon to load Claire's craft supplies. He was a hardworking member of the community, wiry and handsome, and quick with an encouraging word.

"Dad!" Lindie practically flew into Sully's arms and began telling him about her day.

"He's a gem," Leah whispered.

"Isn't he, though?" Claire whispered back with a private smile. "I have a gem in mind for you, too. I'm going to have this hot guy meet you at Rigatoni's tonight at six. I'll tell him you'll be carrying a daisy." She plucked one out of the bouquet Leah had brought her and handed it to Leah.

Who recoiled. "I don't do blind dates. Nobody in Sea Glass Bay should. The town is too small." And everyone knew everyone else, if not personally then at least by reputation. This blind date scheme could be worse than showing up at Charlie and Ashley's wedding solo.

Claire tsked. "When you say you *don't* do blind dates, I hear that you *haven't* done blind dates. Time to try something new."

"No. Please, no." Leah broke down one of Claire's folding tables.

"The least you can do is let me ask." Claire helped Leah carry the table to Sully's wagon. "Go on to The Tipsy Table without me."

"I don't know what you two are cooking up," Sully said, giving them a dazzling smile while holding Lindie, "but it worries me."

"Don't worry about us." Claire had a winning smile of her own for her man. "When we're done packing up, I need to run a quick errand before meeting you at The Tipsy Table."

Am I really going to let her set me up on a blind date?

The alternative was to go to Charlie's wedding dateless. So yes. Yes, she was.

Didn't stop her from experiencing a moment of panic.

Leah grabbed Claire's arm. "Don't tell anyone about this, not even Jazzy and Paige. I'd die of embarrassment. And be sure to tell this guy that I'm—"

"Gorgeous, smart, and funny," Claire finished for her, "because you are."

"Do you think so?" Leah laughed. "Suddenly, I want to date you."

The Tipsy Table had the advantage over other bars and restaurants of having outdoor seating that overlooked a small playground, which worked great when Leah had Owen with her. Though they usually gathered there on Sunday's for their weekly wine and whine session, Paige and Claire had cornered Leah in her booth at the start of the day, convincing her that they should go clothes shopping instead as their market winddown treat for the week. They knew she was dragging her feet on picking an outfit for a wedding she didn't want to go to, let alone dress for, so they'd moved their wine get-together up one night.

Leah sat down at a table with Paige and Jazzy and explained that Claire was going to be late. The daffodil bouquets she brought for her friends lay in the table's center, trying to be cheerful. Leah wasn't sure if Claire could pull off a blind date in such a short time frame, but if she did, Leah was going to have to run home and change out of her jeans and purple Flower Girl T-shirt.

"We waited to order until you showed up." Jazzy rocked an adorable little baby in her arms. "Jeremiah can't make it today." Her significant other. Her *new* significant other.

"We know how picky you are about your wine," Paige added, drinking water and watching Sully push Lindie on a swing. They planned to join the

118

group later when Claire arrived. Paige pushed a lock of short auburn hair behind her ear.

"You say that like picky is a bad thing." Leah tried not to be offended. "At least I'm not high maintenance like 'Mommy Ashley,'" she air-quoted.

They all groaned as if pained, which reminded Leah: "Jazzy—how is your stomach? Pesky parasite gone now?"

Jazzy grimaced a little, readjusting Caleb in her arms. "Yes, the antibiotics are doing their thing, thankfully."

Claire leaned forward in her seat, concern showing. "Should you even be here? It's only been a few days since the hospital, and we would have understood if…"

Jazzy waved her off. "This is the only time I've been out since I got home, and it will only be for an hour or so. Besides, I bailed on our wine and whine session last week to have dinner with Lauren." She beamed. "And then there is Jeramiah—he has been absolutely amazing, looking after Caleb while I recovered. It helps to have a hot guy around. Although, I have to admit, I'm not bouncing back as quickly as I would have…like, say…in my twenties. Why does it feel like guys stay in their prime—smoking hot—long after women do?"

"It's the price of having babies. Or mothering everyone around us. It ages us. We were all hot in our prime," Leah said with a low chuckle, reaching forward to stroke the black hair on Caleb's head.

"We're on fire now," Paige said unconvincingly, making Jazzy and Leah laugh. "Hey, we are! Or at least, Jazzy and Claire are. They have men." She sighed. "Give over that baby, Jazzy, before I talk myself into the pathetic zone."

Jazzy transferred Caleb to Paige's arms. Staring at the baby made Leah long for another child. She'd come from a large family and had always assumed she'd have several children of her own.

"Can we just agree that we're well-aged," Leah suggested, smiling warmly at her friends, despite being unable to forget Claire was setting up a blind date for her this very minute. The intimidation factor of a date with a hot man was making her palms clammy. "We're aged like fine wine.… Speaking of which, it's time to order. Let's order Claire her Syrah. I'm going to have a white wine blend." She waved to their waiter as a bee flew past. "Oh, my gosh. I almost forgot. You won't believe what happened to Ashley this afternoon…"

2

*B*usiness always picked up at Tank's Bar & Grill as the weekend market in the town's historic center wound down.

Hank DeLeon came out of the office to help his brothers with the sudden rush.

But before he reached the host's station, Charlie Martin flagged him down. He held a young boy on his hip and a purposeful look in his eye. "Hank. I set up a meeting with the owner of the buildings across the alley. Bill might be interested in hearing your offer to lease that space we talked about." He glanced around as if concerned someone might be listening.

"The florist space?" It was the perfect size for his mother to open a small restaurant, and the perfect place to keep her under his watchful eye. "Fantastic."

A frown passed quickly over Charlie's face and he cast another furtive glance around the bar. "Yes, the lease is coming up for renewal, or reassignment, next month. I'll send you the details." He left, holding open the front door for...

Hank's mother. She carried a basket of cookies and passed them out to the waiting customers with a broad smile.

Where did she get those cookies? Hank forgot about helping the host seat the peak rush of customers and met her mid-restaurant, taking her arm. "Where have you been? I tried to call you several times today and you didn't pick up."

Mama patted his hand and gently but firmly freed herself, sashaying toward the kitchen. "You know I don't turn on my phone unless I want to call someone, Henry." She was the only one who called Hank by his given name.

Hank tossed his hands, looking around the bar and restaurant for his brothers, who were already converging on him. "But what if we want to call you?"

Roman had followed Mama from the hostess station. "You can't just wander around town without telling us where you're going."

"Dad always knew where you were." Emilio came from behind the bar.

Their brother Sebastian came out of the kitchen, wiping his hands on a white dish towel. "What if something happened to one of us?"

Mama stopped and faced them. "Your father always knew where I was because we ran a restaurant *together*. But he didn't need to know where I was every minute of every day. If something were to happen to me, I'd turn on the cell phone. And if something were to happen to one of you, I'd know it, and I'd call." She turned her back on them and marched into the kitchen.

The four DeLeon brothers looked at each other, shaking their heads. Standing together, Hank was reminded of how alike they were in appearance—tall, broad shouldered, dark hair, and their father's strong chin, which was apparently no match for their mother's stubborn streak.

"I told you not to let her take that apartment in the Sea Glass Bay Retirement Home." Sebastian snapped Hank's arm with his dish towel before returning to the kitchen.

"Or let her keep her car." Emilio poked Hank's shoulder with the point of one knuckle, and then headed to the bar. "Some head of the family you've become."

"She should have moved in with you." Roman gave Hank a disparaging look before heading back to the hostess station. "Then you wouldn't snap at us all the time."

Hank ran a hand over his goatee, mumbling to himself, "Dad wanted us to watch out for her. I didn't think it'd be this time-consuming." He'd thought it'd be simple to set her up in a small restaurant that only served lunch. That would allow her to participate in the retirement home's activities in the afternoon. And then one of her sons would dutifully see she was safely tucked away in her apartment every night. It was the vision their father had for her. A vision he hadn't yet told her about. A plan Hank was finding hard to execute.

Most of the time he had no idea where she was. And Roman was right. Since her move here, all Hank seemed to do was snap at everyone.

So much for the best laid plans.

Mama popped out of the kitchen. "You're not pushing today's special enough, Henry." Clearly, she'd taken inventory of the kitchen with her usual efficiency, one learned from running a restaurant with their father for forty years.

Hank held up a hand in her direction. "Mama, it's a bar more than a restaurant. I'm not going to push breakfast for dinner just because you made a new friend and purchased eight dozen eggs."

"I know a thing or two about the hospitality business." Mama swatted his hand down. "You have to mix up the menu regularly, so your customers find you interesting. Which means having daily specials, and it also means you've got to push the special until it's gone to cover costs. I don't know how you boys have stayed in business so long without me."

"We're more a bar than a restaurant, Mama." He didn't know how many times he'd told her that.

"If you serve food, you're a restaurant." She flounced back toward the kitchen.

Hank leaned against the bar and gestured to Emilio to give him a shot of whiskey. He'd moved to Sea Glass Bay five years ago when he got out of the Army and purchased the bar. It was far enough away from Redding that his folks couldn't interfere, but close enough that he could get home in a day if needed. Sebastian had been a Navy cook and had shown up during the first year Hank was open. The kitchen was his domain, and he was struggling to share it with their mother. When Emilio was done serving in the Marines, he'd come to tend bar, working the taps with Hank on the busiest nights of the week, or holding up the fort when Tank had to disappear into the office to handle all the owner-related upkeep of the business. He had the patience of a saint and could listen to customers talk for hours. And when Roman had enough of the Air Force, he'd also landed in The Bay, as the older locals called their northern California town. He was the pretty brother, and as the face of Tank's, he was a good magnet to draw a crowd. But Hank was finding that five DeLeons were too many for one establishment. He needed to find Mama a place of her own.

"Emilio!" A slender curly blonde—or was she a very light red-head?—hurried up to the bar. Curiously, she had a smear of dark brown paint on her shirt sleeve. "What time do you get off work? I have a huge favor to ask."

"I'm off at six, Claire." Emilio handed Hank a filled shot glass. "Don't tell me you need help moving classrooms again. Or loading your car with bricks for some art project. Or *anything* to do with heavy lifting."

Hank recognized the woman now. She'd helped Emilio pour drinks at an outdoor event they'd held last summer. He downed his shot, letting the alcohol burn away his frustration over managing his wayward mother.

"There's no heavy lifting involved with this favor." Claire sat on a barstool and extended her arms across the gleaming mahogany surface, hands reaching toward Emilio. "My friend needs a date tonight."

Emilio drew back, shaking his head. "I don't do blind dates."

Oh, this is going to be good. Hank grinned.

Claire scoffed. "What a coincidence. She doesn't either." Arms still on the bar, she made a gimme gesture with her hands. "Come on, Emilio. You owe me. Remember that time I pretended to be your girlfriend last summer when that blonde wouldn't stop hitting on you?"

Hank chuckled. He remembered.

Emilio continued shaking his head.

The reddish-blonde straightened in her seat, not taking no for an answer. "This won't be a hardship. Leah is gorgeous, smart, and funny."

Leah. Hank cast about his mental contacts file. Since opening the bar, Hank wasn't much for networking or socializing, unlike his date-happy brothers. He couldn't put a face to the name.

"Come on. What's wrong with her?" Again, Emilio shook his head. "Gorgeous, smart, and funny women don't need blind dates."

"She works all the time and never has a chance to meet anyone." Claire clasped her hands together. "Please."

Hank moved behind the bar to rinse his empty shot glass.

"Leah? The Flower Girl shop owner?" Mama had come out of the kitchen and was barging in on the conversation. "She's adorable. Emilio, you must go."

"Yes." Claire grinned at Emilio, tossing her hair over her shoulder. "See? She's Marisol-approved."

Leah was The Flower Girl shop owner? Hank would love to know if she were open to relocating so that Mama could open a small restaurant in her space.

"Be a good boy and go." Mama came to stand next to Emilio, putting an arm over his shoulders and giving him a gentle shake.

Emilio knew he was trapped and immediately capitulated, although he didn't look happy. "Of course, Mama."

"Fantastic. Leah will be at Rigatoni's at six and carrying a single daisy." Claire slid off the barstool and hurried toward the door.

"You owe me," Emilio called after her.

"No." Claire was adamant. "Now we're even."

Mama returned to the kitchen while Emilio took a few drink orders and Hank thought about this opportunity to talk to Leah. Charlie was the realtor advising Hank in his search for a small restaurant space for his mother, but Hank preferred to gather his information from a more direct source.

"Hey." Hank moved next to his brother. "You've already put in a long day. I'll meet Leah during my dinner break."

"You?" Emilio didn't look up from the two Moscow Mules he was making. "You don't date either."

Hank drew up short. "It's not a date."

"What are you up to?" Emilio's hands stilled. He gave Hank an inquisitive look.

"Nothing." Hank walked away. "And if I was up to something, it'd be none of your business."

"Worst idea ever," Leah mumbled to herself from her seat in Rigatoni's.

Every time the restaurant door opened, Leah smiled and sat up straighter. The flowered, blue jersey sheath she'd chosen to wear with a white sweater was increasingly feeling like it was too casual for the white tablecloth establishment. It was now six-fifteen, her back was beginning to ache, and it was looking more likely that Claire had been unable to find Leah a date.

She got out her cell phone and texted Claire: *My date is late.*

Claire immediately replied: *But he's worth the wait.* She added a smiling emoji holding a rose between his teeth.

Okay. So at least she wasn't being stood up.

"Excuse me." A deep voice. A big hand dragging a chair back. A tall man.

Leah's eyes kept going up. Over the black button-down shirt that covered broad shoulders. Over the black goatee, the straight nose, short black hair, and cool dark eyes that were just as unabashedly assessing her. He was one of the DeLeon brothers who ran Tank's Bar & Grill. But which one? Him not being a native of Sea Glass Bay and she not being nosy, Leah didn't know.

What would Marisol say if she knew they were on a date? Leah didn't know.

She squared her shoulders, wondered if she'd bitten her lipstick off, and flashed her DeLeon date a smile, along with the daisy. "Did Claire send you?"

He nodded, sitting down and leaning back in his chair as if he needed distance to assess her. "I'm Hank."

Hank. *Henry,* as his mother called him. He was the oldest DeLeon and the owner of Tank's.

Leah introduced herself. She couldn't stop staring at him because he wasn't exactly what she'd ordered. Sexiness exuded from every pore, but it wasn't a turn-off. At least, not on her part. Hank was the kind of suave, arrogant man who'd never date her for real. Hank would date women who carried name brand accessories, had regular manicures, and put sophisticated highlights in their hair. They'd be high maintenance, but he wouldn't put much effort toward maintaining them. Why should he? Rumor had it that women hung out at the bar for a chance to date a DeLeon man. Was it a rumor? Hank's presence here seemed to indicate it was.

Best get down to business first, in case Hank wasn't going to go along with the wedding date idea. "I don't know how much Claire told you, but—"

"We'll start with drinks." Hank signaled their waiter. "I'll have a glass of your best Cabernet. And the lady…" His cool gaze sent hot waves over Leah. "She'll have a Moscato."

"Too sweet." Leah grimaced. "I'll have the Sauvignon Blanc from New Zealand." She'd seen it featured on the menu's wine list.

The waiter disappeared.

"You know wine?" Hank quirked those dark eyebrows.

Yes, arrogant was an apt descriptor. Hot, too.

Speaking of which…. It was hot in the restaurant. Leah would have flapped the ends of her sweater if it didn't give away that Hank was the source of the heat. If she didn't get a grip on her self-esteem, she was at risk of melting into a puddle at his feet.

She cleared her throat. "Hey, not only do I know wine, but I know how to change a flat tire, too." Leah tapped her thumb against her chest, where her heart was currently beating an oh-my-he's-sexy, fast-paced cadence. "Divorced single moms need to learn how to take care of themselves."

"You're prickly." He stroked his goatee and Leah could just imagine those dark whiskers scraping across the sensitive skin beneath her ear.

What is happening to me?

"You need the Moscato. A little sweetness smooths away the edges." He tried to signal for the waiter.

Leah's mouth dropped open and the impact of all that sexiness fell to the black and white checkerboard tile at her feet. "Please don't change my drink order."

"You'll thank me later."

She bristled. Her ex never listened to her either. "I think not." Leah reached across the table and captured his raised hand, drawing it down between them and somehow tangling her fingers with his.

They fit, those fingers, even if Hank's attitude didn't fit with hers. And it was that incongruency that slowed everything down until it was as if she and Hank were alone. And holding hands. And staring into each other's eyes over a romantic candle flame. In his eyes, she swore she saw surprise, along with another flare of heat.

I want to kiss him.

Leah swallowed, still caught in that dark gaze.

I am in so much trouble.

Hank loosened his hold and shifted his grip, cradling her fingers in his. "You aren't what I expected."

What was she supposed to say to that? Leah inched her hand free, and with each inch her cheeks grew hotter.

Their wine glasses arrived.

Hank raised his Cabernet toward her. "To the unexpected."

"Please, no. I hate surprises." Leah cast about for a better toast. "To not making a fool of myself." She clinked her glass with his and drank. The wine was cool and refreshing, exactly what Leah needed to reboot this date.

She set her wine down on the white tablecloth, prepared to tell Hank exactly why he'd been asked to meet her. There would be no other dinners before or after Charlie's wedding.

But Hank was already signaling the waiter to return. "We'll start with Caesar salads and then have the linguini with clams."

Leah's ire grew. "You're ordering for me?"

"Yes. It's what Latin men do on dates." Hank sipped his wine as the waiter hurried off, studying her over the rim of his glass. "Rigatoni's is known for their clam dishes. If you look around, half the customers have ordered it. If you're allergic to shellfish, we can change your order. I think you'll like the risotto."

Being Latin was no excuse for being presumptuous and rude. "Do you know what gives me an adverse reaction?"

He shrugged. "How would I know? We've only just met."

Leah drew a calming breath. "I don't like being told what to do or what I should like or how I should run my business." Hello unresolved issues with her ex. Leah tried to soften her words with a smile.

Hank tilted his wine glass toward her. "Who's been telling you how to run your business?"

"My ex-husband for one." Why had she told Hank that? She crumpled the cloth napkin in her lap. "That's not the point. The point is—"

"And what does he say to get your hackles up?"

"That I have too much unused space in my flower shop." Leah loosened her grip on her napkin. "He doesn't understand me or my dreams."

"You like elbow room," Hank surmised, again with that superior voice that should have grated on her nerves. After all, Charlie spoke the same way.

Except he didn't, she realized. Charlie's contempt and tone were meant to demean. Hank's was just a reflection of his self-assuredness.

"If you must know, Hank, I have plans to expand, plus I like my location." Leah sat back in her chair, trying to relax or at least appear so. "How, exactly, did we start this personal conversation?"

"We ordered wine," Hank said simply. "I was wrong. The Sauvignon Blanc is taking the edge off your temper nicely."

"I like my edges. I mean…" What was this man doing to her? Leah sipped her wine. "Everyone says I'm very nice. If anything, the wine didn't soften my edges, it gave me some." She rarely talked back to anyone, including Charlie.

"You don't like your wine?" He glanced around for the waiter.

Her hand instinctively went to his slowly rising arm. This time, her palm covered the back of his hand and brought it gently down to the table. "My wine is fine. Do you always have conversations like this?"

His brow clouded. "About wine? All the time. I run a bar."

The waiter approached with salads and a bread bowl.

Leah drew her hand back. "I'm not sure we're talking about the same things."

"But we are." Hank settled his gaze with more certainty on her. "You have the space to expand your business, but you haven't yet, which means that you either lack the capital or the courage to do so."

"We're definitely not talking about the same things." They weren't even on the same wavelength. Perhaps it was time to steer a course to safer waters. "Are you a sports fan?"

"No." He dug into his salad. "Is that the direction you want to move your business in?"

"No." *I was just trying to make polite conversation.* She took a healthy sip of wine. "Did Claire tell you why I wanted to meet with you?"

"No."

"Good…I mean, it's just a date." The more time she spent with Hank, the more convinced she was that he wasn't the right man to take to Charlie's wedding.

Which left her back at square one.

3

"You should take a day off," Sully Vaughn told Leah early Sunday morning as he dropped off a special order of teapot vases, which he set on her workbench in the back room. "You work seven days a week."

Smiling, Leah opened the box to make sure none of the merchandise had been damaged during shipment, but it all seemed packed well. She tightened the ties of her work apron. "Isn't that the pot calling the kettle black?"

"Maybe." Sully chuckled before taking the back steps to his truck. "Although, I can't say I'm a workaholic now that I'm dating Claire and I have a personal life." With a friendly wave, he was gone.

"I have a life," Leah grumbled to herself. What would Sully say if he knew she had gone on a date last night? Whatever he thought, he'd have had the wrong impression.

The service at Rigatoni's had been efficient. Leah had managed to keep the conversation rolling and had avoided touching Hank a third time. There'd been a disagreement when the bill arrived. She'd wanted to pay or at least go Dutch—Hank would have none of it. And so, she'd ended their date while he settled up the bill, scurrying out the door before having to deal with him wanting to walk her home and facing a worse fate—that awkward moment where the date ends and it's a *Should I/Shouldn't I* game regarding a goodnight kiss. She

129

was convinced that she shouldn't kiss on a first date, even if there'd been enough sparks when they touched to set off a Fourth of July fireworks display.

"The last thing I need is to date a guy just because he's sexy." Leah brought several bunches of flowers from her cooler, preparing to make Mother's Day themed bouquets for the teapots. "The nerve of Hank to think I lack the courage to expand my business."

She drew a deep breath, letting the sweet mix of floral aromas calm her.

She glanced around the workroom, which was divided into four different spaces. A walk-in refrigerated unit, two worktables, a small kitchenette, and Owen's corner with his sand table, blue beanbag chair, and toys. She'd like to hire another florist, at least part-time. And she'd like to grow plants for sale. But while Owen was young, his need for space was her priority. Or it was when he wasn't staying with Charlie, as he was now.

"I have courage. And a strong work ethic." Leah set about preparing the teapots to be filled with short arrangements. She set oasis foam bricks inside, and then began cutting filler flowers and foliage to height. "And I don't show up for a date with a woman intending to put her in her place."

"Did I come at a bad time?" Marisol poked her head in the back door. She had on a flowing magenta blouse and a black skirt. "If you need a few more minutes to talk to yourself about a bad date…" She blinked and entered without finishing her sentence. "You can always talk to me. Vent. Go on."

Talk to Marisol about dating her oldest son? *Not in this lifetime.*

"I was just rehashing a show I watched on Netflix last night," Leah improvised. "Single moms who own flower shops don't have time to date."

"Rules-rules-rules." Marisol tsked and set down a cloth grocery bag on the kitchen counter. "Love is like a wildflower. It needs a little sunshine to bloom. You don't need to read up on the rules of growing for that. And it may come as a surprise to you, Leah, but you won't find sunshine in this workshop."

"I'll get plenty of sunshine when the market opens in…" Leah glanced at the time on her camera lock screen, "oh, less than an hour. I better get moving." She snipped off stems and stuck flowers in teapots.

"Plenty of sunshine but no blooms," Marisol said in that mothering way of hers, gentle but knowing.

"I'll give you blooms." Leah stuck a floral pick that said Happy Mother's Day into the center of a small arrangement in a white and pink striped teapot. And then she brought it over to Marisol. "Cappuccino roses, lavender snapdragons, and pink Gerber daisies. That'll bring a little sunshine to anyone's day, just like you bring sunshine into mine." No male DeLeon needed.

"Do you know what this could use?" Marisol admired Leah's work, smiling. "A trio of wedding cookies tied to the handle."

"It needs a home on your shelf," Leah said firmly, "in your home."

"Nonsense." Marisol unloaded her groceries from her bag. "I get enough enjoyment from working around beauty. I don't need to bring any home."

"Fine, but I left you an envelope on the counter to reimburse you for the cookies you gave away yesterday with my flowers."

"I don't want—"

"Please don't argue. It's what I would have paid a supplier for them."

Marisol frowned at the envelope.

"I can't keep letting you contribute to my business like it's a charity," Leah said softly, turning the teapot and moving it to the back corner of the counter so that Marisol could enjoy it, but it was out of her way. She tucked the envelope beneath it.

"Do you remember the first day I wandered in here?" Marisol's gaze sought Leah's. Her dark eyes were filled with unshed tears. "I was lost and looking for something. I didn't know what. But you talked to me as if you'd known me forever. And little Owen ran to greet me as if we were family. And I felt as if I'd found that something that had been missing since Paulo died." She took the envelope and stared at it. "You didn't blink when I asked to bake cookies here. You didn't blink when I suggested cookies would help sell your flowers. And you shouldn't blink when I give this money back to you." She held out the envelope. "I don't come here out of charity for you. I come here because you welcomed me into a community and introduced me to your friends in the farmers market. I come here because you make me feel at home and not a burden."

It was Leah who was blinking back tears now. She accepted the envelope and gave a small nod. "Okay."

"Yes." Marisol sniffed. "All will be okay. With a bit of sunshine, a few blooms, and a trio of wedding cookies."

A few hours and many bouquet arrangements later, as Leah was setting up for the market, Jazzy popped by, her baby strapped to a carrier on her chest.

Leah tickled his little toes, earning a tentative smile in return. "You're looking healthy enough to tackle the world again."

"I woke up today with no pain—not even a dull ache in my stomach. I feel so much better!"

"And I swear, that baby gets cuter every day."

"I think so, too. But I'm biased." Jazzy shook her head, sending dark curls swinging. "Hey, I had an idea last night. We're at separate street entrances of the market strip. I was thinking that I could feature some of your live plants in my booth, outside my shop, and you might display some of my sea glass crafts in yours? That way we could double our sale potential." Jazzy collected sea glass from the beach that had given the town its name and made art from it. She tilted her head and smiled coyly. "Pretty please."

"Of course." Leah grabbed the now-empty teapot box and filled it with live plants in various decorative planters. "I'll carry these over and you can give me some stuff to bring back. There's a Flower Girl tag with the price on each plant. I have hooks on the patio, so some of your blue-green windchimes would be perfect." She headed to the front. "Marisol, I'll be right back."

Jazzy and Leah hurried down the steps and over to Jazzy's booth toward the other end of the market strip. With a bit of rearranging, the plants found new display homes.

"It's funny how plants make my booth seem more inviting," Jazzy noted, rubbing Caleb's back.

"It breaks up the fragile displays of your exquisite artwork," Leah agreed. "Although I still wouldn't let Owen in here unsupervised."

"Mommy!" Owen ran up to Leah, who swept him into her arms. He smelled like syrup and boy.

"Speak of the devil," Jazzy said softly.

Leah grinned and hugged her son tighter. "Did you miss me, pumpkin?"

"Yep." His little arms wound around her neck. "And Marisol's cookies."

Charlie and Ashley stood at the entrance to Leah's outdoor booth. Ashley drifted to Paige's booth, where she sold a variety of aromatherapy candles. Charlie waved Leah over.

She set Owen down. "Hang out with Miss Jazzy for a minute, pumpkin."

"Okay." Owen reached for Jazzy's hand.

Charlie wasted no time when Leah reached him. "Ashley and I have been talking. We don't approve of Owen being raised in a flower shop."

Leah gritted her teeth. "Would you like to pay for his full-time preschool tuition?" She footed the bill for afternoon sessions.

Charlie pressed his lips together.

"I thought not." Leah returned to Jazzy's booth and picked up Owen, needing her son in her arms. "Did you have a good time, pumpkin?" Leah asked in a voice that felt like it had sharp edges. She was reminded of Hank's heated gaze and softened her voice. "I missed you so much."

Owen sighed and rested his head on her shoulder. He always returned a little pensive from visits with his father. Leah hated that.

"Marisol made those little white cookies you love so much." Leah set Owen's feet on the sidewalk, kneeling to tie one of his blue sneakers. "Why don't you run back to the shop and ask for one."

He pulled at the blond cowlick on his crown, fighting back a smile. "Can I have two?"

What a charmer he was going to be. Leah tipped her head from side to side. "You'll have to ask Marisol." If it was up to Leah, he might get three.

"Marisol!" Owen raced off in that endearing toddler gait of his, more arm swing than fast legs. "Marisol!"

Leah's heart swelled with joyful regret. It seemed like just yesterday that Owen had taken his first steps. "You better watch out, Jazzy. They grow up before you know it." And things change without warning—like Charlie's request for a divorce and the unexpected invitation to his wedding.

"That's what they say. Are you okay?" Jazzy asked softly, having filled the teapot box with some of her sea glass work for Leah to take back. "You look a little worried."

Leah forced a smile. "Oh, you know. It's Charlie's wedding. I hate to go alone." But she was going to anyway.

Jazzy nodded. "I guess the new Mrs. Martin doesn't want a four-year-old running around her fancy-schmancy wedding reception without supervision."

"You've got that right. And since it's being held on a seaside cliff, I don't trust Charlie's parents to watch Owen." They weren't exactly hands-on grandparents.

"You need a man."

From his carrier, Caleb cooed his agreement.

"A capable, successful man." Leah picked up the box with sea glass. "Know of any?"

Jazzy's expression turned mischievous. "I have one in mind. Can I set you up?"

Leah hesitated. She really didn't want to go to Charlie's wedding alone. And it couldn't be as bad as her first blind date, could it? "Okay."

"Really?" Jazzy's eyes widened.

Leah chuckled. "You don't have to sound so surprised."

"I didn't take you for the adventurous type." Jazzy held up a hand. "I mean, until recently, I'd given up on love. I thought we were in the same camp."

"I'm not looking for love," Leah said matter-of-factly. "I'm looking for a plus one."

"All right, then." Jazzy grinned. "I'll text you the details, but I don't know if I can make it happen for a few days."

"You don't have to explain. I understand. But…can this just be our secret? I know I shouldn't feel embarrassed about this, but if word got back to Charlie…"

"Enough said. My lips are sealed."

When Leah had finished setting up Jazzy's windchime display, she went inside her shop. Marisol had given Owen three wedding cookies and a glass of milk in a green sippy cup.

"Did you tell Jazzy about your date?" Marisol sounded hurt at the possibility.

"No." Leah cleaned up her workstation, sweeping discarded leaves and stems into the trash.

"Did you get burned, Mommy?" Owen's mouth was rimmed with powdered sugar. "Miss Claire said you were seeing a hot man."

Marisol's amused gaze met Leah's.

"No, pumpkin. I didn't get burned." But Leah's cheeks heated all the same. She turned away, wiping down the worktable.

"I want to hear about that fire." Marisol stirred batter in a bowl.

About her son? Not on Leah's life! A change of subject was long overdue. "What are you making? You've done four dozen wedding cookies already."

"Polvorones." Marisol tipped her head, smiling the way she did when she was excited about baking. "Which are just sugar cookies with food coloring, but they're meant to lift the spirits."

"Bright cookies. Bright flowers. You're right. All that color will brighten up anyone's mood."

Marisol stopped stirring. "Your husband's marriage is soon. Did you find an escort last night on your hot date?"

"First off, he's my *ex*-husband." As if Leah could forget. "And second, I should be strong enough to go solo."

"Bad move." Marisol went back to stirring her batter. "You should show up at the wedding with a strong man by your side. Someone your husband will measure himself against and maybe be a bit jealous of."

"Marisol!" Leah glanced at Owen, but he was playing with his superhero figurines and making battle noises.

"I'm a widow, but I'm still a woman," Marisol said with sass. "You have more class than that couple. You should let the world know it."

"Show the world," Leah laughed, "by toting around a handsome man?"

"Yes. And wearing a revenge dress that tells everyone what a fool your husband was to let you go." Marisol ran a hand from her shoulder to her thigh, as if showing off that revenge dress.

The idea appealed in theory. It was the execution that was tripping Leah up in the man department. "Doesn't a revenge dress imply that I care what my *ex*-husband thinks?"

Marisol tsked. "A dress like that with a better man at your side means you're over him and don't care what anyone thinks."

Good thing she'd already planned on going dress shopping with the girls that night. "I guess I need a revenge dress."

After the market ended, Leah found herself at Splendiforous with her friends shopping for something too-hot-for-you to wear to Charlie's wedding. She sat in a chair with Owen on her lap while everyone searched for the right dress.

"This one?" Marisol held up a floor-length mauve dress with heavy beading over the bodice. "It's very classy."

"Matronly," Paige whispered from her seat next to Leah, adding in a louder voice. "She has nice legs. She should show them off."

"You're right." Marisol nodded. "I should buy this dress. I can wear it on Trudy's birthday cruise coming up."

Paige nodded. Trudy was her aunt. "You'd look good in that on the dance floor."

Jazzy appeared from behind a rack, pushing Caleb in his stroller with one hand. With the other, she held up a red cocktail dress with spaghetti straps. "How about this?"

"I'd feel more confident if the dress was bra-friendly." Leah's comment earned a double-take from Owen. She covered his ears. "Girl talk, pumpkin."

"I found this one on the clearance rack." Claire held a gauzy white dress up to her shoulders.

"Does it come with a slip?" Leah asked, hands still over Owen's ears. "Or a full body pair of Spanx?" Because it was too revealing. And too white. She was not going to be the bride, so she was sure as hell not going to dress like one. There's a world of difference between getting a revenge dress and being vengeful. The later was not her style.

"What about that dress in the window?" Paige got up and went to find Maddy, who owned the shop, while the others went to the store window.

Leah stood, settling Owen on her hip, and joined them. "It looks expensive."

"Revenge dresses don't come cheap," Marisol said, the mauve evening gown slung over her arm.

Claire put her hand under the hem. "It's not sheer, like the white dress."

"And it's sleeveless, but you can wear a bra," Jazzy noted.

Maddy wound her way through the racks toward them. "I'll give you the friends and family discount."

"She'll take it," Paige said.

"Mama, are you trying to sneak out the back door?" Hank looked up from an email Charlie had sent him with an appointment request to talk terms on the lease to The Flower Girl shop. He'd been crunching numbers all Monday afternoon, trying to find a lease amount that made sense for Mama.

Like his so-called date with Leah, the numbers were fluid and could mean success or failure. He'd asked Sully about her when he brought a special delivery of whiskey. Leah had a reputation as being kindhearted and easy going. All she'd done during dinner was block his questions. And then she'd tried to pay for dinner! Hank respected women, but his father had been a stickler about how they should be treated—like queens. He liked women who let him be in charge. He sighed. He should *only* be thinking about Leah in terms of what it might cost to buy her out of her lease.

But thinking about Leah didn't change the fact that Mama was trying to sneak past him. His office was between the kitchen and the back door. "Mama? Where are you going?"

"Out." His mother backed up, returning to view. She had her hands behind her back.

"What have you got behind you?"

"Tamales." There was a mutinous tone in her voice as she swung the bag around.

"I thought you were making tamales for the special tonight." He narrowed his gaze. "Are you giving those away? What happened to managing inventory to maximize profits?"

"I made extra. I'm having a potluck dinner with my friends from the apartment complex."

"The retirement home," he muttered disparagingly. At the rates they charged, they should keep his mother occupied and at home every day.

"Don't call it that, Henry." Mama shook a finger at him. "I'm not over the hill."

"But you are, currently, retired." His father's life insurance policy and the sale of their restaurant in Redding enabled her to live as she pleased. He just didn't want her to be roped into someone's scheme and taken for all she was worth. She'd once invested a thousand dollars with a door-to-door scammer. Her daily disappearances were worrisome.

Mama scoffed. "I'm retired, but not to a rocking chair."

The back door was flung open. "Hey, Marisol. I was taking a shortcut from my shop and thought I'd come in since I have a minute. I'm looking for Roman." A woman appeared in Hank's doorway. She had black curly hair, an infectious smile, and wore a carrier with a baby strapped to her front. "I have a surprise for Roman." She captured her little one's feet in her hands and held them up, as if the baby was Roman's surprise.

Hank's mouth dropped open. Had Roman...? Was she...? Was that baby...? "Um...Roman?"

"Roman's out front, Jazzy." Mama pointed the baby mama in the direction of Hank's younger brother.

Jazzy continued down the hall toward the restaurant proper.

"Are you sure that was wise?" Hank bumped the corner of his desk in his haste to follow Jazzy.

Mama trailed behind him, clutching those tamales to her chest as if he might take them away from her. "When did you become such a busybody?"

"When I became the head of this family." Hank hadn't thought about it before, but it was true. He was the oldest DeLeon now. It was his job to watch out for everyone. Not just Mama, but his brothers, too. "She's got a baby. Aren't you worried? Or curious?"

"About Jazzy?" Mama laughed. "No. If you spent more time with your downtown neighbors, you wouldn't worry either."

They reached the bar and a spot where Hank was close enough to listen and far enough away to pretend he wasn't. Mid-afternoon business was slow. He set his elbows on the bar top, ignoring Emilio's questioning look.

"You aren't fooling anyone, *mijo*." Mama rolled her eyes.

Hank held up a hand, requesting silence.

"Roman." Jazzy flagged his brother down at the host station. "Surprise! I need a favor."

"Jazzy, you and favors are no surprise." Roman smiled easily at Jazzy as if he wasn't responsible for the precious tyke in her carrier. "You always need something."

Hank drew a relieved breath.

Emilio went to check on a couple drinking on the outside patio.

"I have this friend," Jazzy began, hooking her thumbs in her carrier straps. "And she has an event coming up that she needs a date for."

"Someone sexy," Mama murmured next to Hank. "Roman is perfect."

"You say that like Roman is your only son with sex appeal," Hank grumbled.

"I have an active social life, Jazzy," Roman was saying. "I don't need to be set-up or offered for pity dates."

Mama gasped. "That boy needs to work on his manners."

Hank was experiencing a moment of déjà vu, like the other night when Claire had asked Emilio if he'd meet Leah for dinner.

"This isn't a pity date." Jazzy huffed. "Leah has a lot going for her. But she's super busy with Mother's Day coming up and she really needs some eye candy at this event."

Leah.

Hank relived that jolt of awareness sparked by Leah's touch. That was quickly followed by a wave of heat he attributed to misplaced jealousy. He didn't want Roman to take Leah out. He didn't want Roman to touch Leah's hand and feel a bolt of attraction. And he definitely didn't want Roman to kiss Leah, because he'd been consumed with curiosity about how her lips would taste.

"What happened when Emilio met Leah for dinner? Did he say?" Mama whispered, trying to push past Hank, but he set his arm in her path. "I tried to ask, and Leah implied the date was a dud."

A dud? Far from it. "You shouldn't ask about your grown sons' dates."

"Why not?" Mama demanded, although in a whisper because they were both still half-listening to Jazzy and Roman's exchange.

"Because you might not like what you hear," Hank whispered back. She frowned.

"Jazzy…" Roman warned.

"Now, Roman, we both know you have superpowers when it comes to the opposite sex. I'm just asking you to use them for good for once." Jazzy grinned. "Leah needs a date to make her ex feel inadequate. You should be flattered. I immediately thought of you and—"

"Leah has a revenge dress," Mama muttered, distracting Hank from hearing the details Jazzy went into. "Low-cut cleavage. High cut hem. Midnight as a star-studded romantic evening."

Hank glanced down at his mother. "If your grandkids could see you now…"

"I don't *have* any grandkids." Mama put her nose in the air.

Meanwhile, Roman had agreed to meet with Leah.

My love-'em-and-leave-'em brother is taking Leah out.

Hank's hands fisted.

"Sweet." Jazzy high fived Roman. "Meet Leah at the Cliff House tonight at six-thirty to work out the details for this weekend. I'll text her that you're coming. She's blonde and she'll be carrying a daisy."

"In her teeth?" Roman chuckled.

Hank rapped his knuckles on the bar top as Jazzy headed back their way.

"Hey." Hank stepped into her path. "Jazzy, is it? You should add some mystery to that date. Don't tell Leah who she's meeting."

"Oooo. That's brilliant." Jazzy grinned at Hank, who felt like a jerk for suggesting such a thing, but a plan was forming in his head…

He let Jazzy pass, barely registering that his mother was exiting with her.

And then he walked over to Roman to tell him there was no need to plan on dinner at the Cliff House.

Hank was taking his place.

4

The Cliff House was a fancy steak and seafood restaurant perched on a seaside cliff.

Leah sat at a table near a window overlooking the ocean. Her chair faced the front of the restaurant, but the setting sun was making her squint and she couldn't make out who was entering.

With Owen once again with his father, she'd gone the whole nine yards for this date—straightening her hair, shaving her legs, and donning a green dress with white that made her feel sexy without being "out for revenge" level. She'd ordered a glass of Meritage to take the edge off her nerves and was holding up her daisy like a wand during an incantation, trying to be noticeable without holding up a sign that said: *Your blind date is over here.*

A man stepped out of the glare, stopping at her table.

She squinted up at him, able only to discern his outline—tall in height, broad in the shoulders, the impression of a dark suit jacket over a white shirt.

"I see you're already taking the edge off." A familiar voice.

It couldn't be…

Leah shielded her eyes and was finally able to make out short, dark hair, a black goatee, and a superior smile. "Hank?"

A server lowered the blinds on her window, bringing the man into focus.

Leah drew a deep breath. "Shoo. I'm meeting someone." And it wouldn't look good for her date to see Hank with her.

"Yes. You're meeting me." Hank bent over and kissed her.

She knew as soon as their lips met that it would be marvelous. *I should be shocked.*

She kissed him back. How could she not? This was one of those rare *Twilight Zone* moments where caution was thrown to the wind because all too quickly the kiss would end. He'd leave. And her world would never be the same.

The kiss ended.

Leah felt herself droop like a rose that had experienced full bloom.

Hank sat down across from her, a triumphant smile on his handsome face. "Jazzy sent me."

"Oh?" Leah reached for her wine, but before she could raise her glass for a fortifying gulp, Hank covered her hand with his.

Zing!

She gasped.

Hank's smile broadened. "You feel it too, don't you?" And then his hand lifted from hers. But instead of retreating into his own space, Hank extended his arm and brushed the back of his knuckles over her cheek.

Bazinga!

They both sat back in their seats. Leah forgot about her wine. She forgot about Charlie's wedding. She forgot about special orders from the local greenhouse and the floral supply warehouse. But what she couldn't forget was the drop-dead gorgeous man who'd kissed her.

"This makes no sense," she said finally.

"Why not?"

"Because I'm a single mom and you're one of the DeLeon brothers." Her hands rolled around in front of her chest. "You guys date visiting models and college girls on spring break."

Hank's eyes sparkled. "I think you have me confused with my brother, Roman. I'm too busy to date."

Leah shook her head. "That's my line. Why would you want to date me?"

"Because you're gorgeous, smart, and funny."

"Everything Claire said." The attributes she'd promised to tell Leah's date.

He nodded. "I remember my lines."

"They're well-rehearsed." But he'd kissed her as if they were going off-script.

"Claire may have told me, but I believe all three words apply to you." Hank shook his head. "Why don't we start over? I'm Hank, a transplant to Sea Glass Bay and former Army vet."

"Thank you for your service." Could they start over? If they did, would he ask for a do-over kiss? She drew a deep breath. "I'm Leah. Born and raised here, although my parents retired to Nevada."

A waiter approached.

"I'll have a Napa Cabernet," Hank said, without looking at the wine list. "I'm a red wine drinker in restaurants," he said to Leah.

"But not picky about the red. It took me five minutes to decide on my wine." She shook her head. "You know, we have nothing in common."

"Except elemental chemistry and the drive to work hard." Hank stroked his goatee, which only sparked Leah's imagination about how those whiskers might feel against her skin. "We both like linguini with clams. And wine. And I appreciate the beauty of a flower."

"You seem more like the exotic flower type." The way she imagined he dated more exotic women. She put her daisy in the small vase on their table. It was overshadowed by the single red rose the restaurant had put there. "Why did you come tonight? Our last date was...awkward."

"I couldn't stop thinking about you." He gave a little shrug. "And when the opportunity presented itself again, I thought it was kismet."

She sighed, staring out at the ocean, aware that Hank was staring at her. "I like your mother."

"You know her?" His brow furrowed.

"Yes. She—"

The waiter delivered Hank's wine. Like hers, his wine came in a small carafe. The waiter poured a sample in a glass for Hank to approve. Hank took his time evaluating—staring, sniffing, sipping. Had he assessed her the same way?

"Let's toast to uncovering layers," Hank suggested, unaware of her doubts.

"Uncovering?" Leah's heart pounded. She wasn't the type to jump into bed with a man just because he made her remember she was a woman.

"Uncovering…" His smile was gentle and reassured. "…layers of our personalities, of our lives, of our…"

"Hearts," she murmured.

Rather than answer, Hank raised his glass and tilted it toward hers.

The moment felt heavy with significance. If she toasted, she was committed to revealing pieces of her life, committed to disclosing thoughts and feelings she kept under lock and key in order to make sense of the attraction between them.

Her glass tapped against his, almost of its own volition.

"I'm a workaholic," Hank admitted. "From a long line of workaholics. My parents ran a restaurant for years. We were raised to chip in if we saw something that needed doing. A table bussed, water glasses refilled, tickets that needed cashing out."

"Do you resent your parents?" Leah asked, although she couldn't imagine anyone resenting Marisol. "I only ask because I'm raising my son in a florist shop."

"Worried he'll resent you later in life?" Hank was perceptive. His gaze caressed her face as intimately as a touch.

If she wasn't careful, he'd uncover all her secrets. "Yes."

"I don't resent my parents." He swirled his wine, staring into its depths. "I mean, I wish they might have been able to watch more of my high school baseball games. But I understand why they couldn't. Tank's is my place. I get twitchy when I'm not there, so I'm always there."

"I know." She nodded. "I never turn down an order, even if I know it means Owen and I will get home late. At least, you have your brothers to rely on."

"They don't feel the same way I do about it. They're employees, after all."

"Which makes you feel like you carry the most responsibility."

"Yes. And here you thought we had nothing in common." He extended his glass for another toast. "To overachievers who have problems delegating."

"I'll drink to that." She sipped her wine, letting the layers of flavor sink into her awareness the way the layers Hank was revealing did. She liked him. "But knowing we're similar just means one thing."

"What's that?" He leaned forward, dark eyes sparkling.

"We're not cut out for a long-term relationship."

Hank wanted to refute her statement.

Instead, he made light of it. "We'll have to focus on the short-term then. Your date-makers hinted that you need an escort for an event coming up."

Leah nodded. "I need a plus one. You wouldn't happen to own a tuxedo, would you?"

"I have the next best thing—my army dress uniform. I don't just haul it out of my closet for any occasion. You'll need a special dress."

"My friends helped me pick one out yesterday." Leah chuckled.

He liked the sound of her laughter, along with her quick wit and warm kiss.

And then he heard a familiar laugh—his mother's.

He turned around, searching for Mama. "I thought she said she was going to a potluck. Excuse me." He stood, intent upon finding her. He followed the sound of laughter to the far side of the restaurant.

Mama sat at a table with five other people, a mix of men and women her age. The man across from her had brightly-dyed black hair and a threadbare blue button-down.

"There must be a new definition of potluck." Hank smiled, but it felt more like a grimace. He held onto that expression through introductions and his mother's dirty looks.

"Now that you've all met my son, let's wave goodbye." Mama tugged on Hank's shirt sleeve until he bent over to allow her to whisper in his ear. "Run along. Don't ruin this for me."

"Ruin it for you?" Hank straightened. "Be home by nine. I'll be waiting."

That gave the table a fit of giggles.

Hank walked stiffly back to Leah's table.

"Everything all right?" Leah asked, looking uncertain.

He didn't want her to doubt the feeling that might grow between them. "It's not you. It's—"

"Me," she cut him off.

"No. It's my mother..." Hank began, more tightly wound than he'd been in a long time. "She's too trusting. She's here and sitting with a man who looks like he could use a handout. I'm wondering if that's who she's been spending all her time with."

Laughter emanated from across the restaurant once more. Hank's shoulders bunched.

A warm hand came to rest on Hank's forearm—Leah's. "She'll be fine. Trust her."

"How can you say that?" Hank frowned. "She's probably going to offer to pay for their dinners."

"The way you offered to pay for mine?" Leah rubbed his arm.

He wasn't ready to receive comfort. This was an urgent situation. "She's been swindled before. I worry about her being taken advantage of and overspending. When Mama moved here, we went over her budget together. Since then, she's gone over her grocery budget. Twice!"

"You know she bakes for the community," Leah said quietly, sitting back in her seat and crossing her arms.

"That's got to stop. She's on a fixed income." And he wanted her to open a small restaurant. "She has to think about her future and stop handing out food to charity cases."

"You don't understand her or Sea Glass Bay or me." Leah shook her head, gathering her purse. "We don't have as much in common as you think." She set two twenties on the table.

"You're leaving?" He stood, perplexed. "And paying?"

"Yes. Why don't you join your mother for dinner? If you give her friends a chance, you might not worry so much about her judgment." Leah hesitated, gaze dropping briefly to his mouth before she pressed her lips together and marched toward the door.

Hank was torn on many fronts.

He wanted to go after Leah. He let her go.

He wanted to join his mother for dinner. He sat and drank his wine, watching the ocean and thinking about what he should do next.

5

The morning after his visit to Cliff House, Hank was up early. He parked his truck outside Mama's retirement complex, ready to follow her. He had to know what she did with her days and who she spent her time with.

Mama was mobile by nine a.m., driving through the complex gates. He followed her to the grocery store.

Hank texted his brothers while he waited for her to emerge.

Does anyone know what Mama does all day?

Emilio was the first to respond: *I hope she's making friends.*

Hank sighed. Emilio was no help.

Sebastian replied next: *She always smells of sugar and cinnamon when she comes into the kitchen.*

Hank nodded. Maybe Mama was replenishing her stock of flour and sugar in that store.

Roman sent the googly-eyed emoji: *I can follow her if you give me the day off.*

That forced Hank to admit that he was following Mama, which led to a series of teasing texts.

Twenty minutes later, Mama emerged from the grocery store with a bright smile and two bags of groceries. But instead of heading home, she turned her car toward the center of town.

Had she been baking in Tank's kitchen every morning? Impossible. It was nearly nine-thirty and Hank was usually in the office by ten a.m. to receive deliveries and set up for opening. He'd never noticed evidence of cookie-making.

Mama parked in the small city lot and then carried her groceries down the street.

Hank got out and followed from a distance. He was beginning to feel silly, but he was also determined to uncover the truth about his mother's daily habits.

Mama stopped to chat with Jazzy, who was unlocking the door to a gift shop. And then she was moving on, hurrying up the stairs a few doors down and disappearing inside.

Hank came to a stop in front of The Flower Girl shop. Leah's place?

He walked to the corner and back, waiting. Still no sign of Mama. Had she ordered flowers? Had she gone out the back? Perhaps trying to enter Tank's from the rear entrance?

From the street, the shop was perfect for a small café. There was room outside the door for a few dining tables. His meeting about the lease was scheduled for Friday. He had mixed feelings about the discussion now that he knew Leah better. But family had to come first. And business was just that—business.

Hank checked his watch. Sebastian had offered to show up early to receive deliveries. He should head over there now, just in case Sebastian was delayed.

Curiosity kept him lingering on Leah's street.

Leah placed a bouquet in the window display. She was talking to someone. Mama? Her son Owen?

Hank couldn't stand not knowing. He bounded up the steps and entered the shop. "Hello?"

Leah turned in the doorway to the back room. "Hank? What a surprise." She glanced over her shoulder.

"Who's Hank?" A little boy with Leah's blonde hair and bright green eyes charged through the door on sturdy legs. "He looks like he needs a cookie."

"Always." Leah swung Owen into her arms and tickled his tummy. "And do you know why?"

Owen giggled, shaking his head.

"Because he works too hard." Leah met Hank's gaze. She wore jeans that had dirt smudges on them despite her work apron and a purple T-shirt.

"Cookies aren't ready yet." That was Mama's voice. She appeared behind Leah wearing an apron. "You can come back and keep us company while I bake."

Leah disappeared into the back room.

Hank followed slowly, wondering why the child looked so familiar to him. Then he glanced around, taking in the details of the flower shop. The wrought iron display shelves. The pre-made bouquets and living plants. A small section featuring aromatherapy candles. Leah was using every inch of the room. And it smelled like his grandmother's flower garden, green and sweet.

Mama could squeeze four tables in here.

The thought felt like a betrayal.

He moved through the doorway to the back room and was immediately struck with déjà vu.

The dedicated space to a child. The small kitchen and abundance of counter space. It was similar in set-up to their family restaurant in Redding. And just as she had in Redding, Mama's place was next to the kitchen sink. He felt...at home.

Hank spared Leah a glance. She watched him warily.

"Mama, you're baking here? Why? You could use our kitchen or your kitchen at the retirement home."

"At my *apartment*, you mean," Mama corrected with just a hint of impatience. She brushed a lock of hair from her forehead with the back of her hand. "Do you know that food imparts smells on other foods? If I baked in Sebastian's kitchen, my cookies would smell like barbecued wings and greasy French fries."

"But—"

Mama set her hands on the counter's edge. "Be careful with your next words, Henry."

Leah snipped stems at a worktable. Her son flipped through pages of a book but watched Hank while he did so.

Hank sighed. "Do you come here every day?"

"Yes."

"That's good." It meant she was content in the space. His statement earned him double-takes from Mama and Leah. "I mean, I'm glad you found somewhere you feel comfortable. But the baking is surprising. I guess this means you want to open a bakery."

"It means no such thing," Mama snapped, still clinging to the counter.

"I'm confused." Hank stroked his goatee.

"I have no schedule to keep and no menu to make," Mama said, raising her voice. "This is the way I have fun."

"Fun?" Hank had no concept of fun. There was the daily grind and the satisfaction of a profit at the end of the month. "Giving away baked goods is *fun?*"

"We workaholics rarely have fun," Leah murmured.

Hank frowned.

"Henry." Mama came to him, taking his face in her floury hands. "She's right. There is more to life than work. There are friendships to be made. Joy to be given. Laughter to be shared."

"And you find that here? At a flower shop?" Instead of with family?

"I think I should be offended," Leah murmured.

"I find it here. In the community of Sea Glass Bay." Mama dropped her hands, only to raise them again, this time with a dish towel to wipe at his facial hair, which he imagined was dusted in flour. "This is your home, too. And yet, you hardly know what's outside of the fences bordering your patio dining area."

"I'm too busy—"

"No one is too busy to let life pass them by." Mama returned to her mixing bowl. "Now off with you. I imagine your deliveries are about to begin."

He nodded numbly and headed for the back door and the alley.

Owen ran after him. "Hey, mister. Here. Take this." He held out a small strawberry plant. It had a tiny white strawberry on it. "Mom says plants give smiles. You need one. You need one real bad."

Hank stared down at the plant, feeling ashamed that a kid had marked him as needing to smile more and feeling hurt that his mother had marked him as missing out on life. He'd been in the army. He'd traveled the world in uniform. It was time to plan and save for the future.

But as he raised his gaze to Leah's, as he saw her soft smile when she looked at her son, he realized that he might be wrong.

There might be more to life than work and profits and saving for a rainy day.

Rainy days could be lonely if you didn't have someone by your side.

"Ready to balance your monthly?" Paige swung by The Flower Girl after closing her shop to help Leah with her books.

Owen was in the beanbag chair watching a cartoon on Leah's phone. He'd had a play date with Lindie this afternoon and was tuckered out.

"Paige, you always make accounting sound so fun." Leah crossed her eyes.

"I think it's fun. It's like a puzzle. Everything in its place." Paige took out the stack of papers from a wire inbox on Leah's desk. Her short auburn hair swung across her shoulders as she bent her head to read them.

"Do you think we work too hard?" Leah asked, staring at Owen as he yawned.

"No." Paige didn't look up. "If we lived in mansions and drove expensive cars, my answer would be different."

"But we don't...date." She'd been thinking about Marisol's words about life being too short all day. "And I never take Owen on trips, much less take a day off."

Paige set the invoices down and looked at Leah. "Is this because Charlie's wedding is in a few days? Are you lonely?"

"Not lonely. Aware." Leah sighed. "I'm thirty, divorced, and there are no prospects on the horizon." Her heart wanted to argue that last point, because there was Hank. But Hank was...*not mine.*

"So this *is* a by-product of Charlie's marriage." Paige tucked her short hair behind one ear. "Do you need a pep talk?"

"No. I'm practicing my gracious smile." Leah flashed it toward Paige. "What do you think?"

"You look like you're happy to have another woman take Charlie off your hands." Paige chuckled, sorting Leah's invoices into piles. "Hey, have you thought about bringing a date? That dress you bought says you're datable, not over the hill. Maybe you'll meet someone there."

"I told Ashley I was bringing someone." Leah didn't mention that Claire had described him as hot. "It's not going to be pretty if I show up alone." Ashley would never let Leah live it down.

"Don't you know someone you can ask?" Paige snapped her fingers. "I know. What about that guy who owns the greenhouse outside of town? He's cute. What's his name?"

"Ray. I think he bats for the other team." Although he'd probably go with her as a favor if he didn't have a boyfriend.

"What about Liam? The produce manager at the grocery store."

Leah shook her head. "I think he's dating his manager, Susan."

"I should go through my list of clients and find you a date."

"Or I should just put on my big girl panties and go it alone." Leah sighed.

"Would you…try a blind date if I found someone?" Paige looked hopeful.

"Well…" How much worse could Paige do than Jazzy and Claire?

"Mommy needs someone to eat dinner with," Owen said from his beanbag.

"There you have it." Paige grinned. "I have to find you someone now."

"Can you ask around without using my name?" Leah vowed to tell her circle of friends how each of them had tried to set her up, but only after the wedding.

"I am the voice of discretion," Paige assured her. "Doesn't Charlie have Owen on Thursday night?"

"Not this week."

"I can watch Owen Thursday night." Paige waved a hand as if this was nothing. "Why don't I have my guy meet you for coffee at the Salt and Sea Café after work?"

"You sound like you know a guy…"

Paige nodded. "I do. I don't know why I didn't think of him before. Trust me."

Leah trusted Paige. It was kismet she didn't trust.

"Are you ready for me?" Paige poked her head into Hank's office after the dinner rush.

"Is anyone ready for accounting?" Hank shook his head. He'd created piles for Paige to enter into his accounting program. He moved out of her way, taking the small strawberry plant that Owen had given him and putting it on the high windowsill.

Paige set down her purse, car keys, and water bottle. "I don't know why numbers get a bad rap."

"Because they make most people's head hurt." Hank headed toward the door. "I'll leave you to it."

"I'll start just as soon as I ask Sebastian something." Paige followed him out the door.

"Sebastian? Is he in need of bookkeeping?"

"No. But hopefully he's in need of a date."

Hank stopped in his tracks. It couldn't be.

"Excuse me." Paige edged past Hank in the narrow hallway. "Hey, Sebastian. Are you still a man without a girlfriend?"

Sebastian flipped a dish towel over his shoulder. "Are you still a woman without a boyfriend?"

Paige blushed. "I've taken myself off the market. Answer, please."

Since when did Paige have a flirty relationship with Hank's brother? Was Mama right? Did he have his head so far down in the sand that he wasn't seeing what was going on around him?

"There's been a lot of talk around here about Leah needing a date," Sebastian said, giving Hank a significant look.

"Oh, gosh. Don't tell anyone that," Paige said quickly. "But yeah, she needs a date and I think it'd be best if she had a dry run before the event, you know?"

Sebastian gave Hank the side-eye. "Have you asked Hank?"

"No." Paige sliced her hand through the air. "Everybody knows that Hank has no time for women."

"I think I'm offended," Hank murmured, reminded of Leah uttering those same words.

"Why?" Paige pushed her hair behind one ear. "Everyone respects what you've done with this dive, Hank. We all know you work hard."

"He lives to work." Sebastian flipped some burgers. "Instead of working to live."

"Well, maybe I *should* take Leah on this date." Hank could use it as an opportunity to apologize for barging in on her and Mama this morning. Not that he needed to apologize...

Okay, maybe he did. But mostly, Hank wanted to grab hold of that electric chemistry they had. Wasn't that something worth working the kinks out of?

"A date might be good for you both," Paige said slowly, giving Hank a once over. "But if you mess this up..."

"I won't hurt her, if that's what you mean." Hank wasn't sure he could keep that promise, not with a meeting coming up with the owner of Leah's building.

"Seriously, Hank. I know all your financial secrets." Paige shook her finger at him. "And I know how to use them."

"Seriously?" Hank watched Paige walk back to his office.

"She's kidding," Sebastian reassured him. "Haven't you ever talked to her before about anything other than your balance sheet? Paige would never hurt anyone."

"Right. I knew that."

But it made Hank wonder who else in Sea Glass Bay he should know.

Other than Leah, of course.

6

*T*hursday night, Leah didn't bother changing to meet Paige's assigned date at the Sea and Salt Café.

The coffee shop didn't frown upon sneakers or T-shirts. And she held out little hope that Paige would find anyone willing to be her wedding date forty-eight hours before Charlie's wedding.

She put her back to the door, lay the daisy on the table's edge and put her chin in her hands. And waited.

"If ever anyone looked in need of flowers, it's you, flower girl." Hank set a small planter with blue primroses on the table and then dropped into the seat on the other side of the booth. "Why so glum?"

Leah was both flabbergasted and excited. She'd been so frustrated with him at the end of their last date, but she'd since had some insight into his protectiveness, courtesy of Marisol. "Paige sent you?"

"Yes. Are you surprised that all your friends think of me when they want to find you a suitable date?" He gave her a wry grin.

Leah nodded, dropping her gaze to the primroses. "I can't remember the last time someone gave me flowers." The vase was a thoughtful choice, too. Blue with white script: *Happy Mother's Day.*

"That's just wrong." His voice was deep and sincere. "If we were dating for real, I'd give you something every day to show you how much you meant to me."

155

"You'd shower me with gifts when you don't approve of your mother giving cookies to her friends?"

His gaze dropped to her lips. "When I said I'd give you something, I didn't mean things that cost money." He reached into his back pocket, withdrew a folded sheet of paper, and handed it to her.

She accepted the paper but didn't open it. "What's this?"

"Another gift. Of sorts." His gaze was intense.

She unfolded the paper and read the bold handwriting. "I couldn't stop thinking about you today." Her heart thudded in her chest. She'd been thinking of him, too. "Hank…"

"We're off to a rocky start, but we can figure this out."

A man stomped up to their table. "Oh, you're trying to undercut me now, are you? I should have known."

Leah glanced up. "Charlie?"

Leah's ex wasn't scowling at her. He was scowling at Hank. "We have a meeting tomorrow with Bill Tompkins. What are you doing here with my wife, Hank?"

"*Ex*-wife," Hank said mildly, deceptively casual. Leah could hear the judgement in his tone. "You'd somehow neglected to tell me that detail before you set up this meeting."

Charlie ignored him. "Are you trying to cut out the middleman and sublet Leah's shop? Costing me my commission?"

"No." Instead of looking as perplexed as Leah felt, Hank was looking rather…guilty.

Leah's heart began pounding, but it had nothing to do with her attraction to Hank. "What are you talking about, Charlie?"

"Oh, he's good." Charlie leaned on the table. "But he's not good enough to get anything past me. We have a meeting tomorrow, Hank. And in that meeting, I will be paid for the time I put in." He slapped the table, rattling the primroses. "You may think you've backdoored me, but I have Bill on speed dial." He stomped off, reaching for his phone.

"Sorry about that." Hank ran a hand over his goatee.

"Why do you have a meeting with my landlord?" Leah asked evenly. "And why would Charlie assume you're trying to sublet my flower shop?"

"Leah…"

"The first night we met, you wanted to talk about my business." Pieces of their conversation were coming back to her now. "You were quick to judge

my ability when it came to being profitable or courageous about expanding."
She stared at his face, that handsome face. And those lips, those lying lips.
"And when you came inside the shop the other day, you spent a lot of time
looking around. At first I thought…" She shook her head. "I thought it was
because you were trying to soak in the atmosphere of what I created. But
now…" Her voice thickened with emotion. "Now I realize that you were
imagining how it might look set up differently as…as…" And here her theory floundered. She stared deep into his eyes, willing him to come clean.

"I thought my mother might like to open a restaurant or a bakery
there." His words hung between them thicker than any chemistry,
because finally his repeated attendance as her date made sense.

Leah grabbed her purse, trying to slide out of the booth before
tears slid out of her eyes. "I see where this has all been going."

"Leah…"

"It's all about business to you." She got to her feet.

Hank was quick to get to his. "At first, yes. I wanted my mother occupied and safely within range." He followed her toward the door. "Yours
was the only building in the neighborhood with a lease coming available."

She burst out of the coffee shop, yanking on her sweater.

He pressed the primroses and his note into her hands. "It wasn't
the way you think—"

"You *lied* to me. *That's* what I think. And to your mother, which
is worse." Leah stared at the flowers and the note, emotion crowding
her chest and clogging her throat. She crumpled his note and threw
it at his chest. "Don't come near me. Ever. Again."

"Henry, what are you doing here?" Mama opened the door to her
apartment and let Hank in.

"I just wanted to tell you first." He sank into the big easy chair that
used to be his father's. Mama's apartment was filled with the familiar—a hand-carved secretary's desk, a pine end table, a picture of his
father in front of the family restaurant.

"Who died?" Mama whispered, perching on the arm of his chair.

"No one." Hank scrubbed at his goatee and then ran his hand over
his hair. He couldn't help but think that he'd screwed up something
important tonight with Leah.

"Are you sure no one died?" Mama was still whispering. "You look like you're mourning."

"I am. I should go. I have to make this right." He stood, hesitating. How was he going to do that when Leah didn't want to see him?

Mama stood.

And instead of leaving, Hank blurted. "Dad would be disappointed in me." The words cut him inside.

"Oh, honey. Never." His mother wrapped her arms around him. "He was so proud of you. So proud of you all."

"You don't know…. I thought I was doing the right thing…" Why was it so clear now that helping his mother was wrong if it was at the expense of someone else. Someone who was quickly becoming just as important to him.

His mother took his hand and led him to the couch. "Tell me, Henry. Tell me everything."

And so he did.

He told her how in his father's last few days he'd made Hank promise to watch over the woman he'd loved for forty years so no one would take advantage of her. How Dad had told Hank that Mama wouldn't be happy unless she was running her own place once more. He confessed to consulting with Charlie, a local realtor, to find a place close to Tank's. And how it involved offering the owner of Leah's building a higher monthly lease.

"Stop right there." Mama stood. She paced to the kitchen and back. And then she crossed her arms and stared down at Hank. "Your father loved that restaurant."

Hank nodded.

"And I loved running it *with* him."

Hank nodded again.

"But the thought of being responsible for such a business again… alone…" She shook her head. "I want to have the freedom to get up in the morning and cook what I want—*bake* what I want. Not the same thing every day. And I don't want to be responsible for keeping customers coming in the door so that my employees will be paid. I'm past that. Do you understand?"

Hank nodded. "You put in your time." And he was putting in his.

"Yes." Mama's arms fell to her sides. "Yes. It was wrong of your father to ask such a thing of you."

Hank felt the need to defend Dad. "He did it out of love."

"Yes, he did. But his intentions were misplaced. As were yours." She paced to the kitchen and back once more.

Hank was gobsmacked by the feeling of respect he had for this woman. His mother was amazing. He'd expected her to rant and rail. He deserved her to—

"But you…" Mama swatted him on top of the head, although not hard.

"Ow." Hank ducked in case she felt compelled to swat him again.

"You *knew* it was wrong to plan a restaurant without consulting me. And you *knew* it was wrong to try and take Leah's space in such a way, if you had have stopped for more than two minutes and thought about the ramifications for her life. Business decisions don't just affect business. They impact families." She crossed her arms over her chest again. "Of all the people in town, you asked her ex-husband for advice."

"I didn't know who he was. He was just someone who came into the bar."

Mama leaned forward, eyes narrowing. "You would have known if you were part of the community, not just a man concerned with making money."

That stung. "A man who keeps his family employed."

Mama didn't say anything for a moment, but in that moment, Hank also knew she wasn't letting him off the hook. "Why did you choose to buy a business in Sea Glass Bay?"

"The bar was available. The tourism rates were good. And the town seemed…"

Mama arched her penciled brows. "Yes?"

"The town seemed friendly." He rolled his shoulders back, then sighed. "Especially the business owners who participate in the weekend market. I knew their happy customers would then spill into my bar after the market closed down. Win-win."

"You're still too focused on work." Mama sat in the easy chair, running her hands along the arms. "The locals *are* friendly and kind. They've accepted me into their midst. And what have you done? You haven't even sponsored a local soccer team."

"I know what I have to do." Everything was clear to him now. He stood to go, bending to kiss his mother's cheek. "I'll make it right." With Leah. With the community. With Mama. All he needed was time.

"Henry?"

He turned at the door. "Yes, Mama."

"You're wrong." His heart sank until she added, "Your father would be proud of you."

Friday morning, Leah hung up the phone with Bill Tompkins, reassured that with a slight increase in rent that her lease would be renewed.

She sat with Owen at his child's table in the back of the flower shop. She ruffled his hair. "Everything's going to be okay." Even if it didn't feel okay right now.

Her heart ached every time she thought of Hank and her blood boiled every time she thought of Charlie. Hank had been motivated by concern for his mother, while her ex had been motivated by bitterness. He'd never supported her business endeavors, particularly when she became one of the popular vendors at the weekend market.

But the question remained: *What was she going to do about Marisol?*

There was bound to be tension between them. Her oldest son had tried to displace Leah for his mother.

She looked over her shoulder toward the kitchen, which was sparkling clean, just the way Marisol had left it.

"Mommy." Owen stopped eating waffle squares and picked up his sippy cup. "You don't have to be sad."

Leah's gaze swung back around to her son. "Who says I'm sad?"

He reached out and smoothed the lines in her forehead.

"Oh."

Owen scampered across the room to the worktable. He stretched out his small arms and took the primroses Hank had given her last night. He carried the pot carefully back to her. "You smile when you look at flowers."

"Do I?" She didn't feel like smiling.

But then Owen draped his arms around her neck and gave her a loving squeeze. "That's better."

And it was.

Leah drew back to look at her beautiful boy, smoothing his soft blond hair and smiling. "You're right. There are things around me that make me smile."

Blessings like Owen. Good friends like Paige, Claire, and Jazzy. Suppliers and customers who made it possible for her to create small arrangements that lifted people's spirits. Her heart might feel bruised and her trust broken, but life would go on and get better.

"Hello?" Marisol came into the room tentatively, rather than with her usual confidence.

"Marisol!" Owen ran over to give her a good morning hug.

The older woman's gaze sought out Leah's. In it was an apology. And perhaps a plea. The Flower Girl's kitchen was an important part of Marisol's daily life. She could probably bake in her apartment, but here she was in the center of Sea Glass Bay's community.

Leah couldn't turn her away.

"My son has made many mistakes." Marisol sighed, blinking back tears.

She's not going to stay.

Leah's heartache deepened. She'd become so fond of Marisol, so used to her being here in the kitchen, adding light and energy and laughter.

"Are you gonna forgive him?" Owen asked Marisol, angling his head up to see her face. "Mommy says you have to forgive people and say it's okay. Mommy says sometimes it takes a lo-o-o-ong time after you say okay for you to feel okay."

"I'm going to forgive him," Marisol said slowly. "But maybe it would be easier if your mother did so as well?"

A good question. Leah wasn't ready to forgive. She was still hurting and feeling foolish for allowing the spark of attraction to bring down the barriers she'd put around her heart when Charlie left.

"Is there anything I can do?" Marisol asked, eyes watery. "I could... leave."

"No. We're going to be fine. All of us." Leah got to her feet and realized it was the truth. She tried smiling, because she was certain it had been hard for Marisol to come here this morning. And good friendships were worth keeping even if they sometimes caused you a bump or two in the road. Her gaze caught on the primroses. "We could use some Polvorones today, don't you think?"

Marisol crossed the room and brought Leah into a warm hug. "I was hoping you'd say that."

7

"*D*addy, my clothes look just like yours!" Outside the wedding venue, Owen stumbled in his shiny black dress shoes but managed to right himself in time to leap toward Charlie.

Leah followed at a slower pace. She wore the midnight revenge dress and high heels she'd borrowed from Paige. Marisol was running her booth today, the last Saturday before Mother's Day weekend. She hadn't seen Hank since the disappointment at the café, but it was her ex-husband who was top-of-mind now.

Charlie had avoided her calls (two) and texts (also two) yesterday. She didn't want to have a hard conversation with him on his wedding day, but he'd left her no choice.

"Owen, you look handsome enough to carry my wedding ring." Charlie swung Owen into his arms and tweaked his nose. "Do you think you can do that the way we practiced? No giggles. No questions."

"No fun." Owen fingered his cowlick with a sigh.

"Charlie, can I talk to you for a minute?" The stern tone rasped against Leah's throat. She was being polite. But she wasn't asking. She came to a stop in front of her ex-husband and crossed her arms over her chest. "Owen, can you go give Uncle Carl a hug?"

"I love Uncle Carl." Owen wiggled his feet and was off as soon as Charlie set him on the ground.

Charlie stared over her head. "Now isn't the time, Leah."

"Oh, it is the time, Charlie. And let me tell you why." She drew a deep, fortifying breath because the old Leah, the girl who let Charlie snipe at her, needed the strength to stand up for herself once and for all. "What you tried to do to me was underhanded. Low. Slimy. Like cheating on your wedding vows." Leah held up a hand when it seemed like he wanted to speak. "People in Sea Glass Bay aren't like that. Bill Tompkins was under the assumption that I was going to close up shop and move out of town. You lied to him. And do you know what's worse than a liar? A father who'd put his pride above his son's well-being and happiness."

Charlie's gaze dropped to her face.

"You don't want me to succeed. You never have. But my success gives Owen stability. Kids need stability and love. And they need adults around them who respect others." When Charlie rolled his eyes, Leah raised a finger in the vicinity of his face. "*All* others. Stability, love, and respect are what children need to grow up to be good people. So next time you feel the need to undermine my business or to say something disrespectful to me or about me to Owen, think twice about the example you're setting."

Owen stumbled back against Leah's leg. "I couldn't find Uncle Carl. I love you, Mommy."

"I love you, too, pumpkin." Leah knelt down to his level, which was hard considering the high heels and the burn of adrenaline from telling Charlie off. But she managed it because single moms were modern day superheroes. "Now, you be good for your father. And if you need anything, I'll be sitting in the back."

"Okay." Owen scampered after Charlie, who'd turned his back and walked a few feet away from them.

Leah stood and wished that she could just head back out to her car and collapse. It wasn't every day an inconsequential flower girl stood up for herself. Her knees felt like waterlogged stems about to give way.

Someone came to stand next to her.

She glanced to the right, and then did a double-take. "Hank?"

The man next to her resembled Hank. He was tall. His shoulders were broad. And his hair as dark as the ocean at night, covered by a debonair hat. But he'd shaved his goatee. And he was wearing his dress uniform—a black jacket with bright buttons and medals. Lots of colorful medals.

He glanced down at her from the corner of his eye. "You look lovely, as always."

Her palm—of its own volition—traced the hard line of his smooth jaw. "You clean up nice."

I'm going to miss that facial hair.

Leah snatched her hand back. He'd gone behind her back. He'd tried to sabotage everything she'd worked so hard for. And yet, he'd shown up when she needed someone by her side.

Hank's mouth quirked up at one corner, but only briefly. "I owe you an apology. And also…" He blew out a breath. "…a debt of thanks."

"Thanks?"

Hank turned to face her, stiff with military precision and perhaps something else…regret?

"When my father passed away six months ago, my world became a little smaller. I felt the pressure to work harder and to protect those family members I had left, particularly my mother. I made decisions without consulting anyone. Decisions that ruffled the honor this uniform represents. Decisions my family members would have pointed out were ill-advised. Decisions my mother wouldn't be proud of." He sighed and reached for her hand.

Instead of an unsettling spark, there was warmth.

Hank stared at their hands. "Grief and fear of further loss aren't acceptable excuses. I should have done better. I should have *been* better." And then his dark gaze came up to meet hers. "I will strive to be the kind of man a woman like you deserves, whether you give me a second chance or not."

Leah's grip tightened on his and she knew in that moment that she was going to forgive him. Not because there was chemistry or that they had a thing or two in common. But because Hank was a man who was willing to admit he'd made a mistake, learn from it, and move forward. He was everything a mother hoped her son would turn out to be. And if she opened her heart, someday he could be hers.

"You know, I have very high standards," she told him in a slow, low voice that she hoped sounded sultry and confident, like a woman certain of the man in her sights.

Smiling, Hank threaded her arm through his and steered them at a leisurely pace toward the venue's double doors. "Honey, if you didn't raise the bar every once in awhile, I'd be disappointed."

Family Wanted

by Cari Lynn Webb

"Aunt Trudy, I'm having a baby." *A baby.* Paige Duffy presented the positive at-home pregnancy test to her aunt. Her fingers tingled. The breath trapped in her throat dried her mouth out.

"Such a wonderful birthday present." Aunt Trudy pressed a kiss to each of Paige's cheeks then tipped her head up to look niece in the eyes. "You're going to be a *terrific* mom. You know that, don't you?"

"Yes." Paige's voice trembled with uncertainty her aunt didn't seem to notice.

Paige had suspected she'd been pregnant for a few weeks before she'd taken the test. She knew she wanted a family. But she'd never planned to be a single parent. Still, there was a beacon of hope nestled near her heart that whispered she'd never be a single parent. "I believe life is about to change."

"We're not living if we're not changing. And life is always changing because there are too many dreams to pursue. Can't ever forget that nugget." Trudy touched her newly cropped and tinted lavender-streaked white hair. "Now we have my birthday party to prepare for. You should touch-up your makeup while I put on my face. It's a party, not a funeral tonight."

"Right." Her aunt never left the house without her makeup applied and her clip-on earrings attached. *Self-confidence likes to look its best, too, Paige.* Another of her aunt's favorite nuggets.

"You already have that new-mom glow." Aunt Trudy tucked Paige's hair behind her ears and cupped Paige's cheeks in her gentle hands. The same way she'd been encouraging and comforting Paige since she'd become an orphan at the age of fourteen. "I remember your mom had the same glow when she was pregnant with you. And after your father's death, you were her saving grace."

Until cancer had intruded. Two years and Paige's mother couldn't muster the strength to fight it. But Paige knew the truth. Her mother's heart had never recovered after her father's untimely death chasing his mountain-climbing dreams. Cancer hadn't taken her mother. She had died of a broken heart and broken dreams. And Paige's idyllic family fractured.

Paige turned toward the guest bathroom. "I better finish getting ready. We don't want to be late."

Her aunt shuffled toward her bedroom. "Gavin is sure to notice your glow tonight. It'll be brighter than the sunset."

Gavin Cole. The captain for Aunt Trudy's sunset cruise birthday party tonight. Paige's good friend. And now the father of Paige's surprise baby. Paige tossed the pregnancy test stick into the trash can in the bathroom and dropped onto the closed toilet lid.

She had to tell Gavin about the baby. Had to explain the consequences of their spontaneous one night together after they'd promised each other nothing would ever change their friendship. Not even one spectacular night spent in each other's arms. The next morning, they'd sipped coffee, watched the sunrise from the sundeck of his dive boat, and pretended their friendship remained the same as it had been.

And those emotions—the sticky ones like love that ruined friendships—she'd tucked away, too afraid they were one-sided. She wanted Gavin in her life. If that meant as a friend only, she'd take that. Actually, that was a lie. She didn't want to settle. She wanted a partner in life.

How was she supposed to announce she was pregnant, the baby was his, and expect nothing to change between them?

"Fun fact, Gavin. I'm pregnant. The baby is yours." Paige grabbed her makeup bag from the bathroom counter, unzipped it and dug around for her eyeliner. "But you don't owe me anything."

"That's good, dear," Aunt Trudy hollered from the hallway. The older woman barely brushed the five-foot mark on the height scale. Yet her petite stature never stopped her from making her presence known. "After all, he's already donated his sperm."

Paige cringed. Her aunt's bat-like, supersonic hearing had not dulled with age. Her touch-up forgotten, Paige rushed out of the bathroom. "Aunt Trudy, you have to keep the baby news a secret."

Aunt Trudy rolled her glossy lips together, peered into the floor length mirror in the hallway and swiped more of the glittery gloss across her bottom lip. "I won't tell anyone else."

Paige captured her aunt's clever gaze in the mirror and frowned. "You told Benita, didn't you?"

"Of course." Her aunt tossed her lip gloss into a designer clutch and turned to face Paige. "Benita isn't anyone. She has been my best friend for more decades than you have been alive."

Benita Farrell and Trudy Potts shared a rare friendship. One that had remained strong despite distance, even continents at one time. It was a friendship that had weathered divorce (multiple ones), unexpected loss (miscarriages), and illness (cancer battles and debilitating surgeries). There wasn't a life detail Trudy and Benita did not share with each other. The women had come together to raise Paige, becoming the family Paige had needed.

When the news was exciting, Trudy and Benita all too often overshared with everyone from the postman to the pharmacy tech to the landscapers. Worry pinched the back of Paige's neck. She'd have to keep a close eye on the pair tonight during the birthday party. "You're both going to promise that you won't tell anyone about the baby."

"Fine." Trudy grinned, grabbed her blackthorn walking stick from the couch, and touched her black and gold rose-shaped earrings. "Let's get Benita, make our promise, and get to my party. I want to test out my new boat shoes."

Trudy tapped her walking stick against her fresh-out-of-the-box canvas loafer and managed a quick shimmy. Her aunt's excitement also shimmied against Paige's sudden reserve. Paige locked her aunt's apartment door and walked beside her aunt to the apartment two doors down in the Sea Glass Bay Senior Living community, which provides a little bit extra medical care and health assistance than the adjacent Retirement Home community.

Aunt Trudy pressed the doorbell to Benita's apartment then clutched Paige's hand and squeezed. "You should know Benita and I approve."

Paige gripped her aunt's hand and locked her knees, stilling herself mid-sway. "Approve?"

"We approve of Gavin Cole," Aunt Trudy continued. "For you, that is."

"There's nothing to approve," Paige argued.

"You're pregnant, Poppet." Aunt Trudy released her and set both her hands on her the top of her blackthorn walking stick. "You're building a family now. Gavin will fit right in."

Building a family. This wasn't a new house Paige wanted to build. There were no blueprints. No permits granted. She hadn't planned a contraception failure or her pregnancy. She hadn't arranged to slot Gavin right in as the last piece to her family puzzle. "Gavin isn't…"

Benita's door swung open. "Gavin Cole. Lovely, thoughtful, respectful boy. Perfect choice, Paige."

Paige's stomach rolled, a slow tumble straight into nauseous and lightheaded. She wanted to blame her pregnancy, but she feared it was the two women she adored more than anything in the world.

"Paige has yet to reel Gavin in." Disappointment tinged Aunt Trudy's expressive voice and the small shake of her head.

"What are you waiting for?" Benita's clear cornflower-blue gaze dipped to Paige's still very flat stomach. "Babies are on strict timelines."

Paige glanced at the neighboring apartments and ushered the wonderful, but meddling pair inside Benita's apartment. The one-bedroom unit was an exact replica of her aunt's floor plan. Only warm tones covered Benita's walls and classic leather furniture filled the space. Aunt Trudy preferred to be surrounded by bold paint colors and statement prints from her home to her clothes.

One thing spanned the two apartments: Paige's candles. She created and sold candles that gave the same kind of comfort her aunt and Benita had given her for so many years. If only lighting one of her candles would give her the calm she sought now. She studied the two women. "Ok. Listen. I'm not 'reeling in' Gavin. Or building a family."

Aunt Trudy gripped her cane and pursed her lips.

"I'm having a baby." *A child. Her own child.* Nerves curled around a thread of happy. Nothing she'd planned. But the baby was created out of Paige's hope for something more between her and Gavin.

"We intend to help raise the baby, of course." Benita's voice was matter-of-fact.

Trudy nodded.

"Definitely." Paige grabbed Benita's hand then her aunt's. The baby would expand their family and give Paige someone to guide, support, and love the same way her aunt and Benita had done for her. "I'll definitely want and welcome your help."

"Your mother would be proud of the woman you've become." Aunt Trudy's eyes glistened.

"That she would." Benita tilted her head and considered Paige. "Now you *do* plan to tell Gavin, don't you?"

"Yes." Uncertainty tripped into her voice, suspending the conviction in her words. "I just need to find the right time."

Benita and Trudy shared a look: eyebrows raised, faces set. Paige recognized the this-is-not-settled, we'll-talk-later silent look the pair shared. She quickly added, "Tonight is about Trudy Potts and celebrating her seventy sensational years. Tonight is not about me. The right time is some other time."

It wasn't at a birthday party that happened to be on Gavin's charter boat at sunset. With most of the senior community living within the town limits attending.

"We could..."

Paige intercepted her aunt's offer. "You can help with the baby, *not* with Gavin."

Trudy straightened into every inch of her five-foot frame. Her steely gaze fixed on Paige like a queen commanding obedience. The pair were formidable opponents, but Benita and her aunt had instilled an inner strength inside Paige, too.

Paige added, "Benita, we need Peg. We have to make a promise before we leave."

Benita rushed into her bedroom and returned carrying a worn, faded Platypus stuffed animal, known affectionately as Peg. The glitter was worn from Peg's feet and tail. Her beak bent. Her once plush body was bare in spots. Peg had been the grand prize at the ring toss at the Sea Glass Bay's Mother's Day Festival when Benita and Trudy had been kids. The girls had pooled their money together and won. They'd agreed on shared custody and Peg instantly became a valued member of the family. Present for every important occasion, both the celebrations and the hard times.

The trio had made a pact on Peg after Paige's mother had passed to always be Paige's home. Paige's safe place. They'd never broken their vow.

The women each set a hand on the stuffed platypus. Paige looked at her aunt, then Benita. "You are now promising on Peg that you will not tell Gavin that I'm pregnant with his child."

Benita straightened and kept her gaze connected to Paige's. "I will not tell Gavin your baby secret."

Aunt Trudy lifted her chin and repeated Benita's oath word for word.

Satisfied, Paige placed Peg on the sofa then hugged both women. "Let's get this birthday party started."

2

Money. Gavin Cole's entire life was centered around money. Not a fact he wanted to celebrate. But something he wasn't certain would change any time soon.

Spend more money, Gavin. His real estate agent insisted he had to spend more money on the renovations of his grandfather's beach house. If Gavin wanted to yield a larger return.

He needed a larger return on the house sale to fund his *Head South* account. The very account that would finance his move from Sea Glass Bay to an as-yet-determined coastal town south of the equator at the end of the summer.

But first, there were things he had to do on the 92-foot motor yacht, *Sea Quest,* to ensure a successful sunset charter that evening. Things that would ensure tonight's client paid Maritime Voyages, Gavin's employer. And in turn ensure that Gavin received his paycheck.

One he'd already spent on upgraded wood flooring for the beach house.

Gavin set his cell phone on the polished bar top in the climate-controlled main deck and ignored the text from his real estate agent about a renovation completion date. A new incoming text flashed on his screen.

Paige Duffy. Gavin grinned and replied to Paige's text about their ETA for her Aunt Trudy's sunset cruise birthday party. When he was with Paige, he thought of more than money. He thought of inviting aromas, warmth, and laughter. All the things Paige infused in her handmade candles. All the things Paige was herself.

A box landed on the counter beside Gavin. Then a soft punch landed on Gavin's shoulder from his longtime friend and temporary crewman, Jeremiah Caldwell.

Jeremiah laughed, a booming sound from a big man. "If you stall any longer, you're going to be stuck in the friend zone for good."

"What are you talking about?" Gavin unpacked the box of bar condiments, setting plastic bags of lemons, limes, and pineapple wedges on the bar.

Jeremiah tapped Gavin's phone screen. "Paige Duffy. You. And the friend zone you find yourself in."

"We are just friends," Gavin argued.

Except every time Gavin thought about Paige Duffy, he pictured Paige in the early morning pre-dawn light, her chin-length auburn hair tousled, her hazel gaze soft and her embrace welcoming. He knew he shouldn't have slept with her, but strangely he failed to locate his regret over their one night together.

But Paige wasn't a short-term girlfriend type. And he was leaving in less than four months. For good. He may have wanted to spend another night in Paige's arms, but he valued their friendship too much to jeopardize it for his own selfish wishes.

"But you want to be more than friends with Paige," Jeremiah pressed.

Gavin wanted tonight's charter to be a success. He wanted his summer booked with private charters. And another night with Paige—sure, he wanted that, too. Because he was short-sighted and greedy. But he still won't go there. "I'm leaving in August."

Hank DeLeon, owner of Tank's Bar and the evening's bartender carried a box of liquor bottles behind the bar. "Are you really leaving?"

"That's always been the plan." *Go find what you've been missing, Gavin. Go live your life.* His life was on the open water, sailing to a new coastal town whenever he wanted. That had been his goal for the past year and his dream for the past ten years. Now everything was finally in reach.

"Plans change." Hank unloaded one of the boxes and secured the bottles behind the bar. "Feelings change."

"Paige and I are friends only." Friends who helped each other out. Paige gave him advice on his renovation designs. He helped her make candles in the work shed on Granddad's property on his free time. That he spent his limited free time with Paige wasn't relevant. Gavin checked his watch and focused on his work. The caterer would be arriving any minute. Sully Vaughn was late with the birthday decorations. "The friend zone works for us."

Jeremiah's eyebrows pulled together. His eyes narrowed on Gavin.

"What isn't working are your renovations on your grandfather's house, according to Allie Bruce." Hank crammed lemon slices from one of the plastic bags into the condiment holder on the bar. "Allie lamented over Gavin's slow progress at the bar yesterday."

"You hired Allie." Jeremiah shook his head. "Allie gets results and expects immediate results for anyone she works with. She's the best real estate agent in three counties for a reason and it's not because she's timid or patient."

"I have to work." And make money. There it was again. "It's the charter's busiest season."

"We get it." Hank opened a bag of lime wedges. "Best time to make the money is when the tourists are in town."

Gavin scrubbed his hands over his face. "And the renovation is a bit more complicated than I anticipated."

"I know a guy," Jeremiah offered. "He's a good contractor. Reasonable and fair."

"I can do the work." Granddad had taught Gavin when he was a teen how to work every power tool in his garage. His grandmother had a specific vision for the beach house. After she'd passed, Gavin and his granddad had begun the restoration. Granddad had died before seeing their vision realized. Gavin had vowed to finish it.

"I'll text you my buddy's information just in case." Jeremiah typed on his phone.

"You could have the renovations complete and the house on the market before the end of the season." Hank checked the ice in the undercounter ice machine.

"I know now is the best time to list the house and sell it to a family." Gavin shoved the empty boxes in a cabinet behind him.

This house was made for family, Gavin. Not two bachelors wandering around the empty halls like lost sheep.

His grandparents had planned to fill the large house with grandchildren. Then Gavin turned out to be their only grandchild after Gavin's uncle was killed during active duty overseas and Gavin's parents divorced. Gavin's father skipped through girlfriends and cities while Gavin's flight attendant mother remained stateside long enough for Gavin to receive his high school diploma. Once Gavin had started college, his mother accepted a flight route based out of London and never looked back. She'd claimed it was finally her turn to explore the world. More than a decade later, she hadn't stopped. Simply exchanged one international flight route for another.

"Wait." Jeremiah pointed at him. "The house is like the friend zone you have going with Paige, isn't it?"

"What are you talking about?" Gavin crossed his arms over his chest.

"You're pretending you want to be Paige's friend only." Jeremiah leaned against the polished bar and considered Gavin. "Are you pretending you want to sell your granddad's house, too?"

"I'm not pretending anything," Gavin argued.

With his granddad's passing six months ago, Gavin no longer had any ties to Sea Glass Bay. No obligations holding him back from leaving. Granddad had wanted Gavin to use the money from the sale of the beach house to get his own private charter business established on an island down south. *You looked after your grandmother and me for long enough, Gavin. It's time to look after yourself.*

Yet Gavin couldn't deny his connection to his grandparent's house. Roots had been established in the decade he'd lived there. But the house was too large for one person. Too empty. A family would bring it to life again. "All I've ever wanted was to sail the open seas and anchor wherever I chose."

"I thought all I ever wanted was a successful business. Until I had it and my dad died. Now all I want is a life that is full and makes my family happy." Hank shrugged. "You guys can laugh all you want. People change their minds all the time."

"And their hearts," Jeremiah said.

"My mind is made up." And his heart wasn't the topic. His own wanderlust was in his blood. A trait he came by naturally. "Now, can we get ready for this charter?"

"Only if you admit that you hate the friend zone with Paige," Jeremiah challenged.

He disliked laundry. Despised the aftertaste of peppers. And really liked Paige Duffy. Not that he'd ever admit that. What good would come of it? *I really like you Paige, but I'm leaving soon. For good.*

Paige deserved a long-term commitment and to be put first before dreams of open waters and unfilled wanderlust. Paige was the kind of person his grandparent's house needed. She'd light her scented candles in the rooms, infusing the space with the scent of vanilla, citrus and harmony. She'd transform the house into an inviting home. That was simply her way: open-heart and kind words for everyone around her, including Gavin.

"I'm heading up for a pre-check. Guests will be arriving in less than an hour." Gavin turned and collided with a massive wall of balloons.

"Gavin, I'm changing our deal." The irritation in Sully Vaughn's voice reached him around the balloons. The helium bouquet shifted, and Sully appeared. Pink and purple feather boas were stacked around his shoulders, up past his chin.

Gavin's laughter burst free. Behind, Jeremiah and Hank joined in.

"Sully, that crown is all you." Jeremiah's laughter scrambled his words.

A Sassy and & Seventy crown was perched on Sully's curly blond head. "Jeremiah, you'll be glad to know there are two more dozen crowns to choose from in my truck." Sully guided the balloons into the main dining room. "I wouldn't want any of you to feel left out."

Jeremiah took a candid picture of Sully, shoved his phone in his pocket and headed toward the exit. "I'll just go and get the rest of the decorations from Sully's truck."

Sully untangled his hands from the balloon bouquet and transferred the pile of feather boas to Gavin's shoulders. "I've decided I want a swing and a slide added to Lindie's playhouse."

Gavin flicked a feather off Sully's shoulder. "Does this mean you still want me to design and build the playhouse?"

Sully grinned. "That's exactly what I want. Chop chop."

Sully and Gavin had bartered earlier in the week. Sully would pick up the personalized birthday party decorations Paige had custom ordered in Santa Rosa a two hour drive away. Gavin would help Sully build a boat-themed playhouse for his daughter.

Boas and crowns aside, Gavin was excited to get started on the playhouse. He'd have liked a boat playhouse as a kid. "I'll draw something up later this week."

Gavin headed for stairs and the pilot's house. He'd leave his grandparent's legacy inside the beach house in the town they'd loved and called home for so long. And he'd leave a piece of himself in a boat-themed playhouse for his friend's daughter.

3

"Benita. Aunt Trudy—you two should be dancing." Paige waved to the dance floor behind them. "Marisol is out there leading the cha-cha line dance. That's one of your favorites."

"We like our seats here at the bar." Her aunt accepted a white wine and elderflower spritzer from Hank.

"We have an excellent view of the dance floor and the buffet line. Arthur Denny has passed through the pasta station three times already." Benita stirred the ice around in her drink and pursed her lips. "Arthur claims diet restrictions don't apply in international waters."

"We claim diet restrictions shouldn't apply at parties." Aunt Trudy chuckled. "And we have a view of the bathrooms. This way we can avoid standing in line."

The pair also had a direct view of the stairs leading to the pilot house where Gavin was currently working. The stairs Gavin would use when he came downstairs to check on the guests. "What about watching the sunset from the bow deck?"

"We tallied the number of sunsets we've seen with Hank's help. Hank is better with that calculator on the phone than we are." Her aunt slid a cherry from the plastic toothpick floating in her spritzer. "How many was it, Hank?"

"Over twenty thousand, give or take." Hank shook a stainless-steel drink mixer over his shoulder. "It's impressive."

Not as impressive as the pair's cunning. Paige eyed the two women. "What else have you two been calculating?"

"The odds of Jeremiah and sweet Jazzy having another baby together." Benita finished her spritzer and motioned to Hank for another.

"And the month Hank will get married." Her aunt toasted a surprised-looking Hank.

"I have to ask the woman first." Hank filled two plastic glasses with soda. "And then she needs to say yes."

Aunt Trudy waved her custom printed paper napkin like a fan swishing away his argument. "We've consulted your sweet mama, Marisol, and already decided when you'll propose, too."

Hank dropped the soda sprayer and gaped at the women.

"Sorry." Paige cast the bar owner an apologetic look. "They do this all the time with everyone they meet, even complete strangers. As if they were reliable psychics. They're hardly ever right."

Trudy dabbed her napkin against her mouth and sniffed. "Shows you what my niece knows."

Benita touched her silver-tipped jet-black hair as if Paige's apology had unsettled her. "We have a ninety percent success rate, if you must know."

Gavin came down the stairs and walked through the galley.

Paige caught the crown sliding off her head and her heart. She wanted a one-hundred percent success rate with Gavin. Wanted to believe that whisper inside her. The one that promised her that her own family was within reach.

Gavin grabbed a bottle of water from the undercounter refrigerator and smiled at her aunt. "A ninety percent success rate on what?"

"Calculating important dates." Trudy adjusted her birthday crown and winked at Paige.

Alarm streamed through Paige, slow and steady like a barely turned-on faucet.

"You know, important dates like proposal and wedding dates." Benita fluffed her purple feather boa.

"Due dates," her aunt rattled off. "Don't forget those."

Paige blanched and blurted, "It's just a silly game of theirs."

"Hardly," her aunt muttered.

"Let's test our skills on Hank." Benita smiled.

Paige's patience was already being tested. She wanted to shout for the DJ to play the pair's favorite song and crank the volume until their hearing-aides protested. Perhaps she could relight the seventy candles on the last bit of remaining birthday cake and make everyone sing again.

Hank topped a soda with a lime wedge, handed it to the waiter and grinned at the women. "I'm game. Tell me when you've calculated that I'll propose."

Trudy pressed a hand over her chest. Appreciation warmed her voice. "You always celebrate Mother's Day and your own mama."

"As it should be," Benita beamed. "Then you have an over-the-top Halloween bash at the bar every year."

"Always entertaining." Approval highlighted her aunt's words. "But then there's Christmas."

Benita's shoulders drooped. "You keep the bar fairly plain and boring during Christmas."

"But you can change that." Aunt Trudy aimed her plastic toothpick at Hank and grinned. "A Christmas proposal would give you a new reason to celebrate the season again."

"Bring some joy to the holiday season," Benita offered. "That's our calculation. A Christmas proposal."

Hank rubbed his chin, staring across the dance floor at Leah, his girlfriend and Paige's best friend.

Benita and Trudy high-fived and clinked their spritzer glasses together.

Gavin laughed and tapped his water bottle against her aunt's cup. "That's impressive."

"It doesn't mean Hank will do that." Paige squeezed her forehead. "Or that you two are right."

Her aunt sipped her spritzer and eyed Paige over the rim of her pink plastic cup. "How about we calculate something for you, Poppet?"

Panic rushed through Paige like a spray of cold water down her back. They couldn't tell Gavin. They'd promised on Peg, the platypus. Paige needed to find the words that had lodged in her throat that

183

night on the boat. The same ones she'd failed to say to him again in the morning light. "I have nothing to calculate."

"But if you don't turn the page, you can't get to the next chapter, Poppet." Her aunt wagged her eyebrows and tipped her head at Gavin.

"And the next chapter might be the best one yet," Benita offered, barely contained enthusiasm spread through her voice.

Paige rounded the bar and captured Gavin's attention. His green eyes settled on her, warm and tender. She'd fallen into his gaze on a different night. Then fallen into his arms. And lost herself in a kiss that left an imprint on her heart. She wanted to kiss him again. Tempt the magic to return. Steal another moment. It was wrong. She wanted it to be right.

She never should have pretended that night meant nothing. Her mother had always told her that when it was right, she'd know it. Her mother just never said when it was right, Paige should say something out loud.

Paige stammered, "Do you have more napkins? The buffet is low."

"In the galley." He reached toward her as if he stepped into the same memory. On the same nautical couch at sunset.

He'd tucked her hair behind her ear. Trailed his fingers across her cheek. Leaned in.... Paige remembered their audience and pulled back.

Gavin quickly course-corrected and pointed over his shoulder. "Give me a second to get those."

Paige followed Gavin through the door into the relative privacy of the galley. She heard her aunt call for another piece of cake to celebrate before the door swung shut. She cleared the breathless catch from her throat. "Gavin, we need to talk."

He opened a cabinet and took out a stack of plain white napkins. "There are things we should've discussed before now."

Paige dipped her chin. Her nod, small and indecisive, like the right words she struggled to find.

"I should've told you this before we. . ." Gavin's voice drifted off. "This is awkward."

And not what they'd agreed on. They'd been friends for too long. Paige exhaled. "Gavin...."

Gavin blurted, "I'm selling Granddad's place and leaving Sea Glass Bay."

She'd known he wanted to leave. Paige waited a beat. Then another. Waiting for him to ask her to join him.

Gavin simply watched her.

He offered no more of an explanation. No invite for Paige to go along with him. His was a trip for one. Their night had been one night only. Nothing more to him. Now she knew exactly where she stood. Friends only. Just like her father, the timing was off. Her father had lived his dream to climb Mount Everest, yet he'd waited too long to reach for his oxygen. Now love was slipping through Paige's grasp.

But not Gavin's dreams. She respected him for going after his dreams. And because she loved him, she refused to be an anchor, keeping him landlocked. "I wish you all the luck in the world, Gavin. You know that." Now for her truth, because she still owed him this knowledge. "I'm pregnant and the baby is yours."

"Pregnant." Gavin dropped the napkins.

The napkins floated to the floor. Untouched. Unnoticed. Fluttered softly and silently. Unlike her announcement. Her announcement lodged between them like that anchor she'd never wanted to be.

"I took a home pregnancy test. It was positive." Paige clasped her hands together. "I have an appointment with Dr. Freeman next week."

"I can't go with you." He rubbed his hands across the back of his neck. "I have two early morning dive charters, an overnight to Driftwood Cove and several more day trips next week. I mean, I could go with you, but I have already committed to work those trips and cancelling at short notice—."

"I wasn't asking you to join me," Paige interrupted. The time for asking him to be her life partner had passed with the sunrise on that night they'd spent together.

Paige wanted Gavin to *want* to be with her for her, because he loved her, not because she was pregnant. Not because his honor demanded he stay by her side.

He lowered his arm and eyed her. "What are you asking from me?"

"Nothing." She clasped her hands tighter together. She'd wanted this to be different. That realization sank through her. She'd wanted him to be happy. She'd wanted him to be excited. She'd wanted him to want her. She swayed and let her heart shatter. It was her own fault for falling after one night. She accepted the fallout. "I wanted you to know."

"There has to be something you expect from me." His hands returned to his head, his fingers spearing through his short dark hair. "I'm the father."

"That's just it. I have no expectations." Paige wanted to reach for him. Sooth him. Reassure him. But she had her own heartache to heal. "I want to have this baby. I can raise this child."

"I support that, but…" He lowered his arms to his sides. "Where do I fit into this picture?"

"You have to do what's right for you." What was right for her was having her child. And loving her child the way she would've loved Gavin.

"I'm leaving in August." Regret tinted his words. "It's what Granddad and I always talked about. Always dreamed about. It's what I always wanted to do."

She had known about his dream to travel the open seas. He'd shared it while they'd watched the sunrise after their night together. That Gavin was leaving much sooner than she'd expected surprised her. She'd expected more time before he sailed away for good. This was for the better. More time with Gavin would only make the goodbye that much harder. "I'm not stopping you from following your dreams."

"But you're having my child." His voice unraveled into a whisper. "I'm going to be a father."

But they were not going to be a family. Not like the one she'd had before her dad's death. As it should be. Her parents had been in love. Love had been the cornerstone of her family. She'd love her child enough for two parents. She would make sure that was enough. "You need time to process this. I've had that. I know it's a lot to take in."

"Yeah. It is," Gavin said.

"Take all the time you need." Paige walked toward the galley door.

"Paige."

Paige turned around. He dropped to one knee. Her breath stalled.

But he reached for the napkins, not her.

Paige gathered her heart and her reckless expectations. The ones that bumped her hope forward, but only tripped her up more. "I have to get back to my aunt's birthday party."

4

*I*t was Monday afternoon. And Gavin knew exactly where to find Paige. He knew her schedule for every day of the week. He wondered if she'd be surprised to learn that.

He tossed the last of the sheet rock from the half-bath he'd finally finished demoing into the dumpster in the driveway and tucked his work gloves into the back pockets of his jeans. He'd stalled long enough. Paige had told him to take all the time he needed. He wasn't certain there would ever be enough time to adjust to her big news. He was going to be a father. Ready or not.

And ready or not, he had to talk to Paige.

She was having his baby. There was a lot to discuss. If only he knew where to start.

He headed across the wide driveway to Granddad's work shed.

The very same work shed Granddad had opened to Paige and her candle-making business one year ago. Granddad had refused to charge Paige rent for the space. In return, Paige had supplied Granddad with his favorite scented candles. Granddad had claimed the lit candles brought him peace and a clear, trouble-free mind.

Paige and Granddad were each other's biggest supporters. Granddad was her best salesman around town. And Paige claimed Granddad was her best nose. Together, over the span of a weekend spent inside the shed, they had developed her two best-selling scents.

187

Gavin had lit several of Paige's aromatherapy candles after he'd returned home from Trudy's birthday bash two nights ago. He'd wanted the clear mind his granddad had always boasted about. Last night, he'd spent awake on the sundeck of his boat, watching for a falling star. As if a shooting star and a wish would grant him clarity.

He opened the work shed door and stepped inside.

Paige wasn't stirring melted wax in her oversize pot. Or pouring the scented wax into her apothecary style glass jars. She was seated at the small desk, staring at her laptop screen. "What are you doing?"

"Fixing Maddy's accounting file." She tapped on the keyboard and blew a strand of her hair off her face. "Maddy needs to submit her quarterly taxes for Splendiforous, but the formulas are incorrect."

Gavin walked over to the large workbench and the finished candles lined up in neat rows. "You need to start charging for your bookkeeping services."

She winced. "Maddy is a good friend. I couldn't charge her."

"Then you should be working on your products." Gavin picked up a candle and tipped it over. He peeled off a warning label from the sheet Paige had left on the workbench and stuck it to the bottom of the jar. "And the things that bring in revenue for you."

"I've been working all morning." She frowned at the computer screen. "I've started looking for a place to relocate my shop to as well. When do I need to be out of here?"

Never. Paige was as much a part of the property as his grandparents. Granddad would hate that Paige was being displaced, too. Perhaps Gavin could talk to the new owners. If he finished the renovations and someone placed an offer. He added warning labels to several more candles. "The property isn't even listed yet. Much to my realtor's frustration."

"I would buy this property if I could." Paige closed the laptop, stood, and stretched her arms over her head. "Just as it is. I'm going to miss this place."

I'm going to miss you. Gavin needed his own warning label. Getting attached to Paige wasn't his goal. Had never been his dream. He wasn't meant to stick. He'd never planned to be a permanent part of Sea Glass Bay. He'd only stayed so long for his grandparents. Now he was ready for a new adventure. He'd take the good memories and leave the pain behind. Maybe then he'd stop hurting. "Granddad loved it here."

Paige reached over the table and grabbed his hand. "I miss him, too. So much."

"I still can't believe he's gone." And yet the constant loneliness that shadowed Gavin ebbed and eased, with only the steady touch of Paige's hand in his. He stared at their linked fingers. "A baby, huh?"

"Yeah." She tightened her grip. "What do you think Granddad would say?"

"He'd be thrilled." Gavin lifted his gaze to hers. "Granddad always adored you."

"What do you think?" Her voice was tentative.

"That I want to know the baby. Be a part of the baby's life." Gavin released their hands and paced along the workbench. "But I don't know what that life looks like."

Paige turned a line of candles over. Picking up the sheet of warning labels, she peeled the stickers off and pressed them onto the candle jar bottoms in quick succession. "You don't have to have it all figured out. It's enough that you want to know the baby."

"Is it?" He spun around and faced her. Emotions spilled through him, hard to hold onto like melted wax. Impossible to decipher. Was he afraid to stay or leave? Eager to meet his child or live his dream. Ready to celebrate his freedom or a baby on the way. He eyed Paige. Her hands were steady. her posture confident. How could she be so secure? "You'd be raising the baby alone if I leave."

"That's a choice I'm making." She concentrated on the labels, not him.

"What about your dreams?" He closed the distance. Only the workbench separated them, yet he never felt farther from her. He floundered. She remained poised. "What about your goals for the future?"

"I'm living my dream." She turned the jars over, picked up a yellow candle and spun it until her label was visible. "My goal is to never go back to corporate America and lose myself again."

"But you told me that when your severance runs out, the candle business can't sustain you." And she'd confessed her severance from her corporate accounting job in San Francisco was ending soon.

"I know. Now with the baby coming, I'm hyperaware I need to increase my income stream." She hugged the jar to her chest. Determination strengthened her words. "And I will."

He'd give her money from the sale of Granddad's house. He might not be there to help her, but the extra funds would certainly relieve some of her stress. He should feel better. He pushed his discontent aside. "You could charge for your bookkeeping services."

She frowned. "That feels too much like stepping back into my old job, my old life. Hank's books give me a free lunch when I want it. Leah's books give me organic ingredients. Maddy's gives me a discount on clothes."

"You're good at it." She'd corrected his errors on his own tax returns, saving Gavin from multiple fines and penalties. He wasn't the only one in town she'd assisted.

"I'm a good candlemaker, too. Granddad told me so." Her smile turned wistful before falling into pensive. "I need to open an online shop. Convince more shops outside of town to carry my candles. And triple my sales. That can't be hard, right?"

If she wasn't alone. If she had help. Gavin pressed a dose of optimism into his words. "I think you can make whatever you want happen. I only shop online so I'd likely buy from the online candle shop."

"I'll let you know when it's open." She opened a box of candle lids, added covers to the finished candles and stored them in another box. "You can be my first sale."

"I will be." Gavin set to work and finished adding warning labels to the last row of candle jars. "Have you told anyone about the baby?"

"Aunt Trudy and Benita know." She folded the top flaps of the box closed. "They've been sworn to secrecy."

Gavin nodded. "We should have a story or a plan."

"Do you want me to reveal that you're the father?" Paige asked.

Yes. No. Gavin opened and closed his mouth. He had no idea what he wanted.

"I shouldn't start showing for another month." She touched her stomach. One brief press of her palm against her still-flat belly. "Trudy and Benita believe it's bad luck to announce a pregnancy until after the first trimester. You have time to figure out your story."

"What are you going to say?" he asked.

"It's going to be more than obvious I'm having a baby." She shrugged. But an edge of sadness, not indifference, worked through her words. "I don't think I have to say much more than that. To anyone."

That felt wrong. Paige should be happy. He wanted her to be happy. Gavin rubbed the back of his neck and rolled his shoulders as if Paige's words pushed him out of alignment. He was having a baby. Shouldn't he want to shout that news to the world, not hide it? "I'm sorry, Paige. I feel like I keep getting everything wrong."

She smiled at him. "I told you to take all the time you need to adjust to the news. I meant it."

But adjusting wouldn't put them back to how they used to be together. Relaxed. Easygoing. Carefree. He wanted them back, then maybe he'd know where he stood.

5

*P*aige stepped inside The Flower Girl shop, owned by her best friend Leah Martin, and inhaled a tiny breath of the fresh-cut flower potpourri medley. Her stomach didn't respond. She inhaled deeper, smelling the aromatic blend of jasmine, lilac, and gardenia. Her stomach didn't protest. Her shoulders relaxed.

Yesterday the smell of her coffee brewing had chased her into the bathroom. Later the neighbor's fresh-cut lawn had sent her from her porch back inside her cottage to breath her recycled air.

She walked into Leah's backroom and lifted the to-go carrier from Salt and Sea Café. "I'm here to help. And I have caffeine and pastries."

"I'll take both your hands and the coffee." Leah's Flower Girl apron was tied around her neck and her long blonde hair was tied back. She glanced at the kid-sized sand table in the corner of the room. Beach toys were scattered from the tabletop to floor. "Owen spent the night at his dad's house. Other than the odd customer and Marisol, we should have minimal interruptions."

Paige set the food on the side table and rubbed her hands together. "What do you need me to do?"

"Assemble." Leah motioned to a tall rustic farmhouse pitcher on the worktable. "I've already lined it. Now it needs flowers. I'm thinking tulips, paperwhites. Maybe ivy to drape over the side. Fern leaves. Create and have fun."

The bells on the front door jingled. Leah checked the clock, then headed out of the backroom to help her customer.

Paige picked up the metal pitcher and traced her finger over the words: *Home Sweet Home* etched into the side. Paige's mom had collected items imprinted with that phrase. She had always claimed her favorite place was home with her husband and her daughter. *Nowhere else I ever want to be than with my family.* Paige wanted her mom now for a shoulder to lean on. For an extra dose of courage. She brushed at the tear that spilled free and busied herself picking out tulips in every shade.

Twenty minutes later, Paige stepped back and admired the bright, cheerful pitcher. "It's a celebration of tulips."

Leah glanced over from the sink and the roses she had sorted by color into buckets. "It should sell quickly."

The bells chimed again. Seconds later, Marisol DeLeon swept into the backroom, carrying several tinfoil covered dishes. "I've brought you fresh red chili pork tamales for lunch. Or dinner. Or whenever you need a pick-me-up."

"Did I hear tamales?" Claire Bishop, art teacher and one of Paige's closest friends, lifted the thick strap of her oversized carpet bag over her strawberry-blonde hair and dropped it on a stool. Claire was never without ideas or her beautifully detailed carpet bag that contained everything for any emergency.

Claire accepted a plate from Marisol. "These are my absolute favorites. Lunchtime can't arrive soon enough."

"You have a cold-brew coffee to tie you over until your lunch break." Paige pointed to the to-go carrier on the counter. "The other one is for Jazzy."

"This day keeps getting better and better. I took the day off to take a class at the junior college on decoupage. Now all this." Claire grabbed her coffee and eyed the farmhouse pitcher. "Marisol, your boys need to get you this flower arrangement for Mother's Day. It's perfect for your patio table."

"My boys need to get married and give me grandchildren," Marisol chimed. She winked at Leah and grinned. "That's the Mother's

Day present I'm wishing for. Besides, Leah has already given me a gorgeous arrangement of hers, in that lovely pink and white striped teapot vase over there." And she pointed it out on the side of her workstation.

"Aunt Trudy and Benita predicted Christmas," Paige blurted.

"For what?" Marisol asked, curiosity piqued.

"A proposal."

Leah spun around, her cheeks and roses the same shade of red.

Marisol handed Paige a tamale plate. Paige lifted the tinfoil and inhaled. The mash-up of chipotle, chilies, and cumin-seasoned pork confused her senses. Her stomach rolled, then lurched. She thrust the plate back into Marisol's shocked hands, slapped her palm over her mouth and sprinted for Leah's bathroom.

Fifteen minutes later, Paige emerged from the bathroom and accepted she looked paler than Leah's paperwhite flowers. Leah guided her onto a stool beside the worktable. Marisol ran water over a stack of paper towels she held in the kitchen sink.

Claire dug inside her bag and pulled out a small vial. She uncapped the vial and waved the essential oil blend under Paige's nose. "Inhale deep. The peppermint scent will take the edge off."

"I haven't seen a reaction like that since I was pregnant with Henry and smelled onions sautéing on the stove." Marisol pressed the damp paper towels against Paige's forehead. "Never touched onions until I gave birth to my last son."

Leah dropped onto a stool beside Paige and looked her in the eyes. "Paige? Is there something we should know?"

I'm pregnant. Gavin doesn't love me. And I can't stop him from going after his dreams. Paige squeezed her eyes closed. Aunt Trudy believed it was bad luck to reveal a pregnancy too soon. Gavin wanted a story. Paige took that as code Gavin wanted her to keep quiet about her baby news. But these were her best friends. Marisol wrapped her arm around Paige's shoulders, requiring no explanation and offering only support.

Claire picked up Paige's coffee cup and sniffed. "This isn't your usual triple expresso macchiato." She sniffed again and frowned at the cup. "This is chamomile tea."

Leah's eyebrows rose. "You have a caffeine addiction worse than anyone I know."

"I thought I'd try something new." Paige rested her cheek against Marisol. "Change things up."

"You haven't changed your coffee order since we met." Claire stood behind Leah and studied Paige.

"Or your red wine order." Leah's words stretched into thoughtful. "Except last week."

"When you didn't have any wine," Claire added.

Leah grabbed one of Paige's hands.

Claire took Paige's other hand. Concern worked across her face into her voice. "What aren't you telling us?"

Marisol dabbed the paper towels against Paige's forehead.

"I'm not supposed to tell anyone." Paige glanced at her two friends.

Leah's eyes widened. "But we can guess."

"It's obvious she's pregnant." Marisol touched Paige's cheek. The older woman's smile softened into kind and understanding. "Paige has that new-mom glow even though she's sicker than a passenger on boat in a storm-tossed sea."

"Pregnant. That's amazing." Claire gasped and pressed her hands against her cheeks. "It's amazing, isn't it?"

Paige straightened and reached for a genuine smile. "I'm excited despite my stomach's current revolt."

"I have the best cure." Marisol pressed the damp paper towels into Paige's palms. "I was going to make cookies here. Instead I'm going to fix you a Greek lemon soup with chicken and orzo. Delicious and pregnancy approved. I ate it during my pregnancies. Give me an hour. Girls, watch over her."

Marisol bundled up the tamales and breezed out of the floral shop the same way she'd breezed inside: like a burst of sunshine and wisdom.

"Now that we guessed the truth, we need the details." Leah cleared the cuttings from the worktable and set a distressed white milk can on the worktable. Leah was constantly in motion. As a single mom, wasting time wasn't in her vocabulary. Leah glanced at Paige. "When? How?"

"Who." Claire pulled another stool closer to Paige and sat.

"I'll skip the how. You're both old enough to know that part." Paige tore the damp paper towel into pieces in her lap. "It happened on St. Patrick's Day."

"We started at Hank's and then joined the block party in the historic district." Claire tapped a finger against her cheek. "It was a girl's night out."

"Until it wasn't." Leah aimed a spray of lavender at Paige. "Until Gavin talked you into line dancing on the pier."

"Gavin is the who." Claire grinned and nodded as if offering her approval of Paige's choice.

"Gavin knows." Paige gathered the paper towel pieces into her hand. "I told him the night of Aunt Trudy's birthday party."

"What did he say?" Leah added three pale pink roses to the milk can.

"He was shocked." Paige gave them the short version of his reaction. She curled her fingers into her palm, crushing the paper towel, but not her lingering disappointment. But she had no right to be hurt. The baby wasn't planned. Gavin wasn't hers.

"But he's excited, too?" Claire tipped her head and studied Paige.

"Does it matter?" Paige stood and tossed the ruined paper towel into the trash. She brushed her hands on her pants, brushed away her hurt and thoughts of Gavin. "I'm excited. Isn't that what matters? I'm going to have a baby."

"Of course, that matters." Leah added another rose to the bucket and edged around the worktable. She took Paige's hand. "And we'll be here to help you with whatever you need."

"I'm counting on it." Paige gripped her friend's fingers, steadied her balance, and released the full truth. "The co-parenting thing won't be happening. But it's fine. It's good. It's really good."

"Gavin doesn't want to be involved?" Claire shook her head. "That's wrong. How can he be like that?"

"It's not that simple," Paige quickly added. "Gavin is leaving Sea Glass Bay at the end of the summer. And I want him to go."

Doubt crossed Leah's face. Irritation tinged her words. "Where is he going?"

"To follow his dream of sailing the world." Paige clutched Leah's hand as if that would help her friend understand. And if her friend understood, maybe then Paige would be convinced Gavin's leaving was for the best. "Isn't that great? I think it is great. More people should follow their dreams, but they don't get the chance. Gavin has that chance. He needs to take it."

"But what do you need?" Leah squeezed Paige's fingers.

"From Gavin?" Paige asked.

Leah and Claire both nodded.

"Nothing." Paige tugged her hand free and held her arms out. "Come on, you guys. I'm happy. Please be happy for me."

"We just want the best for you," Claire said.

"I appreciate that," Paige said. "It's not the way I would've planned things. But I'm here now and I intend to make it the best. That includes being the best mom I can be."

"We all have advice for how to do that," Leah said. "Including Jazzy. She'll have all kinds of tips."

Claire nodded. "We got your back. Always."

The bells chimed. Jazzy's cheerful greeting bounced through the floral shop, announcing her arrival. Jazzy appeared in the workroom doorway. "Sorry I'm late." Her all-too-perceptive gaze skipped from Leah to Claire to Paige. "What'd I miss?"

"Tamales." Leah grinned.

Claire shrugged. "Nothing other than baby news."

Jazzy gasped.

Paige looked at her dear friend, speared her arms out to the sides and released only her excitement. "I'm pregnant."

Jazzy lunged forward and wrapped Paige in a warm hug. Leah and Claire joined in.

Paige held onto her friends and her hope. "It's going to be a Mother's Day to remember."

6

"Thanks for coming with me." Gavin opened the door to Harrell's Tile, Kitchen and Bath Store for Paige. "I've second-guessed every design choice I've made for the house."

And if he were honest, he was second-guessing every choice he'd been making for the past four days. Ever since Paige announced she was pregnant with his baby. This gave him a benign excuse to see her. Work out more than tile choices.

"This worked out. I was done helping Leah at her shop anyway." Paige tucked her phone into her purse. "And I discovered three more boutiques on the drive here for my To-Be-Contacted list. Just one boutique outside of Sea Glass Bay selling my candles would be more than I have right now."

"What about the online store?" He headed toward the bathroom design area.

"I want a custom website, but that costs money. Then there are shipping costs, sales taxes, and website hosting fees to factor in. The new fees will adjust my pricing model." Paige grimaced. "I want to launch my online store the right way, and that's going to take time."

"I can help," he offered.

"I think you have enough to do with your house renovations and work." Paige turned and greeted the design director of Harrell's. "We need tiles for the floor in a guest bathroom."

The design director led them into an alcove and pointed out the popular tile options. She slipped out to greet other customers and offered last minute instructions to call if they needed assistance.

Paige's dismissal of Gavin's offer to help stung like a splinter under a fingernail. Even though she made a good point: he *was* busy. But he'd never been too busy for Paige before. She was his friend. Friends helped friends. It was as if she already started *not* to rely on him, because he was leaving. He should be relieved. Instead irritation twitched through him.

Paige walked over to the wall of tiles. More tile samples were spread out across a large island and stacked around the design space. "What's the feel you're looking for?"

He wanted to feel confident in his decision to follow his dreams. To leave Paige and his child behind. He wanted to feel like selling Granddad's house was right, too. Gavin stared at the dizzying array of tile options. "It's a small half-bath. Tucked away in an alcove. Does it need to feel any particular way?"

"Okay, I'm thinking Granddad's place is a modern beach house that also gives a nod to a vintage beach cottage feel." Paige spread her hands out in front of her. "But it isn't so pretentious that no one wants to go inside. It's a house that wants people to come in and stay for a while. That's how your Granddad was. Everyone's instant friend."

His granddad had been larger-than-life. Always ready to laugh. And always generous. Granddad would've insisted Paige move into the beach house. *Because it's where family belongs, Gavin.* But Gavin belonged on the open waters, exploring and traveling.

Gavin set his hands on his hips and stared at Paige. "How do we find that particular feeling in floor tile?"

"We just have to look." Paige laughed and sorted through tile samples on the wide countertop. "When we see the right tile, we'll know it. We'll feel it."

"You don't seriously believe a tile is going to awaken something inside us, do you?" His voice was dry and deadpan.

"If it's the perfect one, it will." Grinning, Paige held up two patterned tiles then discarded both. "If it's the right one, you'll see it perfectly in the space."

Like a vision. Maybe that's what he should try. Envisioning his life on the water. Then his life in Sea Glass Bay. Neither one was perfectly clear. Gavin shook his head, concentrated on selecting a tile and picked up a dark gray and blue tile. The pattern of wiggly lines appeared to have been scribbled on the entire tile by a child. "This one says please leave."

"Can you imagine walking into a room tiled with that?" Paige touched the porcelain square and winced. "You'd get so dizzy from looking at the floor, you'd forget why you walked into the room in the first place."

"How about this?" Gavin held up an ocean-blue-colored tile.

"Yes, for a kid's bathroom with a sea-life-printed shower curtain, a whale-shaped bathmat and an octopus toothbrush holder." Paige moved several more tiles aside. "But not for the guest's bathroom."

"That's incredibly specific." Gavin chuckled. "Did you have a sea-life themed bathroom growing up?"

"No, but my friend did." Paige's hands stilled on the sample tiles as if she'd stepped into her memory. "I loved spending the night over there. She also had a tree house inside her playroom. It was every kids' dream in the neighborhood."

He'd have a child soon enough. With dreams, too. How would he make those dreams come true if he wasn't in town? Gavin cleared his throat, bringing the carefree back into his tone. "Sounds like your friend's house was the place to be."

"It's what Granddad's house should be, too." Paige reached over and touched his arm. "The place to be. That was Granddad's vision."

Gavin was beginning to wonder where his place was. More and more, he began to wonder if it was beside Paige. But love required trust. His parents had trusted in their personal dreams and goals more than their love for each other. Gavin wasn't certain he could love Paige like she deserved. And what about all those plans he and his granddad had envisioned for his life? *All those one-day imaginings. One day Gavin, you'll find your place in this world.* That one day was finally arriving.

Gavin chose another gaudy patterned tile. "So, you don't think this was Granddad's vision?"

Paige grabbed his arm and tugged him playfully closer to her. "Leave those patterned samples alone and join me over here. I feel like our tile is in this pile."

Our. Gavin liked that. Yet that word belonged to couples and partners. Not two friends who'd found themselves becoming parents after one spontaneous night together. He sorted through tiles, building a discard pile.

Too many tiles later, Gavin and Paige reached for the same deep navy mosaic tile.

"That's the one." Paige's fingers skipped over Gavin's hand to grab the tile.

Gavin wanted to grab her hand. Hold on and holler: *you're the one.* He pulled back, crossed his arms over his chest and considered the tile, not Paige. Not his chaotic feelings. "That's our accent tile set inside pure while porcelain tiles. Simple."

"And stylish." Paige gripped his arm. "Can you see it? I can. It's perfect."

He pictured the finished half-bath. Every detail, including one of Paige's Bewitching Sea Citrus candles on the floating shelve above the toilet. "Yeah. I'm starting to see it."

7

*W*ednesday nights were reserved for family night dinner at Aunt Trudy's house. Paige always prepared dinner, Benita always baked a delicious dessert, and her aunt always created a cocktail that paired perfectly with the menu. Wednesday night had been their tradition for more than a year. Nothing had disrupted their Wednesday night dinner fest until now.

Until Paige's pregnancy put alcohol on the not-to-have list and altered Paige's response to food. Now, her mouth watered, not in anticipation of Benita's salted caramel and double chocolate tart. But rather of a constant queasiness.

"I'm thinking takeout for dinner tonight." Paige gathered the to-go menus piled in Aunt Trudy's kitchen drawer and waited for the women's disappointment.

This was the pair's highlight of the week. They scoured recipe books every day. The menu was decided a week in advance. It was their one night a week to expand their culinary tastebuds.

"Takeout is fine, Poppet." Aunt Trudy placed a stack of magazines on her kitchen table. She hummed a tune from her favorite musical, *Mamma Mia.*

Takeout was fine. Paige narrowed her gaze on her aunt. Takeout had never been acceptable before. The evening had to be about the whole experience. Takeout wasn't an experience.

"I agree. Takeout works." Benita carried more magazines and swayed her hips as if listening to the same soundtrack as her aunt. "Gives us more time to find our inspiration."

Paige searched for their disappointment. Her aunt hummed louder and swished around the table, sorting magazines. Beside her, Benita sashayed.

"Don't be upset, Poppet." Her aunt glanced up and moved to Paige's side. She slid her arm around Paige's waist and squeezed. "We'll get back to our dinners once you can trust your stomach again."

"In the meantime, we have the perfect distraction." Benita added another handful of magazines to the table. "We can look through these magazines for inspiration."

"Inspiration for what?" Paige asked.

"For the baby's nursery." Aunt Trudy guided Paige over to the table. "The one we're going to build at your cottage, Poppet."

Paige glanced from Benita to her aunt, taking in their barely contained joy.

The doorbell chimed. The interruption saved Paige from deflating the women's delight. She wasn't against a nursery. She simply wanted to slow the pair down.

Paige opened the front door and gaped at Gavin. "What are you doing here?"

"It's Wednesday night dinner fest." The upbeat confidence in Gavin's voice widened his grin as if he had always been included, too.

Trudy called out, "Who is it, Poppet?"

"Gavin," Paige replied.

"What a wonderful surprise." Her aunt shuffled to the entryway. "Gavin, your timing couldn't be more perfect. Come in. Come in."

Paige opened the door wider and allowed Gavin inside. But her aunt and Benita only knew the abbreviated version of Paige's baby announcement. Worse, she'd told the pair that Gavin and she were on the same page. She'd never elaborated on *what* page. This wasn't good.

"I hope I'm not intruding." Gavin stood in the living room, shopping bags gripped in both of his hands.

"Not in the least." Benita hugged him.

"We're discussing nursery design ideas." Her aunt clasped her hands together.

"It's nothing." Paige gathered the magazines.

"A nursery is not nothing." Aunt Trudy frowned and tugged the stack away from Paige. "Besides, you told us we could help."

"You can't take that back." Benita arched an eyebrow as if daring Paige to try.

"I'm not taking it back," Paige said. "I do want your help. But we have time to discuss a nursery."

"But Gavin is here now," Trudy wrapped her arm around Gavin's. "He's good with his hands and knows how to build things."

But Gavin wouldn't be there much longer. And Paige didn't want to get used to including him as if he was going to be involved fulltime. Or even parttime.

"He can advise us on our project," Benita said. "And give us a budget."

"We need one of those." Trudy nodded. "Gavin can give us one."

Gavin locked his gaze on Paige. "I can try."

"Wonderful. We'll discuss everything over dinner." Trudy motioned to Paige. "We're ordering takeout, Gavin. Cooking turns Paige's stomach at the moment. What would you like?"

Gavin held up several shopping bags. "I had a different dinner idea, if you are okay with it."

"What's in the bags?" Trudy leaned forward.

"Fresh caught salmon." Gavin walked to the kitchen island and set the bags down. "And everything I need to make maple Dijon salmon, strawberry spinach salad, and herb roasted potatoes."

Benita clapped her hands together. "I approve."

"Me too." Trudy peered into a shopping bag. "You have any soup in there? Paige doesn't have her usual appetite."

"I have a ginger tea blend. It was my grandmother's go-to when she was sick." Gavin pulled a can from one of the bags. "Chicken soup. Vegetables and dip. I read when you're pregnant it can be better to eat cold meals."

Gavin had read on up on pregnancy. Paige was impressed. And he'd brought her special tea and soup. Now she was grateful and touched. And those sticky feelings she had for him got stickier.

"Let's give Gavin his space to create his culinary masterpiece." Trudy swept her arms toward the table as if gathering her flock.

"The kitchen is all yours after I make a cup of your grandmother's tea." Paige filled the tea kettle with water.

Gavin paused and studied Paige. "How are you feeling? Really?"

The concern in his gaze and face wrapped around her insides. Paige skipped her gaze over the array of food on the counter and away from Gavin. "I'm okay. But all bets are off once you start cooking. I don't know why, but certain scents aren't working for my stomach."

Gavin pulled a container from another bag. "Then you're definitely going to need this tea."

"Maybe we should take our magazines onto the porch," Benita suggested.

Paige motioned for her aunt and Benita to remain at the kitchen table. "The tea has a wonderful aroma. It should block everything else."

Paige pulled a large coffee mug from the cabinet and smiled. "I remember when Gavin's granddad and I attempted to replicate the scent of the tea in a candle."

"Marshall Cole always had a good nose," Trudy said.

"Did you succeed?" Benita asked.

"We never quite captured the right essence." Paige took the whistling teapot off the burner and filled her mug.

Gavin scooped a blend of dry herbs into the stainless-steel tea leaf holder and clipped it onto the mug. "Maybe now that you're drinking the tea, you'll discover what was missing."

Gavin would be missing in her life. Soon.

"You could create the candle in Marshall's honor," Trudy said.

Gavin held a roasting pan and looked at Paige. "Granddad would have loved that."

From the catch in Gavin's words, Paige knew Gavin would like it, too. She concentrated on her tea, inhaling the aroma, then taking a tentative sip, letting it linger in her mouth. The ginger was there, but there was a subtle touch of something else. Paige sipped again.

Gavin dropped the salmon into a frying pan and Paige immediately forgot about dissecting the nuances of the tea. Instead, she kept her nose inside the steam to keep her stomach from revolting.

"You should ask Dr. Freeman for nose plugs tomorrow." Trudy refilled Paige's mug.

"Surely there's a nose stopper for women sensitive to smells." Benita returned from opening the patio door to allow the ocean breeze inside and the salmon scent out.

"It's not a reflection of your cooking," Paige said to Gavin. "I know how good of a cook you are."

"I'm not offended." He set three plates on the island and moved easily from the stove to the island. "I'm just sorry you have to go through this."

"The second trimester is supposed to be better." Paige's smile wavered.

Gavin set artfully assembled dinner entrees in front of Benita and Aunt Trudy as if he'd been a waiter, not a boat captain, all his life. He set his plate on the table and sat across from Paige. "Are the scents too overwhelming? I can take everything onto the patio."

Paige appreciated his offer. Even more she appreciated his thoughtfulness. But she had to stop appreciating Gavin. He was leaving, and she wanted him to fulfill his dreams. "I'll be fine. Opening the patio door helped."

Gavin eyed her as if still not convinced she was fine. "When are you going to the doctor again?"

"Late tomorrow morning." Paige swallowed more tea. "Do you have a morning charter?"

Gavin shook his head. "It was changed to the afternoon."

"Then Gavin should go with you, Paige." Trudy speared a red potato on her fork.

"You two should share the experience." Benita sipped her white wine spritzer. "It's important to be together for these moments."

As if they were a real couple. A real couple who'd decided to have a baby together. Not two people who'd spent the night together and were now adjusting to the consequences. But Gavin was the father of her child. How could she refuse to let him go? "Do you want to join me?"

"You'll learn the baby's due date," Trudy inserted. "That's a date we must have."

"It's vital to our nursery timeline," Benita added.

Gavin kept his gaze on Paige.

Paige shifted in her chair, trying to unstick her feelings for him. Trying to remember his dreams mattered. And her heart would eventually heal.

Finally, he smiled. "I can't think of any place I'd rather be."

8

"*D*o you have your list of questions ready?" Gavin stretched his legs out and tipped his head toward Paige. They were the only ones sitting in Dr. Angie Freeman's waiting room.

"Yes." Paige patted her purse resting on her lap. "Even the ones from Benita and Aunt Trudy."

"Are you going to ask about nose plugs?" he teased.

"Neither of us is asking about nose plugs. Got it?" She eyed him, her face set, her back ramrod straight. She sat on the edge of the cushioned chair as if poised to bolt at any moment.

"That's fine. We don't need the doctor's advice." He kept his tone serious and turned his cell phone toward her. "I did some research last night and found you a suitable pair."

Paige's laughter erupted into the empty waiting room. She covered her mouth, catching the residual laughter in her palms. "Tell me you didn't order those for me."

Finally, her shoulders relaxed. Finally, that spark in her gaze returned. Gavin studied his phone rather than Paige. "What's wrong with these nose plugs? The lime green color suits you. And the foam is extra dense."

Paige shoved him on the shoulder and sobered. "I'll wear those if you agree to cook once a week for Benita and Aunt Trudy."

"Done." He never paused to consider her request. "Just added them to my cart."

"You're serious," she said, surprised.

"I like Benita and your aunt a lot." *And you.* He shifted in the stiff chair to face her. "I can step in on Wednesday nights and continue the tradition until your nose decides to play nice."

"That could be a while." She frowned and rubbed the back of her hand under her nose.

"That's fine." He'd enjoyed the evening too much not to want a repeat. He hadn't realized how much he'd missed cooking for his granddad. Even more, he'd missed the entertaining conversation and laughter over a good meal. But mostly, he liked feeling a part of something again. Liked feeling as if he belonged.

"What about the nights you have an overnight charter?" she asked.

"We'll have to move their dinner to another night." Gavin scratched his cheek. "Do you think they'll mind?"

"Not if you cook salmon again." Paige fiddled with the strap of her purse. "Aunt Trudy was still raving about dinner this morning. I'm jealous I wasn't able to sample it."

"Next week, I'll make something you can sample," he offered.

"You don't have to go to all that trouble."

But I want to. For you. Gavin noted the hesitancy in her voice. He waved his phone between them. "Back to these nose plugs. They come in banana yellow or neon pink. Would you prefer one of those colors instead?"

The laughter returned to her face. "How about you choose?"

He would choose her, if not for his dreams. Every day. Every time. Gavin blinked and stared at his phone, surprised at the turn in his thoughts. He'd agreed to join Paige for her first doctor's visit. He hadn't agreed to give his heart free rein.

A door opened across the waiting room and a nurse called Paige's name. The nurse motioned Paige through the door. Then the woman, her colorful scrubs as bright as her smile, promised to return for him when it was time.

The door softly closed, and Gavin waited. He wasn't sure what the nurse had meant. Time for what? Baby name ideas. A lecture on how to prevent surprise pregnancies. A conversation about what it meant to be an involved father. Suddenly the chair bit into his spine and forced him to straighten. He considered walking outside.

He could claim he'd gotten an important call. Or forgotten something at home. He'd sort of inserted himself into the appointment anyway. But he'd wanted to be there. For Paige.

Everything kept coming back to Paige. They'd been friends for a while. Companions and confidants. He valued their friendship. But now he wanted...what?

Seeking a distraction, he grabbed a home and living magazine and flipped through the pages, quickly discovering it was the annual baby edition. He stopped on the section about over-the-top nurseries and compared the photographs to his memory of Trudy and Benita's off-the-wall nursery ideas from last evening. Given a construction crew, he could build the foundation of his nursery in a few days. But that required capital and would take away from the money he needed to sail away.

Ten minutes later, he asked the receptionist for a pen and piece of scratch paper, and began to sketch the nursery he imagined. The nurse reappeared before he could finish.

The paper folded and tucked into his back pocket, he returned the pen to the receptionist and followed the nurse into an exam room. Paige reclined on an exam table. A hospital gown was tied around her neck and a blanket covered her from her waist to her feet. Her gaze met his then flickered away as if as uncertain as Gavin. And that awkward feeling they'd both wanted to avoid washed through the exam room like a tidal wave.

After a quick handshake and introductions, Dr. Freeman asked, "Are we ready to hear the heartbeat?"

"We can hear the baby's heartbeat?" Gavin glanced at Paige then back to the doctor. His own pulse picked up. "Now?"

Dr. Freeman smiled. "Let me set a few things up."

Gavin stepped beside Paige. He wasn't sure what to do with his hands and opted for shoving them in his pants pockets. Paige's focus remained on the doctor. She propped one hand behind her head and bunched up her hospital gown in the other.

The doctor squeezed gel onto Paige's bare stomach then pressed a wand against her skin. Dr. Freeman adjusted a button on her machine. A rapid thump filled the silence.

Paige moved her fist from behind her head against her mouth as if she meant to quieten her small gasp.

Gavin covered Paige's other hand. "Is that. . ."

"The baby's heartbeat." Paige's whisper dissolved into tears leaking from each eye. Her fingers shifted and linked around his.

Thump. Thump. Thump. The baby's heartbeat. Gavin's own. Everything inside him raced like a speedboat reaching eighty knots.

"Looks like you'll have an early Christmas present this year." Dr. Freeman adjusted the monitor to face them and smiled. "Your baby is due on December first."

"A holiday baby." Paige's laugh was muted and waterlogged. "Aunt Trudy is going to be thrilled to have a holiday baby."

Christmas present. Christmas was one of Gavin's favorite times of the year. He adored the traditions and the spectacle. Without Granddad to share in the festivities this year, dread had crowded out Gavin's usual anticipation. But now there was Paige and the baby's arrival. New traditions to start.

If he stayed.

Gavin blinked, tried to focus on the screen Dr. Freeman pointed at. Tried to listen to Dr. Freeman's kind voice and her explanation of the image.

All he heard was his baby's heartbeat. All he felt was Paige's hand in his, steady and strong. And all he knew was that his life was about to change.

And for the first time since Granddad's passing, Gavin didn't want to run. Didn't want to leave.

All because of Paige. He dropped his gaze to their joined hands. Suddenly he couldn't recall a time she hadn't been beside him. His best friend. The one he'd always turned to, after he—they—had lost Granddad. The one who'd always turned to him.

The baby was a gift. Paige was the treasure. *Never leave a treasure, Gavin, otherwise you'll spend the rest of your life looking for it.*

Granddad had always repeated that life advice, kissed his two fingers and pressed them against a photo of Gavin's grandmother. Now Gavin knew why.

"I'll give you two a moment. Then you can let me know if you have any questions." Dr. Freeman set the printed photograph of the baby on a side table and slipped out.

"I forgot everything I planned to ask." Paige lifted her tear-soaked face to Gavin.

Gavin forgot every reason he'd wanted to leave. Every reason he shouldn't listen to his heart. He wiped the tears off her soft cheeks. Then leaned down, pressed his lips against hers and released into the kiss every emotion he couldn't find the words for.

If he chose to stay, he'd find those words later.

9

*P*aige walked outside Dr. Freeman's office, the picture of the baby tucked inside her purse, her hand tucked inside Gavin's. They walked toward the pond and quaint park across the street from the medical offices.

Hearing the baby's heartbeat had overwhelmed her. So much joy. So much happiness. So much love. It was all so much to contain.

Now her heart raced on. Her cheeks remained warm. Her steps were light as if she floated. She wanted to blame her bundle of emotions on the pregnancy. But she knew the truth.

One kiss from Gavin and she'd been swept away.

She'd surrendered completely to their kiss. Her knees had buckled, even though she'd been reclining. And her heart had claimed Gavin as if it was her right.

But Gavin wasn't hers to claim.

Now she had to get her feet back on the ground. Falling in love with Gavin wasn't a small stumble either. And the landing was going to hurt. Hearts never broke softly. Or gently.

"I can't do this." Paige pulled her hand out of Gavin's and crossed her arms over her chest. "We can't pretend like we're a couple."

Or pretend they were going to be a family. She had to let him go.

"Do you think I'm pretending?" he countered. "Do you think the kiss we just shared was all pretend, too?"

She didn't *want* to think about that kiss. It was *all* she could think about. His touch. His calm presence. *Him.* An ache pulsed inside her chest like that first catch of a bare toe against a rock. "I think you got swept up in the moment. Hearing the baby's heartbeat was powerful. Overwhelming. I don't blame you."

"So, we just got swept up in another moment, like we did that night on the boat," he challenged. "That moment had nothing to do with the baby."

She winced. Of course, she got caught up in the moment. And in his tender, devastating kiss. Like she had that night, too. And she'd gotten stuck, her heart and all. That was why she had to press pause now.

Before she convinced herself what they shared was real and lasting. Before she believed she could keep on pretending she had the family she'd always dreamed about.

One day the pretense would shatter and what would she be left with?

"I can't stand in the way of your dreams. That's all you and your granddad talked about." *I love you. And I have to let you go.* That ache spread. And Paige saw the fall coming. Knew the impact would hurt more than she'd ever imagined.

"What if I stay?"

"So you can resent us one day?" She shook her head. "You'll be full of regret for not following your dreams when you had the chance."

"I won't resent you." The honesty in his low voice wound through her, bumping her even more off balance.

She pressed her hand against her chest. Nothing stalled the ache deep inside her. "That's not a chance I can take."

"You told me when it's right, I'll feel it. I'll see it." He closed the distance between them. His gaze locked on hers, earnest and open. "Well, I do."

She had to remember the fall. Better a broken heart now, then a shattered one later. "I was talking about tiles for your Granddad's house."

"You don't believe I want to stay in Sea Glass Bay for you and the baby." He straightened. The smallest of moves. Yet the distance between them expanded.

Now she hurt, every bone. Every breath. "No."

"What now?" His gaze shuttered as he closed himself off.

"We stop pretending to be something we aren't." No future dinners. No more holding hands. No more breath-stealing, heart-tripping kisses. That pain clogged her throat. Her words came out in a rasp. "I have to learn to do this alone." *But I'll keep a piece of you with me always. The baby will be my saving grace.*

"But that's just it." He tipped his head and watched her. "You don't have to be alone. I can be here. For you and the baby."

"You always wanted a different future." She pressed her folded arms against her chest. The ache pulsed harder.

"You won't try because you're scared," he challenged.

His words jabbed against her. She clenched her teeth together.

He added, "You're scared it might work out between us and you'll have to risk your heart."

Was she scared? Definitely. This was about protecting her heart. She was never his dream, and nothing could change that. "If you wanted to be with me, you'd have invited me to go with you on your travels."

He blinked. His mouth opened and closed. "Is that an option?"

"No." She threw her hands over her head. "Don't you see? That was never a consideration for you." He only considered her now because of the baby. That wasn't enough to build a family on. To stake a future on. "I was never a good reason for you to stay before I got pregnant. That hasn't changed."

He rubbed his chest as if her words stung. "But..."

"You have to follow your dream, Gavin." She turned away then glanced back. One last promise for him. For herself. "We will be fine."

214

10

*G*avin walked inside Tank's Bar & Grill and stepped around the guests waiting for a table. The crowd was rowdy and lively as if they'd all collectively agreed to start their weekends at noon. Gavin headed for the bar and the empty stool reserved at the far end of the bar.

Hank already had a full pint glass waiting for him on the bar top.

Two sips in and Jeremiah and Sully arrived and flanked him on either side.

"Thought you could use some support." Hank dropped napkins on the bar and their usual drinks.

Gavin glanced at his friends. "You all heard what happened then."

"Leah shared her version last night." Hank filled a pint glass from the taps.

"Jazzy, too." Jeremiah ordered empanadas and pretzel sticks.

"Claire had opinions." Sully added ultimate nachos with double guacamole to the order. "Strong ones at that."

Gavin rubbed his palms over his faces. "Here's what happened."

He ran his friends through Paige's baby announcement to the doctor's visit and the resulting hiccup at the park. He stuck to the facts. To the specific events.

He skimmed over how her family had treated him as one of their own during dinner. How he hadn't wanted the evening to end.

215

He skipped over how right Paige's hand felt in his. How much he liked just being with her. How often he thought about her in one day. Every single day.

He left out how he'd accused her of being scared. Too scared to love him. And how it'd hurt to breath.

Gavin paused, turned his pint glass around in his hands and stared into the deep amber liquid.

"Let me get this straight." Hank leaned on the bar top and eyed him. "You told Paige you love her, and she told you to sail on out of The Bay all by yourself?"

Love her. Love Paige. Air rushed into his lungs. Everything inside him lifted and settled. Gavin flattened his palms on the polished bar top. Not for balance. Not to steady himself. The truth was all he had to recognize to right his own world. He *was* in love. In love with Paige Duffy. "That's not exactly how it went."

"Which part did I get wrong?" Hank asked.

Gavin had gotten everything wrong. He'd been scared, not Paige. He had to fix things. He had to tell her.

Jeremiah's hand landed on Gavin's shoulder, yanking Gavin's focus to his friend. "Gavin never told her."

Sully shook his head and winced as if in pain, too. "You never gave Paige the words."

Gavin blanched. He'd only just admitted to himself he loved her. "No."

"Man, you have to go big now." Jeremiah tapped his pint glass against Gavin's. "Really big."

"And give her the words." Sully thanked the waitress for their food. Picked up a loaded tortilla chop and stared at Gavin. "But you have to tell Paige in an epic way."

Gavin's shoulders drooped. "You're telling me the words aren't enough?"

"They would've been enough," Hank frowned and tossed more napkins on the bar. "had you used them yesterday. But definitely not now."

"What am I supposed to do now?" Gavin asked.

Jeremiah painted guacamole onto his empanada. Sully ordered another beer. Hank wiped an invisible spot from the polished bar top.

"Come on guys. This is serious." Gavin clenched his pint glass. "We're talking about my future with the woman I love."

Jeremiah wiped his hands on his napkin, pulled out his phone and tapped the screen. "Let me hit the internet for some inspiration."

Gavin already had inspiration. It was Paige. It always had been. He finished his beer. "I've got it."

Jeremiah lowered his phone and considered Gavin. "No offense, but are you sure?"

Sully nodded. "You kind of messed it up the first time."

"I'm not getting it wrong this time." Gavin dropped cash on the bar to cover their food and drinks.

Hank collected the money. "What are you going to do?"

Gavin backed toward the exit and found his first real smile since he'd heard his baby's heartbeat. Kissed Paige. "Simple. I'm going to show Paige our future."

11

"You've lost your glow, Poppet." Aunty Trudy pressed her fingers against Paige's cheeks. "Benita, our girl has lost her glow."

Benita rushed from the kitchen to Aunt Trudy's entryway and gripped Paige's cold hands in her own. "This won't do. We have to get it back."

Paige reached for a smile, the smallest of grins to reassure the worried pair. Her lips trembled. "I'm fine."

Or she would be fine. Once she stopped hurting. That had to be soon, right? She'd walked away from Gavin before her heart broke completely. That was supposed to be a good thing. Why did she ache so much now?

Trudy wrapped her arm around Paige's waist and guided her through the kitchen. "I think we need fresh air."

Paige had already tried that at her cottage. Then she'd taken a long walk on the beach. It hadn't worked. Everywhere she was, she saw Gavin. Missed Gavin.

Even now in her aunt's kitchen, she saw him wearing Aunt Trudy's hot pink apron and lip-syncing with a wooden spoon at the stove. She squeezed her eyes closed, forced her tears back.

The easy thing wasn't always the right thing. Aunt Trudy had taught her that. Saying good-bye to Gavin hadn't been easy, but it'd been right. She grasped onto that thought and glanced around the kitchen.

Plates, salad bowls, silverware and napkins were displayed on the table. Full appetizer trays and a variety of dessert stands waited on the kitchen island. The ice bucket on the side bar was full. The red wine bottle opened and set to breath. The white wine chilled in a marble cooler.

Paige slowed. "I've interrupted your evening. It's Friday video-game night and you're hosting."

Benita waved her hand as if the pair hadn't been setting up for the past few hours. Or planning the menu for weeks. "We've got everything ready. You're what matters."

"Come on, Poppet." Trudy tugged Paige toward the patio. "You're looking even more pale."

"I should head home anyway." *I don't want to be alone.* Paige dropped into the cushioned chair.

Benita patted her hand. "I'm going to make you a nice cup of tea."

"There's a canister on the counter." Her aunt sat beside Paige, leaned forward, and tucked Paige's hair behind her ears like she'd been doing since Paige had lost her own mom. Affection and compassion flowed from her, easy and natural. "The tea will settle your stomach."

What would settle her heart? Paige sagged into the chair. "When are your guests arriving? I can slip out the back."

"You'll do no such thing," her aunt scolded. "Besides, you should consider joining us. We've quite mastered the bowling. Tonight, we're car racing, team canoeing, and line dancing. We could really use new competition."

Benita returned and set a large mug in front of Paige. She sat across the table and studied her. "It helps to talk. We may not have taught you much, but we know you learned that."

"You taught me everything about life." Paige gripped the wrought-iron arm rests. "Now, can you teach me not to hurt?"

"That's love, Poppet." Her aunt set her hand on Paige's arm. "Love gives you the highest of highs."

"And the sharpest of lows," Benita added.

"Then who wants to be in love." Not Paige.

Aunt Trudy laughed. "Everyone."

Benita nodded. "Love gives life meaning."

"Love gives life color." Aunt Trudy touched the vibrant yellow lilies on the table and sighed as if her memories filled her. "Love adds adventure. Thrills. And makes the journey that much better."

"Until it doesn't." Paige arched an eyebrow at her aunt.

"That's no reason to avoid it." Aunt Trudy touched her heart-shaped earring and dismissed Paige's argument.

"Is that why you both married multiple times?" Paige asked. "Because you liked the thrill and the adventure."

Benita chuckled. "I married for love and for loneliness."

Aunt Trudy nodded. "I always believed it was love I was marrying for."

"How did you know the difference?" Paige sat up and curved her fingers around the tea mug. "How did you know when it was real?"

"You want a guarantee, Poppet." Aunt Trudy brushed her lavender-tint hair off her cheek. Her smile was pensive. "Unfortunately, life doesn't come with those."

"You just have to take the risk." Benita's voice was matter-of-fact as if risks were no cause for concern.

Paige sipped her tea, searching for something to ease the chill inside her. "And then what?"

"And then you know you're living," Aunt Trudy said. "You can sit on the sidelines and watch life happen. Or you can grab it with both hands and experience more than you ever imagined."

"What if it all falls apart?" Paige countered. What if she hurt more than she did now?

"Then you'll know that love wasn't real," Aunt Trudy said. "Better to have no regrets, than to always wonder."

"I've always wondered about Kirby Patton." Benita ran her fingers through her short hair, loosening her silver-tipped curls. "If I'd accepted his offer to marry him and become the fifth Mrs. Patton, would I be spending my golden years flying on private jets and living in presidential suites."

"Kirby Patton lost everything in a series of very unfortunate and entirely unwise investments shortly after he'd proposed to you." Trudy's voice was dry. "And you'd be working right now."

"Poor Kirby, never had the head for a good business deal." Benita grinned. "I'm much better where I am now."

Paige eyed the older women. Wisdom fanned from the lines around their clever eyes. Their experience slipped into every conversation. And their love for Paige never faltered. "You truly have no regrets?"

"None." Aunt Trudy reached over and grabbed Paige's hand. "I've buried three husbands. Grieved for each one in my own way. But I wouldn't have the pain if I didn't first have the love and the fun."

"We've lived Paige." Benita's voice dipped into insightful and sage. "It's not always perfect. It's not always easy. But it's always worth fighting for the life you want."

"Be fearless, Poppet." Her aunt squeezed her fingers.

Paige's pulse picked up. "But it's my heart we're talking about risking."

"It's the biggest risk there is," Benita said.

"With the biggest return," Aunt Trudy added.

Paige held onto her aunt. "It's time to live."

The doorbell chimed. Benita rose. "It's also time to get our canoe rowing."

"Are you joining us?" Aunt Trudy rose and looked at Paige, a challenge in her stance and her words.

"I believe I will." Paige grinned at her. "I'm feeling lucky."

"What about that life you want?" Aunt Trudy asked.

"I'm going to get that, too." Paige linked her arm around her Aunt's. "I was hoping with all the life experience inside your house tonight, someone might have the perfect way for me to do that."

Aunt Trudy's burst of laughter rolled around the patio. "You can always count on us."

Paige was grateful for that. They'd given her a foundation to grow from as a child. Now she had to trust in herself. Trust she truly could be everything Gavin wanted.

12

*P*aige placed the last box of her special blend Mother's Day candles in the trunk of her car she'd parked close to her work shed. Yesterday, she'd sold out. She hoped the same happened today on Mother's Day. The sun had barely risen, and The Bay was only now awakening. She'd been on Gavin's property inside the work shed for almost an hour, packing up candles and supplies. And fortunately, Gavin hadn't appeared.

She'd walked away a champion at car racing last night at Aunt Trudy's, determined to make the most of her future—whatever that might hold for her.

Footsteps crunched on the gravel behind her. Paige inhaled and closed her trunk.

"Paige." Gavin's voice curved around Paige like an embrace. He asked, "Do you have a minute?"

Paige shoved her hands in her jacket pockets and faced Gavin. "I need to get my booth ready to open. Judging from yesterday, it's going to be another busy day."

"I only need five minutes." Gavin held up his hand, his fingers splayed. "I finished the guest bathroom and wanted your opinion."

"I'm sure it looks wonderful." He looked tired. Paige wanted to reach for him. Hold onto him.

"Please, Paige. I promise I won't keep you long," he urged. "I know it's Mother's Day and the crowds won't wait."

Paige nodded. She followed him inside his grandfather's house. He turned toward the stairs and Paige paused. "I thought we picked out tile for the half-bath downstairs."

"Change of plans." He headed up the curved staircase. "I worked on the bathroom and bedroom upstairs instead."

Paige stepped into the bedroom and gaped. A white four-poster bed took up one wall. A plush pale blue blanket had been draped across the foot of the bed and pillows, plumped and stacked, leaned against the headboard. Leah's milk can flower arrangement they'd made the other day, with its Home Sweet Home message, sat on a matching white dresser. The plantation shutters had been opened, granting a view of the ocean from every vantage point. A glider rocking chair and footstool, like the one she'd pointed out during the dinner fest at Aunt Trudy's, invited her to sit and enjoy the view. She could imagine using it, while nursing.

"Do you like it?" Gavin asked.

"It's everything a bedroom should be." She trailed her fingers over the plush blanket. She really wanted to stretch out on the bed and listen to the ocean waves. "It's inviting and comfortable."

"Then it's a place you'd want to stay in for a while?" He opened a door and turned on a light.

"Definitely." Paige walked over to the doorway where he stood and peered inside. The bathroom had been fully renovated. Waterfall sink faucets, a walk-in shower, and the deep blue accent tiles they'd picked came together in harmony. "This is an oasis."

"A place for a new mom like you to recharge and restore," Gavin said.

She searched his face. "What are you saying?"

"There's one more room I want you to see. It's right next door," Gavin said. "Then I'll explain everything."

Gavin crossed the hallway and opened another door. Paige walked in the bedroom and gaped. The room was in the beginning stages of becoming a nursery. But not just any bland nursery like Benita and Aunt Trudy had shunned. This nursery incorporated the wistful wishes and musings of Paige, Aunt Trudy, and Benita, then brought those daydreams to life.

An unpainted castle captured one entire wall. Beside one tower, a tree filled the far corner. Its bright green leaves exploded around the ceiling. Bookshelves had been inserted in the wide, thick tree trunk. One long hand-carved branch extended away from the wall. Crocheted ropes hung from the branch and attached to a padded oak seat. "Is that a working tree swing?"

"Yes. It was Aunt Trudy's idea. I had a lot of help from Hank, Jeremiah, and his contractor friends." Gavin set the swing in motion. "Want to try it?"

She wanted to explore. She wanted to discover if the castle door really opened. She wanted to stay for longer than a minute. Longer than an hour. She walked over to the swing and sat, her legs suddenly unsteady.

It was a wonderland drawn from her own imagination. And created by Gavin.

If this wasn't a sign he truly cared—truly wanted them in his life—she didn't know what was. He'd renovated his Grandfather's house for them! He was not going to sell it!

He rubbed his chin and considered her. "When the baby arrives, we could put a rocking chair in place of the swing, if you preferred."

We. Paige kept the swing still. Inside, her stomach dropped out, allowing those butterflies to take flight. "You built an indoor tree, a tree swing and a castle in a nursery for us."

"We can go princess if it's a girl." He rubbed the back of his neck and looked around the room as if seeing it for the first time. "Knights if it's a boy. All kids like castles."

So did Paige. And she really liked Gavin. Loved him. "It's an actual castle."

His grandfather's beach house had always had mansion proportions, with its vaulted ceilings, so the castle had two stories. A pair of towers. A walkway. And from her seat on the swing, she could see the staircase hidden inside the gatehouse, leading to the "second floor" of the castle.

"It's not finished. There's a lot of painting and refining to do over the next few months. There will be a slide into the adjoining playroom from the parapet. And rooms to design inside the castle." Gavin motioned to the empty side of the large bedroom. "We need a crib and all the baby things to complete the other half of the nursery."

We. There it was again. Paige curved her fingers around the crocheted ropes and held on. Still her heart lifted with imaginary butterflies.

"Unless you don't like any of this." Worry curved from Gavin's face to his words. "Nothing is permanent. It can all be changed."

"It's amazing. Better than I could've imagined." Paige stood and turned in a slow circle, taking in the space. Marveling at Gavin's detailed work. At his words. "Why? Why did you do this?"

His eyes softened. "It's your first Mother's Day—it deserves to be memorable. But also, I wanted to show you what I envisioned," he said. "For our future with our baby. Our children."

Our baby. Our children. Paige's breath stalled. Her heart skipped, tripping her pulse into rapid speed.

"Granddad told me to go find what I'd been missing. To go live my life." Gavin walked to her. His green gaze, warm and unwavering, locked on her. "Turns out, I haven't been missing anything. You've been beside me the whole time."

Everything inside Paige slowed. And that risk she'd feared no longer scared her.

"You are my life." Gavin took her hands. "I love you, Paige Duffy."

Love wasn't a risk. Love was the reason. Paige closed the distance between them. Her heart fully open. Swept away, or her feet firmly on the ground, it didn't matter. Her heart was safe with Gavin. After all, it had always been with Gavin.

"I should've told you sooner. I should've told you the first day we met at your candle booth. I should've told you every day after that." Gavin squeezed her fingers. Regret thickened his voice. "But I was too afraid."

"You were right. I was terrified, too." Paige found her voice. Found her words. Her truth. "I fell for you the day you bought a dozen of my candles for you and your Granddad. I've been falling for you ever since."

"Let's be brave together," Gavin said. "Let's embrace our life—the one we make together."

"I love you, Gavin Cole." Paige framed his face in her hands and leaned forward.

He met her halfway, one of his hands splaying across her stomach protectively, as if to also extend the love he was feeling to their child.

Then their lips met in a tangle of emotions still yet to be voiced. They showed each other how important this moment was to them with their bodies, as Gavin deepened the kiss, almost breathing her in to his soul.

Promises were made and given. Hearts were joined. And a future started.

Paige pulled away and tucked her head against his shoulder. "You're the family I always wanted."

Epilogue

by Cari Lynn Webb

$\mathcal{T}$rudy and Benita sat beneath a large oak tree and sipped on their Shirley Temple drinks Hank had carried over. The tree's thick branches had offered much needed shade earlier in the day, granting the two women a nice reprieve from the hustle and bustle of the Mother's Day festivities. Now the sun had set, evening had settled in and a deep contentment had settled inside Trudy.

Marisol joined them, shifted her basket from one arm to the other, and glanced at the large tree. "Trudy, do you and Benita want to move for a better view of the fireworks?"

"I already have the perfect view." Trudy smiled and tipped her chin toward the group gathered around the picnic table only a pebble's throw away. A large sheet of paper had been spread across the wide table and colored markers had been dumped from the box, within easy reach of the onlookers. On the far end of the table, a collection of stuffed animals, won at the various carnival games, watched over the proceedings like a private cheering section. Trudy wanted to cheer herself. She tapped her chest. "This view touches my heart."

Marisol sat in the empty chair beside the two ladies and cradled her basket on her lap. Her grin widened into a satisfied smile. "What are they up to?"

"Designing their dreams." Benita chuckled.

Hank and Sully sat side-by-side at the table, each held a marker and studied Gavin's drawing of Lindie's future playhouse. Jeremiah stood behind the pair, Caleb fast asleep in the carrier attached to his chest, and offered his own ideas to enhance the playhouse. Laughter trickled across the table, spilling around the grass like welcome spring raindrops.

"If they keep going, they're going to need to relocate the playhouse from Sully's backyard to the park." Marisol shook her head.

"At the rate they're going, they're going to have playhouses for generations to come." Benita pulled the cherry from the drink and popped it in her mouth.

Generations. The idea warmed Trudy from her head to her toes. They were building so much more than swing sets and slides.

Lindie climbed onto Claire's lap. Claire began working the little girl's dark hair into pretty braids. Every now and then, Claire bumped her shoulder into Sully's to offer her own suggestions. Paige guided Owen onto Gavin's shoulders, earning a delighted squeal from the four-year old. Hank took Leah's hand and urged Owen's mom onto the bench beside him, pulling her tightly into his side. Jazzy rested her head on Jeremiah's shoulder. Jeremiah's arm wrapped protectively around Jazzy's waist before he kissed her head then Caleb's.

Trudy's heart swelled even more. "They're all going to make wonderful fathers and mothers." They were going to build something that lasted.

Gavin circled the table, his grip secure on Owen and his gaze fixed on the drawing. "We've created a playground, not a playhouse."

"Sully, your backyard is going to be the neighborhood hangout," Jeremiah teased.

"This is good for the kids." Hank rubbed his chin and tapped his marker against the paper. "But I think we need a firepit for the adults."

"And swings rated for adults." Paige laughed and eyed the group. "What? I like to swing, too."

Lindie clapped her hands. "Swinging is awesome. We definitely need more swings."

That laughter, full of joy and affection and love, swirled around the group like silk ribbon connecting them all together. More suggestions were tossed out: an outdoor kitchen. Larger patio. An outdoor projector for movie nights. Another blank sheet of paper landed on the table. More markers were picked up and the dreams got bigger.

"Do you think they realize what they've really done?" Marisol opened her basket and handed tamales to Benita and Trudy. "What they have really created is a family. And that's worthy of a celebration."

"Family is the strongest of foundations." Benita sighed, wiped at her eye, and took the tamale from Marisol.

Trudy tapped her tamale against the others in a toast. "It's the best gift we could've gotten this Mother's Day."